FAIRY TALES FROM ALL NATIONS.

BY

ANTHONY R. MONTALBA.

———◆———

WITH TWENTY-FOUR ILLUSTRATIONS BY RICHARD DOYLE.

LONDON:

CHAPMAN & HALL, 186, STRAND.

MDCCCXLIX.

ISBN 978-1-4357-4931-3

TO

THE ILLUSTRIOUS PATRON OF LETTERS

THE RIGHT HON. THE EARL FITZWILLIAM,

This Little Book

IS HUMBLY INSCRIBED,

AS A MARK OF SINCEREST GRATITUDE AND RESPECT,

BY HIS MOST OBEDIENT AND DEVOTED SERVANT,

A. R. MONTALBA.

PREFACE.

———◆———

THE time has been, but happily exists no longer, when it would have been necessary to offer an apology for such a book as this. In those days it was not held that

Beauty is its own excuse for being;

on the contrary, a spurious utilitarianism reigned supreme in literature, and fancy and imagination were told to fold their wings, and travel only in the dusty paths of every-day life. Fairy tales, and all such flights into the region of the supernatural, were then condemned as merely idle things, or as pernicious occupations for faculties that should be always directed to serious and profitable concerns.

But now we have cast off that pedantic folly, let us hope for ever. We now acknowledge that innocent amusement is good for its own sake, and we do not affect to prove our advance in civilisation by our incapacity to relish those sportive creations of unrestricted fancy that have been the delight of every generation in every land from times beyond the reach of history.

The materials of the following Collection have been carefully chosen from more than a hundred volumes of the fairy lore of all nations; and none of them, so far as the Editor is aware, have been previously translated into English.

The Editor cannot close this brief Preface without expressing his grateful acknowledgments of the enhanced attraction imparted to his little work by Mr. Richard Doyle's admirable Illustrations.

CONTENTS.

———◆———

CONTENTS.

The Illustrations drawn by RICHARD DOYLE, and engraved by G. DALZIEL, E. DALZIEL, ISABEL THOMPSON, C. T. THOMPSON, RICHARD THOMPSON, and W. T. GREEN.

FAIRY TALES FROM ALL NATIONS.

THE BIRTH OF THE FAIRY TALE.

WHEN nursery tales and entertaining stories did not yet exist—and those were dull times for children, for then their youthful paradise wanted its gayest butterfly — there lived two royal children, a brother and sister. They played with each other in a garden allotted to them by their royal sire. This garden was full of the most beautiful and fragrant flowers; its paths were overspread with golden sands and many-coloured stones, which vied in brilliancy with the dew

which glistened on the flowers, illuminated by the splendour of an eastern sun. There were in it cool grottos
with rippling streams; fountains spouting high towards
heaven; exquisitely chiselled marble statues; lovely
arbours and bowers inviting to repose; gold and silver
fish swam in the reservoirs, and the most beautiful birds
flitted about in gilded cages so spacious that they scarcely
felt that they were confined, whilst others at full liberty
flew from tree to tree, filling the air with their sweet
song. Yet the children who possessed all these delights,
and saw them daily, were satiated with them and felt
weary. They looked without pleasure on the brilliancy
of the stones; the fragrance of the flowers and the
dancing water of the fountains no longer attracted
them; they cared not for the fish which were mute to
them, nor for the birds whose warbling they did not
comprehend. They sat mournful and listless beside
each other; having everything that children could desire
—kind parents, costly toys, the richest clothing, every
delicacy the land could furnish, with liberty to roam
from morning until evening in the beautiful garden,
—still they were unsatisfied and they knew not why!
—they could not tell what else they wanted.

Then came to them the queen, their mother,

2

beautiful and majestic, with a countenance expressive of love and gentleness. She grieved to see her children so mournful, meeting her with melancholy smiles, instead of gaily bounding to her embrace. Her heart was sorrowful because her children were not happy as she thought they ought to be, for as yet they knew not care; and, thanks to an all-good Providence, the heaven of childhood is usually bright and cloudless.

The queen placed herself between her two children. She threw her full white arms round their necks, and said to them with endearing maternal tenderness, "What ails you, my beloved children?"—"We know not, dear mother!" replied the boy.—"We do not feel happy!" said the girl.

"Yet everything is fair in this garden, and you have everything that can give you pleasure. Do all these things then afford you no enjoyment?" demanded the queen, whilst tears filled her eyes, through which beamed a soul of goodness.

"What we have and enjoy seems not to be the one thing which we want," answered the girl.—"We wish for something else, but we know not what it is," added the boy.

The queen sat silent and sad, pondering what that

3

might be for which her children pined. What could possibly afford them greater pleasure than that splendid garden, the richness of their clothing, the variety of their toys, the delicacy of their food, the flavour of their beverage? But in vain; she could not divine the unknown object of their desire.

"Oh, that I myself were again a child!" said the queen to herself with a deep sigh. "I should then perhaps discover what would impart cheerfulness to my children. To comprehend the wish of a child, one should be a child oneself. But I have already wandered too far beyond the boundaries of childhood where fly the golden birds of paradise; those beautiful birds without feet, that never require the repose of which all earthly creatures stand in need. Oh, that such a bird would come to my assistance, and bring to my dear children that precious gift which should dispel their gloom and make them happy!"

And, behold, the queen had scarcely formed this wish, when a wondrously beautiful bird, whose splendour surpassed all that can be imagined, bent its flight from the ethereal sky, and wheeled round and round until it attracted the gaze of the queen and her children, who on beholding it were filled with astonishment, and with

4

one voice exclaimed: "Oh, how wonderful is that bird!" And wonderful indeed it was, and gorgeous to behold as it gradually descended towards them. Like burnished gold blended with sparkling jewels shone its plumage, reflecting the seven colours of the rainbow, and dazzling the eye which it still rivetted anew by its indescribable charms. Beautiful as it was, the aspect of the bird inspired them with a kind of awe, which, though not unpleasing, increased when they felt the wafting of its wings, and suddenly beheld it rest in the lap of the queen. It looked on them with its full eyes, which, though they resembled the friendly smiling eyes of a child, had yet in them something strange and almost unearthly; an expression the children could not comprehend, and therefore feared to consider. They now observed also, that mingled with the bright coloured plumage of this unearthly bird, were some black feathers which they had not before perceived. But scarcely was a moment permitted to them for these observations, ere the wonder-bird again arose, soared aloft higher and higher till it was lost to the sight in the blue and cloudless ether. The queen and her children watched its flight in amazement until it had entirely vanished, and when they again looked down, lo, a new wonder! The bird had deposited in the mother's lap an egg which beamed like the precious opal with many-coloured brilliancy. With one voice, the royal children exclaimed: "Oh, the beautiful egg!" whilst the mother smiled in an extacy of joy; for a voice within her predicted to her that this was the jewel which alone was wanting to complete the happiness of her children. This egg, she thought, within its thousand-coloured shell, must contain the treasure that would ensure to her children that which has ever been, and ever will be withheld from age—CONTENTMENT;—the longing for that treasure and the anticipation of it would charm away their childish melancholy.

The children could not gaze their fill on the splendid egg, and soon in admiring it, forgot the bird that had bestowed it on them. At first they hardly ventured to touch their treasure, but after a while, the maiden first took courage to lay upon it one of her rosy fingers, exclaiming whilst a purple blush of delight over-spread her innocent face: "The egg is warm!" then the royal youth, to try the truth of his sister's words, cautiously touched it also, and lastly the mother placed her beautifully white and taper finger on the costly egg, which

6

then separated into two parts, and there came out from it a being most marvellous to behold. It had wings, and yet it was no bird, nor yet butterfly nor bee, though it was a combination of all these infinitely and indescribably blended. It was in short, that multiform many-coloured childish Ideal, the *Fairy Tale*, dispensing pleasure, and happiness, and inspiration to infancy and youth. The mother thenceforth no longer beheld her children pining with melancholy, for the Fairy Tale became their constant companion, and remained with them till the sun which shone on their last day of childhood had set. The possession of this wondrous being from that day endeared to them garden and flowers, bowers and grottos, forests and valleys; for it gave new life and charms to all around them. Borne on its wings they flew far and wide through the great measureless world, and yet, ever at their wish, they were in a moment wafted back to their own home.

Those royal children were mankind in their youthful paradise, and nature was their lovely serene and mild mother. Their wishes drew down from heaven the wonder-bird, PHANTASY, most brilliant of plumage although intermingled with its feathers, were some of

the deepest black : the egg deposited by this bright
bird, contained the GOLDEN FAIRY TALES: and as
the affection of the children for Fairy Lore grew
stronger from day to day, enlivening and making
happy the time of their childhood, the stories themselves wandered forth, and were welcomed alike in hall
and palace, castle and cottage, ever growing in charms
and novelty, till they at length received the mission
of pleasing manhood also. The grave, the toil-worn,
and the aged, would listen with pleased ear to their
wonderful relations, and dwell with fond recollection on
the golden birth of those Fairy charms.

SNOW-WHITE AND ROSY-RED.

[Danish.]

———◆———

IN a far-distant land, there reigned a queen, who was one day driving in a sledge over the new fallen snow, when, as it chanced, she was seized with a bleeding at her nose, which obliged her to alight. As she stood leaning against the stump of a tree, and gazed on her crimson blood that fell on the snow, she thought to herself, "I have now twelve sons, and not one daughter; could I but have a daughter fair as that snow and rosy as that blood, I should no longer care about my sons." She had scarcely murmured the wish, before a sorceress stood beside her. "Thou shalt have a daughter," said she, "and she shall be fair as this snow and rosy as thy blood; but thy twelve sons shall then be mine; thou may'st, however, retain them with thee, until thy daughter shall be baptized."

Now, at the appointed time the queen brought into the world a daughter, who was fair as snow and rosy as blood, just as the sorceress had promised, and on that account she was called Snow-white and Rosy-red; and there was great joy throughout all the royal household, but the queen rejoiced more than all the rest. But when she remembered her promise to the sorceress, a strange sensation oppressed her heart, and she sent for a silversmith, and commanded him to make twelve silver spoons, one for each of the princes; she had one made for the princess also. On the day that the princess was baptized, the twelve princes were transformed into twelve wild ducks, and flew away, and were no more seen. The princess, however, grew up, and became wonderfully beautiful; but she was always wrapped in her own thoughts, and so melancholy, that no one could guess what was the matter with her.

One evening, when the queen was also in a very melancholy mood, thinking on her lost sons, she said to Snow-white and Rosy-red, "Why are you always so sad, my daughter? If there is anything the matter with you, tell it me. If there is anything you wish for, you shall have it."

"Oh, dear mother," she replied, "all around me

seems so desolate; other children have brothers and sisters, but I have none, and that is why I am so sad."

"My daughter," said the queen, "you also once had brothers, for I had twelve sons, but I gave them all up in order to have you;" and thereupon she related to her all that had occurred.

When the princess heard what had befallen her brothers, she could no longer remain at home in peace, and notwithstanding all her mother's tears and entreaties, nothing would satisfy her but she must and would set off in search of her brothers, for she thought that she alone was guilty of causing their misfortune; so she secretly left the palace. She wandered about the world, and went so far that you would not believe it possible that such a delicate maiden could have gone to such a distance. Once she strayed about a whole night in a great forest, and towards the morning she was so tired that she lay down on a bank and slept. Then she dreamed that she penetrated still farther into the forest, till she came to a little wooden hut, and therein she found her brothers. When she awoke, she saw before her a little beaten path through the moss, and she followed it till in the thickest of the forest she saw a little wooden hut, just like that she had dreamed of.

She entered it, but saw no one. There were, however, twelve beds and twelve chairs, and on the table lay twelve spoons, and, in fact, there were twelve of every article she saw there. The princess was overjoyed, for she could not but fancy that her twelve brethren dwelt there, and that it was to them that the beds, and the chairs, and the spoons belonged. Then she made a fire on the hearth, swept the room, and made the beds; afterwards she cooked a meal for them, and set everything out in the best order possible. And when she had finished her cooking and had prepared everything for her brothers, she sat down and ate something for herself, laid her spoon on the table, and crept under the bed belonging to her youngest brother.

She had scarcely concealed herself there, when she heard a great rustling in the air, and presently in flew twelve wild ducks; but the moment they crossed the threshold, they were instantly transformed into the princes, her brothers!

" Ah, how nicely everything is arranged here, and how delightfully warm it is already," they exclaimed.

" Heaven reward the person who has warmed our room so nicely, and prepared such an excellent repast for us;" and hereupon each took his silver spoon in

12

order to begin eating. But when each prince had taken his own, there was still one remaining, so like the others that they could not distinguish it. Then the princes looked at each other, and were very much astonished.

"That must be our sister's spoon," said they; "and since the spoon is here, she herself cannot be far off."

"If it is our sister, and if she is here," said the eldest, "she shall be killed, for she is the cause of our misfortune."

"Nay," said the youngest, "it would be a sin to kill her; she is not guilty of what we suffer; if any one is in fault, it is no other than our own mother."

Then they all began to search high and low, and at last they looked under all the beds, and when they came to the bed of the youngest prince, they found the princess, and drew her from under it.

The eldest prince was now again for killing her, but she entreated them earnestly to spare her life, and said, "Ah, do not kill me; I have wandered about so long seeking for you, and I would willingly give my life if that would disenchant you."

"Nay, but if you will disenchant us," said they, we will spare your life; for you can do it if you will."

13

"Indeed; only tell me then what I am to do, for I will do anything you wish," said the princess.

"You must collect the down of the dandelion flowers, and you must card, and spin, and weave it; and of that material you must cut out and make twelve caps, and twelve shirts, and twelve cravats, a set for each of us; but during the time that you are occupied in doing so, you must neither speak, nor weep, nor smile. If you can do that, we shall be disenchanted."

"But where shall I be able to find sufficient down for all the caps, and shirts, and cravats?" asked she.

"That you shall soon see," said the princes; and then they led her out into a great meadow, where were so many dandelions with their white down waving in the wind and glittering in the sun, that the glitter of them could be seen at a very great distance. The princess had never in all her life seen so many dandelions, and she began directly to pluck and collect them, and she brought home as many as she could carry; and in the evening she began to card and spin them into yarn. Thus she continued doing for a very long time; every day she gathered the down from the dandelions, and she attended on the princes also; she cooked for them, and made their beds; and every evening they flew home

14

as wild ducks, became princes again during the night, and in the morning flew away again, as wild ducks.

Now it happened one day when Snow-white and Rosy-red had gone to the meadow to collect the dandelion-down—if I do not mistake, that was the last time that she required to collect them—that the young king of the country was hunting, and rode towards the meadow where Snow-white and Rosy-red was collecting her material. The king was astonished to see such a beautiful maiden walking there, and gathering the dandelion-down. He stopped his horse and addressed her; but when he could get no answer from her, he was still more astonished, and as the maiden pleased him so well, he resolved to carry her to his royal residence, and make her his wife. He commanded his attendants, therefore, to lift her upon his horse; but Snow-white and Rosy-red wrung her hands, and pointed to the bag wherein she had her work. So the king understood at last what she meant, and bade his attendants put the bag also on his horse. That being done, the princess, by degrees, yielded to his wish that she should go with him, for the king was a very handsome man, and spoke so gently, and kindly, to her. But when they arrived at the palace, and the old queen,

15

who was the king's stepmother, saw how beautiful Snow-white and Rosy-red was, she became quite jealous and angry; and she said to the king:—"Do you not see, then, that you have brought home a sorceress with you? for she can neither speak, nor laugh, nor cry." The king, however, heeded not his stepmother's words, but celebrated his nuptials with the fair maiden, and lived very happily with her. She, however, did not cease to work continually at the shirts.

Before the year was out, Snow-white and Rosy-red brought a little prince into the world. This made the old queen still more envious and spiteful than before; and when night came, she slipped into the queen's room, and whilst she slept, carried off the infant, and threw it into a pit which was full of snakes. Then she returned, made an incision in one of the queen's fingers, and having smeared her mouth with the blood, she went to the king, and said:—"Come now, and see what sort of a wife you have got; she has just devoured her own child." Thereupon the king was so distressed that he very nearly shed tears, and said:—"Yes, it must be true, since I see it with my own eyes; but she surely will not do so again; this time I will spare her." Before the year was out the queen brought into the

16

world another prince, and the same occurred this time, as before. The stepmother was still more jealous and spiteful; she again slipped into the young queen's room, during the night, and, whilst she slept, carried off the babe, and threw it into the pit to the serpents. Then she made an incision in the queen's finger, smeared her lips with the blood, and told the king that his wife had again devoured her own child. The king's distress was greater than can be imagined, and he said:— " Yes, it must be so, since I see it with my own eyes; but surely she will never do so again; I will spare her this once more."

Before that year was out, Snow-white and Rosy-red brought a daughter into the world, and this also the old queen threw into the serpent hole, as she had done the others, made an incision in the young queen's finger, smeared her lips with the blood, and then again said to the king: " Come and see if I do not say truly, she is a sorceress: for she has now devoured her third child." Then the king was more distressed than can be described, for he could no longer spare her, but was obliged to command that she should be burnt alive. Now when the pile of faggots was blazing, and the young queen was to ascend, she made signs that twelve boards should be laid round the pile. This being done she placed on them, the shirts, caps, and cravats, she had made for her brothers; but the left sleeve of the youngest brother's shirt was wanting, for she had not been able to finish it. No sooner had she done this than a great rustling and fluttering was heard in the air, and twelve wild ducks came flying from the wood, and each took a shirt, cap, and cravat in his beak, and flew off with them.

" Are you convinced now that she is a sorceress ?" said the wicked step-mother to the king : " make haste and have her burnt before the flames consume all the wood."

" There is no need of such haste," said the king ; " we have plenty more wood, and I am very desirous to see what will be the end of all this."

At that moment came the twelve princes riding up, all as handsome and graceful as possible, only the youngest prince, instead of a left arm, had a duck's wing.

" What are you going to do ?" asked the princes.

" My wife is going to be burnt," said the king, " because she is a sorceress, and has devoured her children."

" That has she not," said the princes. " Speak now, sister ! You have delivered us, now save yourself."

18

SNOW-WHITE AND ROSY-RED.   P. 19

Then Snow-white and Rosy-red spoke, and related all that had happened, and that each time she had a child, the old queen had slipped into the room, taken the child, and then made an incision in her finger, and smeared the blood upon her lips. And the princes led the king to the serpent hole, and there lay the children, playing with the serpents and adders, and finer children than these could not be seen. Then the king carried them with him to his stepmother, and asked her what the person deserved who had desired to betray an innocent queen, and three such lovely children.

"To be torn in pieces by twelve wild horses," said the old queen.

"You have pronounced your own doom, and shall suffer the punishment," said the king, and forthwith the old queen was tied to twelve wild horses, and torn to pieces. But Snow-white and Rosy-red set off with the king, her husband, and her three children, and her twelve brothers, and went home to her parents, and told them all that had happened to her; and there were rejoicings throughout the kingdom, because the princess was saved, and that she had disenchanted her twelve brothers.

THE STORY OF ARGILIUS AND THE FLAME-KING.

[Slavonic.]

—•—

N a certain distant land once reigned a king and queen, who had three daughters and one son. As the king and queen were talking one day together about family matters, the king said to his consort: "Whenever our daughters happen to marry we shall be obliged to give to each of their husbands a portion of our kingdom, which will thereby be greatly diminished; I think therefore that we cannot do better than marry them all three to our son, and so the kingdom will remain entire. In another eight days, harvest will be over, and then we will celebrate the nuptials."

The son overheard this discourse, and thought within himself, "that shall never come to pass."

Now the king and queen having gone to a distant

farm to superintend the reapers, some one approached the window, knocked at it, and said to the prince: " Little prince, I am come to marry your eldest sister."

The young prince replied: " Wait a moment, you shall have her directly." He called his eldest sister, and as soon as she entered the room, he caught her in his arms, and threw her out of the window. She did not, however, fall to the ground, but on a golden bridge, which was very, very long, in fact it reached to the sun. Her unknown lover took her by the hand, and led her along the golden bridge to his kingdom in the centre of the sun, for this unknown happened to be the Sun-king.

About noon some one else knocked at the window and said, as the former had done: " Little prince, I want to marry your second sister."

The little prince replied: " Wait a moment, you shall have her directly." He went into his second sister's apartment, lifted her up, and threw her out of the window. She did not fall to the ground either, but into a chariot in the air. Four horses, which never ceased snorting and prancing, were harnessed to it. The unknown placed himself in the chariot, and as he brandished the whip, the clouds spread themselves out

21

so as to form a road, the rolling of the chariot wheels was like a storm, and they disappeared in an instant. The unknown was the Wind-king.

The little prince was right glad to think that he had already established two sisters, and when toward evening some one else knocked at the window, he said: "You need not speak, I know what you want:" and out he threw his youngest sister. She fell into a silvery stream. The unknown took her by the arm, and the waves bore her gently to the moon, for her lover was no other than the Moon-king. The young prince then went well pleased to bed.

When the king and queen returned the next day they were very much surprised at hearing what their son had done; but as they had got three such powerful sons-in-law, as the kings of the Sun, Wind, and Moon, they were well satisfied, and said to the young prince: "See how grand your sisters are become through their husbands. You must try also to find some powerful queen to be your wife."

The prince answered: "I have already fixed on one Kavadiska, and no other shall be my wife."

The king and queen were quite shocked at this audacious speech, and endeavoured to dissuade him from

22

the thought by all kinds of rational arguments; as, however, they in no wise succeeded, they at length said: "Well, then go forth, my son, and may Heaven guide thee in thy rash enterprise."

The old king then took two bottles from his chest and gave them to his son, with these words: "See, my son, this bottle contains the water of life, and this the water of death. If thou sprinkle a corpse with the water of life it will be restored to life, but if thou sprinkle a living being with this water of death, it will immediately die. Take these bottles, they are my greatest treasure; perhaps they may be serviceable to thee." Now all the courtiers began to weep excessively, especially the ladies, who were all very partial to the prince. He, however, was very cheerful and full of hope, kissed the hands of his royal parents, placed the bottles about his person, that of life on the right side, and that of death on the left, girded on his sword, and departed.

He had already wandered far when he reached a valley which was full of slain men. The young prince took his bottle of the water of life and sprinkled some in the eyes of one of the dead, who immediately rose up, rubbed his eyes, and said: "Ha! how long I have

23

been sleeping." The king's son asked him, "What has taken place here?" to which the dead man replied: "Yesterday we fought against Kavadiska and she cut us all to pieces." The king's son said: "Since you were so weak as not to be able to defend yourselves against a woman, you do not deserve to live;" and then he sprinkled him with the water of death, on which the man fell down again, dead, amongst the other corpses.

In the next valley lay a whole army in the same condition; the prince again re-animated one of the dead, and inquired: "Did you also fight against Kavadiska?" "Yes," returned the dead. "Why did you make war upon her?" resumed the prince. "Know'st thou not, rejoined the dead, "that our king desires to marry her, but that she will have no one for her husband, but him who shall conquer her? We went out against her with three armies: yesterday she destroyed one; this morning at sunrise the second; and she is at this moment fighting against the third?" The prince sprinkled the speaker with the water of death, and immediately he also fell to the ground.

In the third valley lay the third host. The re-animated warrior said: "The fight is only just now ended; Kavadiska has slain us all." "Where shall

24

"I thank thee, dear brother-in-law, for having given her some relief; pray carry me to her," said Argilius.

"Right willingly," rejoined the Wind-king: so he gave a great puff, and he and Argilius, together with the horse of the latter, stood the next moment in the presence of his Kavadiska. Her joy was so great that she let all the kitchen utensils fall into the fiery stream; but Argilius, without stopping to talk much, lifted her on his horse and rode off.

The Flame-king was at that time in his own apartment; he heard an extraordinary noise in the stable, and on going into it he found his horse Taigarot prancing, neighing, biting the manger, and pawing the ground. Taigarot was a very peculiar kind of horse; he understood human language, and could even speak, and he had nine feet!

"What mad tricks are you playing?" cried Holofernes; "have you not had enough hay and oats, or have they not given you drink?"

"Oats and hay I have had in plenty," said Taigarot, "and drink, too; but they have carried off Kavadiska from you."

The Flame-king shivered with rage.

29

"Be calm," said Taigarot; "you may even eat, drink, and sleep, for in three bounds I will overtake her."

Holofernes did as his horse bade him, and when he had sufficiently rested and refreshed himself, he mounted Taigarot, and in three bounds overtook Argilius. He tore Kavadiska from his arms and cried out, as he was springing home again :—

"Because you set me at liberty, I do not kill thee this time; but if thou returnest once again, thou art lost."

Argilius went back very melancholy to his three brothers-in-law, and related what had happened. They took counsel together, and then said :—

"Thou must find a horse which is still swifter of foot than Taigarot; there is, however, but one such horse existing, and he is Taigarot's younger brother. It is true he has only four feet, but still he is decidedly swifter than Taigarot."

"Where shall I find this horse?" inquired Argilius.

The brothers-in-law replied :—

"The witch Iron-nose keeps the horse concealed under-ground; go to her, enter into her service, and demand the horse in lieu of other wages."

"Carry me thither, dear brothers-in-law," said Argilius.

"Immediately," said the Sun-king; "but first accept this gift from thy brothers-in-law, who love thee dearly."

With these words he gave him a little staff, which was half gold and half silver, and which never ceased vibrating. It was made of sunshine, moonshine, and wind.

"Whenever thou standest in need of us, stick this staff in the ground, and immediately we shall be by thy side."

Then the Sun-king took his little brother-in-law on one of his beams, and carried him for one day; then the Moon-king did the same for a whole night, and finally the Wind-king carried him for a whole day and a whole night too, and by that time he reached the palace of the witch Iron-nose.

The palace of the witch was constructed entirely of deaths'-heads; one only was wanting to complete the building. When the old woman heard a knocking at her gate, she looked out of the window, and rejoiced: "At last another!" exclaimed she, "I have waited three hundred years in vain for this death's-head to complete my magnificent edifice: come in, my good youth!"

31

Argilius entered, and was a little startled when he first beheld the old woman, for she was very tall, very ugly, and her nose was of iron.

"I should like to enter your service," were his words.

"Well," replied she, "what wages do you ask?"

"The horse which you keep under-ground."

"You shall have him if you serve faithfully; if you fail however once only, you shall be put to death."

"Very well."

"With me,"—these were witch Iron-nose's last words,—"with me the year's service consists of only three days; you may begin your service at once. You will attend to my stud in the meadow, and if in the evening a singleone is missing, you die."

She then led him to the stable. The horses were all of metal, neighed terribly, and made the most surprising leaps.

"Attend to your business," said Iron-nose, and then locked herself in her apartment. Argilius opened the covered enclosure, threw himself on one of the metal horses and rushed out with the whole troop. They were no sooner on the meadow, when the horse on which he rode threw him into a deep morass, where he sank up to the breast. The whole troop scattered themselves here and there, when Argilius stuck the little staff his brothers-in-law had given him into the ground, and at once the sun's rays struck with such heat on the morass, that it dried up instantly, and the metal horses began to melt, and ran terrified back to the shed. The witch was very much surprised when she saw they were all driven in again. "To-morrow you must tend my twelve coursers," said she; "if you are not home again with the last rays of the sun, you die: they are more difficult to manage than the metal horses."

"Do your duty," said Argilius, "I shall do mine."

The twelve coursers soon ran all different ways. Argilius set his staff in the ground, and a fearful storm arose. The wind blew against every horse, and let them rear and prance as they would, the wind got the better of them, and they were all obliged to return to their stable. Argilius immediately shut the stable door, and at that moment the last rays of the sun went down just as Witch Iron-nose reached the stable. She was quite astonished when she saw the horses and Argilius.

"If you do your work well this night, to-morrow

33

you shall be free. Go and milk the metal mares, and prepare a bath of the milk, which must be ready with the first rays of the sun."

Argilius went to the metal shed, and as he had a misgiving that this would prove the hardest task of all, he was about to set his staff in the ground, when he was met by his brother-in-law, the Moon-king.

"I was seeking thee," said he. "I know already what thou needest. Where my light shines, just by the

34

metallic horses' shed, dig about three spans deep, and thou wilt find a golden bridle, which, whilst thou holdest in thy hand, will cause all the mares to obey thee."

Argilius did as he was desired, and all the metallic mares stood quite still and suffered themselves to be milked. In the morning the bath was ready, the smoke and steam rose up from the milk, which now boiled. Witch Iron-nose said: "Place thyself in it."

"If I stand this trial," replied Argilius, "I shall ride away immediately after; let the horse therefore be brought out for the possession of which I bargained."

The horse instantly stood by the bath. It was small, ill-looking, and dirty. As Argilius approached to enter the bath, the horse put his head into the milk, and sucked out all the fire, so that Argilius remained unhurt in it, and when he came out he was seven times handsomer than before. Witch Iron-nose was much charmed by his appearance, and thought within herself: "Now I in like manner will make myself seven times handsomer than I am, and then I will marry this youth."

She sprang into the bath. The horse, however, again put his head into the milk, and blew back into it the fire he had previously sucked out, and Witch Iron-nose was immediately scalded to death.

Argilius sprang on his horse and rode away. When they had got beyond the Witch's domain, the horse said: "Wash me in this stream."

Argilius did so, and the horse became the colour of gold, and to each hair hung a little golden bell. The horse at one leap cleared the sea, and carried his master to the cave of the Flame-king. Kavadiska was again standing by the side of the fiery stream, washing the kitchen utensils.

"Come," cried Argilius, "I will rescue thee."

"Ah!" exclaimed she, "Holofernes will slay thee if he overtakes thee."

Argilius had, however, already lifted her on his horse and ridden off. Taigarot again set up a wonderful noise in his stable.

"What's the matter?" cried the Flame-king.

"Kavadiska has escaped," replied Taigarot.

"Well then, I will again eat, drink and sleep; in three bounds thou wilt overtake her as before," said Holofernes.

"Not so," rejoined Taigarot, "mount me directly, and even then we shall not overtake them. Argilius rides my younger brother, and he is the swiftest horse in the whole world."

36

ARGILIUS AND THE FLAME-KING.

Holofernes buckled on his fire-spurs, and flew after the fugitives. It is true, he got sight of them, but he could not come up with them. Then the horse of Argilius turning back his head called out: "Why dost thou let those fiery spurs be stuck in thy side, brother? They will burn thy entrails, they are so long; and yet thou wilt never come up with me. It would be much better that we should both serve one master."

Taigarot perceived this, and the next time Holofernes stuck the spurs in him, he threw the Flame-king. As they were very high up in the air, (in fact, they were as high as the stars), Holofernes fell to the ground with such force, that he broke his neck. As for Argilius, he brought Kavadiska back to her castle, where they again celebrated their nuptials, lived very happy; and, if they have not died since, they live there to this very day.

PERSEVERE AND PROSPER.

[Arabic.]

E that seeketh shall find, and to him that knocketh shall be opened," says an old Arab proverb. "I will try that," said a youth one day. To carry out his intentions he journeyed to Bagdad, where he presented himself before the Vizier. "Lord!" said he, "for many years I have lived a quiet and solitary life, the monotony of which wearies me. I have never permitted myself earnestly to will anything. But as my teacher daily repeated to me, *'He that seeketh shall find, and to him that knocketh shall be opened,'* so have I now come to the resolution with might and heart to *will*, and the resolution of my *will* is nothing less than to have the Caliph's daughter for my wife."

The Vizier thought the poor man was mad, and told him to call again some other time.

Perseveringly he daily returned, and never felt disconcerted at the same often-repeated answer. One day, the Caliph called on the Vizier, just as the youth was delivering his statement.

Full of astonishment the Caliph listened to the strange demand, and being in no peculiar humour for having the poor youth's head taken off, but on the contrary, rather inclined for pleasantry, his Mightiness condescendingly said : " For the great, the wise, or the brave, to request a princess for wife, is a moderate demand; but what are your claims? To be the possessor of my daughter you must distinguish yourself by one of these attributes, or else by some great undertaking. Ages ago a carbuncle of inestimable value was lost in the Tigris; he who finds it shall have the hand of my daughter."

The youth, satisfied with the promise of the Caliph, went to the shores of the Tigris. With a small vessel he every morning went to the river, scooping out the water and throwing it on the land; and after having for hours thus employed himself, he knelt down and prayed. The fishes became at last uneasy at his perseverance;

and being fearful that, in course of time, he might exhaust the waters, they assembled in great council.

"What is the purpose of this man?" demanded the monarch of the fishes.

"The possession of the carbuncle that lies buried in the sluice of the Tigris," was the reply.

"I advise you, then," said the aged monarch, "to give it up to him; for if he has the steady will, and has positively resolved to find it, he will drain the last drop of water from the Tigris, rather than deviate a hair's breadth from his purpose."

The fishes, out of fear, threw the carbuncle into the vessel of the youth; and the latter, as a reward, received the daughter of the Caliph for his wife.

"He who earnestly *wills*, can do *much!*"

THE PRINCE OF THE GLOW-WORMS.

[German.]

———◆———

N O ! I 'll bear it no longer, you good-for-nothing vagabond ! " screamed the old woman to little Julius. "When you should be sitting with your book in your hand trying to learn somewhat, if I do but turn my back off goes the dunce to the wood, and stays there for whole days, frightening me out of my wits ! What business have you in the wood, pray ? You ought to stay at home and learn your book or help me in my work. And then you let one have no peace by night either. What's the use of my telling you ten times over all the stories I know about the black man and the grim wolf? You godless child you ! You care for none of the things that frighten good pious children almost to death; but in the dead of the night off you go into the dark forest, through hedges and brambles, making me fine work to wash and patch your clothes. This is the last day I'll put up with it. The very next time I'll turn you out of doors; and then you may go far enough before you'll find anybody to take pity on you, you lazy foundling, and feed you, as I have done, out of sheer humanity!"

"I cannot say much for your food," replied the boy shortly and carelessly, as he sat dreamily in a corner playing with a wild flower.

"What!" shrieked the old woman in a still sharper key; "you ungrateful viper! Is that the thanks I get for so often cooking something on purpose, because our nice savoury potatoes and nourishing black bread are not good enough for you? And so, forsooth, the gentleman must have milk porridge and honey cakes,— and even these he pecks at as if they were not delicate enough for him, the beggarly ingrate!"

"One might as well eat mill-stones and wood-choppers as your vile hard potatoes and sour bread," said Julius in the same tone of indifference.

The old woman fell into such a rage that her breath

failed her for further utterance; so her husband, who was making bird-traps at the table, began in his turn.

"You rascal! do you dare to blaspheme God's good gifts, when, if we did not feed you out of charity—you must starve! And what return do you make us, you stray vagabond? When the fellow wants to slip out at night, truly he can be as sharp and cunning as any fox; but place a book before him, that he may learn to be pious and wise, and he loses his senses at once, and stares as stupidly at the letters as a cow at a new gate. Does he suppose I picked him off the road for love of his paltry flaxen hair and his blue goggle eyes? Fool that I was for my pains! Mark my words, and let every one beware of having anything to do with a child that is not his own flesh and blood! Why was I such a goose as not to let the child lie where I found him, kicking and screaming in the forest?"

"Well, why did you not?" said Julius. "I should have fared much better beneath God's bright sky, than in your nasty smoky hovel."

At this, the old pair—he with a stick, and she snatching up a broom—rushed furiously on the boy, screaming and scolding as if they had a wager who should make most noise. But the child, light and active as a roe-buck, bounded away. He fled to the wood; and when at last the old people had calmed down a little they heard him singing in the distance—

" You ill-favoured couple, adieu to you now !
I 'm off to the forest where waves the green bough.
The bees, they know neither to read nor to write,
Yet they gather sweet honey in sun-shine bright ;
Though the little birds never were taught how to spell,
Full many a blithe song they warble right well ;
The flowers are not fed on potato-roots vile,
Yet through the long summer's day sweetly they smile.
The butterfly, he has no tailor to pay,
Yet he never feels cold,—and who dresses so gay ?
The glow-worms at eve show a lovelier light
Than the dim lamps that mortals consume through the night.
So adieu, ye vile pair, whom no more I shall see,—
To the wood ! to the wood ! there I 'm wealthy and free ! "

Fearlessly ran Julius about in the forest, and the further he penetrated into it the lighter grew his heart. The dark night came on; and many a child would have been frightened, and fancied the tall dark trees with their strangely contorted branches were giants with long arms, or black dragons with twisted tails. But Julius was accustomed to wander by night, and went gaily on. When, however, it began to rain, and it was so dark that he found difficulty in walking, he sang in a clear sweet voice :—

" You glow-worms bright,
        You leaf-clad trees,
    That shine in the night,
        And that bend in the breeze ;
Hither I came, for I trusted that you
Would lighten my darkness and shelter me too.
Come, glow-worms ! light me to my mossy bed,—
Branches ! keep off the rain-drops from my head ! "

Then, a light shone suddenly through the thick tangled bushes and wild plants ; and a multitude of glow-worms came clustering round his footsteps like little torch-bearers, and guided him along a smooth and pleasant path to a retired spot, where the bushes and trees were entwined so as to form a little airy cave, the ground of which was covered with soft moss.   Julius, being very tired, stretched himself on the moss ; and the branches closed over his head, making such a thick covering with their leaves that not the smallest rain-drop could penetrate it.   Then, he sang :—

" Now, glow-worms, let your tiny torches gleam
To light my chamber with their emerald beam ;
In mazy dances round and round me sweep,
Shedding your radiance o'er me whilst I sleep,

45

THE PRINCE OF THE GLOW-WORMS.

That I may gaze in slumber's vision fair
On heaven's bright stars and breathe earth's perfumed air!"

At these words, a thousand glow-worms at the very least came from all sides. Some hung themselves on the leaves like little coronets of lamps. Others lay like scattered gems on the moss; whilst others again circled round him executing the most intricate figures. A great number fixed themselves in the boy's fair hair, —so that he seemed to wear a starry crown. So, in the gold green twilight, sat Julius on the soft green moss, amongst flitting lamps, and concealed by arches and columns from which streamed forth a green radiance, whilst the mild and perfumed air played around him, and he heard the rain drip and the wind murmur mysteriously—but neither could approach him. He gazed smilingly around; when he suddenly heard a murmuring sound that soon formed itself into whispered words. It proceeded from a glow-worm that had perched on the rim of his ear, and spoke to him thus :—

" If thy thoughts are pure and mild,
Such as beseem a holy child,
A wondrous tale will please thee well,—
And such a tale I now can tell."

To this Julius replied :—

THE PRINCE OF THE GLOW-WORMS.

"I seem to myself like some legend strange,
    So thy tale I shall gladly hear:
  So it be but one of wild chance and change,
    Come whisper it in mine ear."

Then, the glow-worm began her story:—

"As glow-worms bright we now appear, but little
nimble elves we were; in form and in figure much like
unto thee, but many hundred times less were we. In
India was our dwelling-place, far—oh how far!—away;
where midst green leaves and blossoms bright we
sported all the day. We scaled the petals of the flowers, within their cups to lie: and rocked by zephyrs,
passed the hours in dreamy phantasy. Our food was
the Aroma sweet exhaled by blossoms fair; and to and
fro we darted fleet, light as the ambient air. 'Twas thus
in careless mood we lived, nor good nor ill did we;
when lo! an earnest man arrived, and a holy tale told he.

"He told us how Creation's Lord had with His own
made peace; because His son His blood had poured, to
make His anger cease. For that life-blood, He willing
gave, had slaked the flames of hell; and His hard-wrung
victory o'er the grave had broken its fierce spell. And
not the human race alone,—all things that breathe
and move, and e'en the insensate-seeming stone, were

rescued by such love. Hence, through all nature's vast domain a universal tremor ran; a thrill like that of death's fierce pain shot through the ransomed race of man.

"'Twas thus the old man daily urged, in high and holy speech, and gently led us to accept the creed he came to teach:—till at length we let him sprinkle us with pearly drops of dew; and he hailed us then a Christian race, and blessed us all anew. And in token of that blessing, as we bent before him low, he gently laid his finger light upon each fairy brow; and as the consecrating sign his finger traced,—lo! there up sprang on each a brilliant star like that which now I bear. Then did the old man in the ground a cross of pure white place,—and calling us around him, spake in words of truth and grace.

"' Revere this holy symbol; and as ye have lived for pleasure and ease, without a creed,—by some good deed henceforward strive your Lord to appease. There are men living in this land who still in sin and blindness stand; they lay their dead in the forest's shade, and scatter o'er them flowers fair, but seek not their poor souls to aid by holy song or prayer. Wherefore, in night's still secresy, for the service of the dead, be ready aye to watch and pray and your little light to

48

shed. That ye this pious work may do, lo! this fair star is given you!'—And many more high words he spake ere his departure he did take. Thenceforth we led a holy life, as he command had given; and often in the silent night, we prayed that through our song and light, the cleansed soul might win its way to heaven."

"How could you do that? You cannot sing, surely," interrupted Julius. To which the glow-worm answered: - "Thou canst no other voices hear but such as thundering reach thy ear. Thou little dull-eared earth-bound wight, thou canst not e'en perceive by night the stars' majestic music sounding, through the azure vaults rebounding, with such a full and mighty voice, that though we listen and rejoice, our delicate nerves shrink tremblingly beneath that storm of harmony. Think'st thou 'tis without sense and feeling, that in our spark-twined dances wheeling, some of us darting radiance throw, whilst others burn with steady glow? But thou knows't not how closely bound by mystic tie are light and sound.

"Now hear my story on.—

"Not all of us became Christians; and one of our orders in particular, which had learnt from a Greek the philosophy of Epicurus, still held to its doctrines. This

49

was the butterfly-tribes,—who like ourselves were also elves. A light and godless race they were, thinking nothing worth their care but how to appear in colours gay; and to their sensual maxims true, they would drink deep of ambrosial dew, and then for hours would sleep; whilst we, the star-adornéd nation, sucked of the flowers' sweet exhalation just so much from the humid air as for our nourishment we needed. But those light creatures far exceeded. The fragrance-breathing rose they courted, and with the young field-lilies sported, till at length of their strength and their perfume bereft, the poor wasted flowers to perish were left. By their uncertain zig-zag flight, dear child, thou well may'st see, that they have drunk more than is right and their senses clouded be.

"We wore a garb of simple green; but they were ever to be seen in jackets with ribbons all gay bedight, and in every idle fashion light,—so that we sometimes laughed to see their folly and their vanity.

"That is evident enough if you only look at their patch-work clothing put together without the slightest taste. The foolish fellow with the swallow-tails thought he had done a vastly clever thing when he appended to each wing a tail like that the swallows have; and after all, this monstrous affectation is but a trumpery imitation of that which nature to the swallows gave. Then, that insufferable ass, the Peacock's Eye, must copy him in his folly, and wear great spectacles of coloured glass, which are so far from helping him to see that his own clear eyes look dim, owing to that fantastic whim. Thou thinkest, perhaps, the one who wears a mantle grave like a funeral pall is far above such senseless airs,—but he's the greatest fool of all! That garb of sorrow is but worn wonder and pity to excite, to seem as if condemned to mourn—a sorrow-stricken wight. Others there are who on their jackets gay, cause numbers to be traced; no doubt, you'll say, to mind them that the years unheeded go and teach them how to value time. But no! Those youths are your Don Juans, and the numbers show in pride how many flowers by them brought low have pined and died.

" The king who then did o'er us reign thought of a method somewhat strange, by which their licence to restrain and work a beneficial change. He caused to be enforced throughout the nation, a most peculiar kind of education. He shut the youthful butterflies within a narrow case of skin, wherein they were so tightly bound they could not turn their bodies round

—and there close prisoners they remained till they a certain age attained. I must confess, the principle to *me* seemed very wrong,—and so it proved to be; for so far from the matter being mended, we had just the reverse of what the king intended. The closer they were mewed in prison, the more they longed for liberty, —and only waited to be free, to plunge in deepest revelry.

"But angry thoughts are leading me astray,—I 've wandered from my theme too far away. To speak of many things I am beguiled which must be meaningless to such a child.

"Thou now shalt hear the sequel of my tale. There was one set amongst the butterflies more worthless than all the rest. These were the confirmed old topers, who had imbibed so much of the ambrosial dew that their bodies had grown fat and unwieldy, and had very large stomachs. Such clumsy butterflies as these had little chance the flowers to please; and so whenever one approached, each bent aside its calyx bright in mockery of the uncouth wight. Or if by chance one clambered up to reach the blossom's nectar-cup, its stem would bend beneath his weight, and down the awkward creature straight would go, and all its members dislocate. So then their evil deeds they did under the cover of the night. When every flower was soundly sleeping, they came like midnight robbers creeping,—then drew them softly to the ground, and sucked from their lips their nectar breath; so that many a flower at morn was found, lying pale in death and sinfully robbed of all its wealth, that had closed its leaves in rosy health.

"Now, my child, thou may'st be sure, full little could those elves endure that we, on our holy mission bound, the silence and darkness should chase away by our song, and our prayer, and our emerald ray,—hoping by that solemn sound to give the dead repose.

"Those who had drunk deep by day, roused by it could not sleep away the ill effects of their carouse, so they with aches and fevers rose. But those deceitful spoilers of the flowers, who trusted by night's shade protected to work their purpose undetected, had now to fast,—for as we passed, the flowers who loved to hear our song saw by our light, that pierced the night, their foes come creeping stealthily along. This with the jealousy within their hearts that glowed, because the star had not on them, too, been bestowed, between our tribes raised feud and jar,—whence bitter grief has grown. They had a king, to whom was known full many a spell of gramarye; 'twas said, that he a league had made with spirits lost, and by their aid could read the scroll of destiny. And there he found this dread decree, which told our coming misery:—

"'When the star-adorned race, shall fall from innocence and grace,—when their first murder shall be done,—when their monarch's first-born son by the waves of the sea shall swallowed be;—then vain shall be rendered their song and their prayer,—from amongst them the white cross shall disappear,—and to insects transformed they shall flutter and creep, doomed far from their own land to wander and weep. The fatal spell may be undone only by their king's lost son; but ere even he can set them free, he must their chosen sovereign be.'

"The king of the butterflies, when he heard this, began to consider how he might contrive to bring us to endless wretchedness; and as by magic he could appear in any form he chose to wear, an angel's guise he took one day, and neared the spot where our king lay deep sleeping in a tulip's cup. He by the rustling wakened up, was struck with wonder and pious awe, when he the angel near him saw; who thus in wicked words began:—

"''Thy loving wife shall bear a son to thee, of

54

whom 'tis written in the Book of Fate, that if he be not whelmed beneath the sea, the elfin nation shall be desolate, and from their native country driven:—such is the mysterious will of Heaven. Therefore must thou this offering make for the elfin nation's sake; else thy people's love for thee, will turn to hatred when they see thou wilt not save them from their misery; and thou thyself a shameful death shalt die.'

" This said, the guilty wretch departed. No longer slept the king; but heavy hearted, he musing lay, till break of day. And lo! just as the sun his radiance bright o'er earth began to shed, the queen gave birth unto a child, lovely and innocent and mild, and small as a pin's head!

" The king looked on it, but no pleasure glowed in his heart at this new treasure; and as he gazed, an icy chill through all his members seemed to thrill; for love of his people, and desire to save his own life, did inspire his thoughts with a ferocious plan.

" He had a faithful serving-man, to whom his secret he confided; and to him command he gave to plunge the child beneath the wave, there to find a watery grave. The boy, however, did not perish:—how he escaped I shall tell thee hereafter.

55

"Thus no murder yet had stained the nation; and the white cross still remained amongst us, and we dwelt unchanged in our accustomed spot. But the servant, by remorse urged on, revealed the murder he had done. Then, loyal as was hitherto the nation, the crime so raised our indignation, that our duty we forgot.

"In the first tumult of their ire some of our fiercest spirits did conspire their monarch's blood to spill. They tore the thorns from the stem of the rose, and the strongest and longest and sharpest they chose to work their wicked will. Beneath their mantles green they hid the spears; and sought their king, the curse-beladen one, who again in the tulip lay alone in sorrow and in tears. Wildly they the stem ascended, and in their rage they struck the deadly blow; they pierced him till his heart's blood forth did flow,—and with his life, his sorrow ended.

"Now the sinful deed was done,—now our innocence was gone! Heaven withdrew its sheltering hand. The white cross the old man had given, the token of our bond with heaven,—vanished from the land! And as we flocked together trembling, we heard a rushing through the air, as if fierce winds in conflict were. Devouring grief our hearts distracted; our delicate

THE PRINCE OF THE GLOW WORMS.　　　P. 56.

limbs all suddenly contracted, and into ugly worms we turned!

"Yet as we were not guilty all of the vile crime that caused our fall, the fair light still upon our foreheads burned. And as we sat in fear and gloom, a shrill voice thus pronounced our doom.

"'Henceforth as homeless worms, away, away!—wander and stray, here and there, and up and down, until at length ye place the crown on the brow of the child who by your king's decree was sunk amid the waves of the foaming sea. Far, far from hence is his dwelling-place, and he seems like a child of the human race,—but him ye shall know by the star on his brow.

"'Your lost cross, too, ye must find once more, which he is destined to restore; when your king and your cross shall again be found, your penance shall end and the spell be unbound.'

"The gay-dressed elves who had their king deceived by treachery and lies, were, like ourselves, transformed, and became butterflies.

"Soon as we heard our melancholy doom, we fled, and traversed many a distant land,—ever peering through the gloom, into each little sleeping-room; peeping about us all the night, in hope to see the twinkling light on the brow of some fair boy. And we looked on many a blessed child, who in his sleep so sweetly smiled, that we would have chosen him with joy,—but the star was wanting still."

"Poor worms!" said Julius; "and thus you still are seeking now, the boy with the star upon his brow?"

"Oh! no my child! by Heaven led, we have found the child with the light on his head; and now I will tell what him befel.

"In his death-struggle with the waves, unto a leaflet green he clung which floated on the tide, and with a lightsome bound he sprang upon its upturned side. Contented thus he lay at rest, swayed by the billows here and there, safely housed and free from care, in the leaflets' soft green breast. His only food was the radiance bright which the stars shed down on him by night, and by that delicate food sustained he made a voyage long.

"But why dost thou stare so fixedly?—why dreamily gaze before thee so?"

Then Julius said :—

"A dreamy sense is o'er me stealing, of moments long gone by :—when I in a green leaf thus was laid, gazing upwards on the sky, whilst the dancing waves around me played. I was rocked by the sea as it

58

rippled lightly,—fed by the stars which shone o'er me brightly; and on I sailed right merrily! And feeding thus on the delicate light by the bright stars downward shed, my nature grew unfit to live by the grosser human bread."

"Now that the light is o'er thee breaking, now that thy memory is awaking,—hear me further," said the glow-worm.—"For four long months the billows bore the child, until he reached the shore of a far and distant land, where they left him on the strand. A stork came proudly stalking by,—well pleased when

he such prize did spy; for by the garment green
deceived, a tree-frog he the child believed. And he
resolved the morsel rare to carry home unto his wife,
who lovéd almost as her life, such choice and tender
fare. He took him in his fine long beak, and with him
mounted in the air; but had not travelled far nor long,
when he beheld an eagle strong flying towards him
in might; and being somewhat of a coward, surprised
at this event untoward, his bill he opened in a fright,
—and down the elfin child from high fell to the earth
again.

"Why dost thou start as if some pain shot through
thee? Why on thy breast are thy small hands pressed?"

The boy replied:—

"I feel an icy chill through all my members thrill.
It must have been a dream, but unto me doth seem
that I had such a fall one day,—and such a piercing
blast right through my breast then passed, its very
memory takes my breath away."

Then the glow-worm said:—

"Oft we mistake some vision vain for life's reality,—
and view the wild creations of our brain as things long
past but true. But listen, now, while I conclude my

tale. Thou think'st perhaps the child, in falling, his limbs would break or dislocate ; but as a feather would descend, light fell that child on the foliage green, and not a tender leaf was seen beneath his weight to bend. Giddy with spinning through the air, and breathless for awhile he lay ; but soon to sense he did awaken, and found that he no harm had taken. Above his head, full, bright, and red, a strawberry hung, green leaves among, and its fragrance o'er him shed. Whether the child was of wit bereft, or that, deprived of the starry spark, he had fasted so long in the stork's bill dark, that hunger did his sense betray, is more than I can think or say ; but the berry to him seemed ruddy and bright, as if woven with a web of light. This when the foolish elf-child saw, he strove with all his might to draw the unwholesome earth-fruit to the ground, which he no easy labour found ; then round his little arms he threw, and to his lips the fruit he drew and sucked its ruby juice. A weary task the boy did find, to penetrate the tough hard rind ; then for a second's space he drained the nectar which the fruit contained,—one hundredth part at least he drank,—and mastered by its potency, upon the earth he sank.

"But alas! all was now lost, that earthly food was unto him fell poison. Soon each little limb unseemly swelled and spread. His floating golden locks, as fine as the slight thread that spiders twine, became as coarse as hay; and every nerve and sinew grew thick and unsightly to the view. The berry's power had changed him into a child of man; and he now began to scream and cry and make such direful noises, as would have drowned the united sound of a thousand elfin voices."

"Ah woe is me!" exclaimed Julius, sobbing; "if I had not so madly sucked the deadly juice of that coarse berry, I still should feed on the perfumed air, and never have known vile human fare."

Then the glow-worm, greatly excited, whispered to him :—

"Know, child beloved, I am thy mother:—the elfin queen, entranced with joy at finding thee, dear human boy! Alas! that thou shouldst so gigantic be and I so very small, that we cannot rush into each other's arms to seal the charms of meeting by a kiss! Thou bearest the light upon thy brow that dull-eyed mortals cannot see; but we have found thee, child, and now from the magic thrall both we and those shall soon be free.

"List, and hear me, while I tell how thou may'st unbind the spell. First, thou must the white cross find; which, when withdrawn from us by Heaven, was to a holy hermit given. Wandering in the north, he bore it,—toiling in the south, he wore it,—whilst many a wonder by its power he wrought : and when his pious mission the holy man had ended, he took it to a church where as a relic 'tis suspended. The church full often hast thou seen when wandering in the forest green ; and thither must thou go this night, nor sound nor sight must thy heart affright, and nought must make thee in thy purpose falter,—but boldly take the cross from the high altar. Nought of evil shall come to thee—'tis only fear that can undo thee; for the Butter-fly King will strive, from fright, to make thee turn again, and all thy hopes our race to right, by magic to render vain. The cross hangs to a rosary, and a lamp burns before it unceasingly. Now, off to thy work without delay, and to the chapel gate on thy steps we will wait, to light thee on thy way."

Then up sprang Julius joyously. "How light feels my bosom, my heart how strong!—'tis as if I had known this all along. Hurrah! I'm the Elfin King. Little care I for the false butterfly. The white cross from the church I'll quickly bring. Come, light me, light me on the track!—triumphant soon you will see me back!"

Then his mother, attended by all the other glow-worms, lighted him on his way, and he followed with bounding steps. They drew up outside the church-door whilst he entered alone; cold blasts blowing down upon him from the lofty, pale, glimmering dome. Onward he went without fear. A great hideous bat fluttered round his head twittering: "Return; go not to the altar high, for if to spurn my threat thou dare, I will stick my claws into thy hair, and tear thy locks out one by one, until with pain thou shalt cry and moan, and thy curly head shall be bald as a stone."

"For this coarse straw I little care, soon I shall have much finer hair," said Julius;—and on he went cheerfully.

Next came a great black owl, with very sharp beak and claws, and sparkling eyes. He also fluttered round Julius, till the tips of his frightful wings scratched the boy's forehead, whilst he screeched aloud: "Return,

return, go quickly back, else thy blue eyes I will claw and hack till thou shalt cry in agony, and blinded thou shalt be."

"My eyes are not so very fine; I shall soon have some that will softer shine," answered Julius, as he approached the altar before which stood the undying lamp.

Then suddenly up rose a pale rattling skeleton, round whose scraggy neck hung the rosary with the white cross; and as the spectre glared at him from its eyeless sockets, it said with a hollow voice: "Forbear, forbear, audacious boy! Ere that cross thy prize can be, thou must conquer it from me. I am Death, the strong, the mighty; no mortal yet has vanquished me."

Julius shrank, and for a moment hesitated; but he heard his mother whisper from the church-door: "Away with fear, 'tis all delusion, magic art and vain illusion. Fearlessly upon him look—thy gaze the phantom cannot brook; by thy mild look and gentle eye, thou shalt win the victory. Seize the cross and banish fear, the spectre so shall disappear."

Julius then regained courage; he rushed up to the skeleton and grasped the cross! Instantly the phantom vanished, and all was still around him. He returned thoughtfully and without running. The elves were waiting for him at the door, and lighted him back to the place whence they had come. He then set up the cross on a little mossy hillock ; and all the glow-worms formed themselves into a circle round it, and prayed and sang songs of gratitude,—which, however, were inaudible to Julius.

His mother then seated herself on the tip of his ear, and whispered: "Ere our deliverance full can be, thou must once more become as we. The charmed drink already in thy veins is working. Four elements it contains: the sound of my voice, the forest's cool air, the fragrance of the flowers by night, and the brightly-coloured light which thou didst so eagerly inhale whilst we were dancing round thee. If that thou dost desire once more thy coarse fat body to restore to its once delicate form, then know, thou must henceforth to eat forego, save of the rays from the bright stars beaming, save of the sweets from the young flowers streaming. Now, sleep in peace, and by to-morrow's light thy limbs will be more delicate and slight."

Julius stretched himself on the moss, and slept. The

next morning he did not waken until it was late; and then he felt himself so wonderfully light that he fancied he must be able to jump as high as the heavens. In order to try his strength, he made a spring, intending to clear a little ant-heap which he mistook for a hill; but he fell in the midst of it, and had great difficulty in extricating himself, so small had he already become. He ate nothing all that day; and at night, was lighted to bed by the glow-worms who danced round him whilst he slept.

On the second day he had already become so diminutive that he was obliged to stand on tip-toe to smell a yellow primrose. When he awoke on the third morning, he saw high in the heavens the sun with its golden disk surrounded by silver-white rays. But it did not dazzle him in the least, let him look at it as steadfastly as he would; and, to his great surprise, he observed an entirely green rainbow which stretched down from it to the earth. He went close to it; and then discovered that the rainbow was only a thick stem, which he grasped with both hands, and by a great effort shook,—when behold! the sun moved a little out of its place. He could not help laughing at himself; for he now perceived that what he had taken for the yellow

67

sun with the white rays and the green rainbow, was only a large daisy on its stalk.

He had now diminished to the proper dimensions of an elf. When evening came, therefore, all the glow-worms assembled round him on the moss to swear fealty to him. The peers of the realm brought with them a crown of pure star-light ore, very delicately and taste-fully wrought, with which they solemnly crowned Julius, and no sooner was the crown placed on his head, than in a moment, as if by magic touch, they were all changed into little graceful elves, and on the brow of each was a star. They then took the oath of fidelity, and Julius swore to maintain the constitution. This done, the re-joicings began, and they shouted and huzzaed until the noise was as great as that which the grass makes when it is growing in the sweet spring time.

Julius and his mother embraced and kissed each other. She could not repeat too often how pretty and slight he was, and how very much he resembled his father:—and then she shed oceans of tears for her murdered husband.

The elves rejoiced the whole night through; but when the morning dawned, they said to each other with some uneasiness: "How are we to get back to India, to our beautiful native land?" Then a light breeze murmured amongst the branches, and shook down a hundred-leaved rose, so that all its delicate curved petals were scattered to the ground—and a voice was heard, saying :

"There your carriages, light as air, you to the spicy east shall bear,—and the cross you shall find in your own bright land, already borne there by an unseen hand."

All the elves now seated themselves in the rose leaves, —Julius and his mother and the court occupying the finest. Then a gentle zephyr sprang up ; which raised all the rose leaves into the air, and wafted them softly in the morning dawn home to the east,—the elves singing :—

To India, to India, the land of our birth !
    Where the zephyrs blow lightly,
    And the flowers glow brightly,
And the atmosphere scent-laden floats o'er the earth ;
Where under the wide-spreading leaves we find shelter,
Nor care how winds whistle, nor how the storms pelter.
    Over our heads
    Their green roof spreads—

THE PRINCE OF THE GLOW-WORMS.

And safe within their vernal bowers
   We elfin spirits dance and play,
   While some soft and holy lay
Is sung by the tall and fragrant flowers
   On their green stems bending,
   And heavenward sending
Angel hymns of joyous blending.
In solemn pomp again we 'll tread,
   By our tapers' light,
   In the still dark night,
To bring to their resting-place the dead !
—Away then, away! carried swift by the wind,
At the dawning of day to our native Ind !

THE TWO MISERS.

[Hebrew.]

———•———

A MISER living in Kufa had heard that in Bassora also there dwelt a Miser — more miserly than himself, to whom he might go to school, and from whom he might learn much. He forthwith journeyed thither; and presented himself to the great master as a humble commencer in the Art of Avarice, anxious to learn, and under him to become a student. "Welcome!" said the Miser of Bassora; "we will straight go into the market to make some purchase." They went to the baker.

"Hast thou good bread?"

"Good, indeed, my masters,—and fresh and soft as butter." "Mark this, friend," said the man of Bassora to the one of Kufa,—butter is compared with bread as being the better of the two: as we can only consume a small quantity of that, it will also be the cheaper,—

and we shall therefore act more wisely, and more savingly too, in being satisfied with butter."

They then went to the butter-merchant, and asked if he had good butter.

"Good, indeed,— and flavoury and fresh as the finest olive oil," was the answer.

"Mark this also,"—said the host to his guest; "oil is compared with the very best butter, and, therefore, by much ought to be preferred to the latter."

They next went to the oil vendor :—

"Have you good oil?"

"The very best quality,—white and transparent as water," was the reply.

"Mark that too," said the Miser of Bassora to the one of Kufa ; "by this rule water is the very best. Now, at home I have a pail-full, and most hospitably therewith will I entertain you." And indeed on their return nothing but water did he place before his guest,— because they had learnt that water was better than oil, oil better than butter, butter better than bread.

"God be praised !" said the Miser of Kufa,— "I have not journeyed this long distance in vain !"

PRINCE CHAFFINCH.

[French.]

HERE was once a king and queen who ruled with the greatest kindness and simplicity imaginable; and their subjects were just such good folks as themselves, so that both parties agreed very well. As, however, there is no condition in the world which has not its cares and sorrows, so also this king and queen were not free from them; in fact, the peace of their lives was considerably disturbed by a fairy, who had patronised them from their earliest years. Fairy Grumble-do—that was her name—was incessantly finding fault, would repeat the same words a hundred times a day, and grumbled at every thing that was doing, and at all that had been done. Setting aside this little failing, she was in all other respects the best soul in the world, and it gave her the greatest satisfaction when she could oblige or serve anybody.

The union of the royal pair had hitherto proved childless, but whenever they besought Fairy Grumble-do to give them children, she invariably replied :—" Children ! what do you want children for ? To hear them squalling from morning till night, till you, as well as I, will be ready to jump out of our skins with the noise? What's the use of children ? Nobody knows what to do with them ; they only bring care and trouble ! "

Some such remarks were all the king and queen got for their entreaties; and the fairy's ill-humour, and the snuffling tone in which she uttered these speeches made them quite unbearable. The good king and queen, however, never lost their patience, so that at last the fairy lost hers, and, in a pet, she all of a sudden gratified them with seven princes at a birth.

The queen remarked in her usual mild and quiet manner, that she had now a great many children, to which Fairy Grumble-do answered, snarlingly :—" Well, you wished for children, Madam queen, and now you have got them according to your wish, and in order that you may have enough of them, I shall just double the number."

74

No sooner said than done, and the queen brought into the world seven more princes at a birth. The royal pair were now quite in trouble; fourteen princes of the blood are, in fact, no joke; for however rich one may be, fourteen princes to nurse, educate, and establish handsomely, costs a good bit of money. Fairy Grumble-do was quite right there; fourteen princes do require a good deal of waiting on, and so she found plenty to do all day, with finding fault, and scolding first this attendant, then that nursemaid, then this servant, or that preceptor; and when she once got into the children's apartment, no one could hear himself speak, for the noise she made. Still at bottom she meant very kindly, and she promised the anxious queen that she would take good care of the princes, and one day provide for them all. Those old times were very good ones, and things were managed in royal residences with great simplicity. The young princes played all day with the children of the towns-people, because they went to the same school with them, and no one had a word to say against it, which would hardly be the case now-a-days, for kings and everybody else are grown much grander than they were then.

Quite close to the palace dwelt an honest charcoal-burner, who lived in his little cottage contentedly on what he earned by the sale of his charcoal. All his neighbours esteemed him as the worthiest man in the world, and the king himself had great confidence in his capacity, and would often ask his counsel in matters of government. He was called the coal-man throughout all the country, and no one within ten miles round would have any coals but from him, so that he had to serve every household, even those of the nobility and the fairies. Wherever he carried his coals, he was a favourite, and even little children were not afraid of him, and no one ever said to them, "Behave prettily, else the charcoal-burner will take you away." After working all day at his business, he went to his little cottage at night to rest, and to enjoy his freedom, for he was sole master in the house. His wife had been long dead, and had left him only one little daughter, called Gracious; for she was the prettiest creature in the world.

He loved this child beyond all measure; and, indeed, not without reason, for a prettier little maiden could not be found on earth; in spite of the coal-smoke that enveloped her, and her poor clothing, she always appeared charming and agreeable, and no one could

76

PRINCE CHAFFINCH.   P. 76

help loving her on account of her wonderful amiability. The king's youngest son, little Prince Chaffinch, who was as sprightly as he was pretty, was extremely attached to Gracious, preferred her to all the other children of his acquaintance, and would play with no one but her, so that they were always seen together, and indeed, they could not live without one another. Meanwhile the worthy coal-man, who felt old age approaching, grew very anxious about the fate of Gracious, after he should have ceased to live; for the partiality of the king for him did not seem to him sufficient to put him at ease about her. "The king," he would say to himself, as he pondered on the subject, "has a large family of his own, and is obliged to ask so much of the fairy for his own necessities, that he surely will not have courage to put in a good word for my child. Even if he were to promise to do so, I should not depend on him. For"—thus he ever concluded his self-conferences, "the poor king, is in fact, worse off than I am; he has fourteen to provide for; I only one. His are princes; mine is only a poor burgher maid. Mine therefore will be easier to provide for. A poor girl like her can manage to get along in the world; she stands alone; but a poor prince never; hundreds hang about him, draining him, and consuming all his substance." Now, after thinking it over and over, he grew quite unhappy at heart, and he knew not what to do. So he went one day, head and heart full of care, to a very beneficent fairy, who had always behaved very kindly to him. She was called Fairy Bonbon; she it was, who, in order to please epicures, both small and great, invented those sweets which now bear her name. When the good fairy saw the coal-man in such trouble, she asked him what ailed him; and after he had given her a highly sensible reply, she promised him in good earnest, that she would take Gracious under her own care, and desired him to bring the child to her the following Sunday.

The coal-man obeyed punctually, and when the time came he made little Gracious put on her best clothes, and the new coloured little shoes he had bought for her the day before, and set off with his dear little daughter. Gracious skipped before him, then ran back to him, and took hold of his hand, saying :—" We are going to the castle, we are going to the castle!" for her father had not told her anything further about it.

When they arrived, Fairy Bonbon received them very kindly, but notwithstanding all was so fine in the castle, and that she had so many bonbons and other nice things, Gracious could not be happy when her father went away and left her behind. For the first time in her life she began to cry, and could scarcely leave off again. This touched the fairy extremely, so that she grew quite fond of Gracious, and all who were present said :—" My daughter would not cry so if she were obliged to part from me." But in time little Gracious became reconciled to her new residence, and was so obedient and docile that the good fairy Bonbon never had occasion to reprove her, nor even to tell her twice of the same thing, so that she took great delight in her.

When her father came to visit her, the pretty child always ran to meet him, and threw herself into his arms without fearing to soil the fine clothes which the fairy had given her. After kissing and caressing her dear papa to her heart's content, she always inquired after her friend, Prince Chaffinch, and sent him her best bonbons and toys. The coal-man always carried them very conscientiously to the prince, who never failed to send his thanks and a message to say how earnestly he longed to see her once again.

Thus Gracious lived till she was twelve years old, and

then Fairy Bonbon, who was extraordinarily fond of her, took her father one day into her boudoir, and desired him to be seated, as she did not like to see the old man standing up in her presence. The coal-man excused himself at first, but the fairy insisted, so that at last he was obliged to obey, although it seemed to him a very strange thing to sit down in his clothes all covered with coal-dust on a white taffeta arm-chair, and he could not think how he should manage to prevent his jacket from leaving marks on it.

At last, however, the fairy constrained him to be seated; and she then said to him, " Old friend, I love your daughter."

"Honoured madam," replied he, " you are very kind; but indeed you are much in the right, for she is a very dear child."

" I wish now to consult with you what I shall do," said the fairy; " for you must know I shall be obliged shortly to travel for a considerable time in another country."

" Ah, madam, then do have the goodness to take her along with you," rejoined the coal-man.

" That is not in my power," answered she. " I can, however, provide very well for her. Only tell me what would be most agreeable to you that I should do for her."

"Then I would most humbly beg," replied the coal-man, "that you would have the kindness to make her queen of a little kingdom, just such a one as may please your ladyship."

Though gratified by this request, the fairy represented to him, that the higher the station, the more cares and sorrows it has; but the coal-man assured her in return, that cares and sorrows are to be found everywhere, and that those of royalty are the easiest to bear.

"I do not ask of you, most gracious madam fairy," continued he, "to make me a king. I prefer remaining a charcoal-burner; that is my trade, which I understand, and as for the trade of royalty, I do not think that I understand that at all. But Gracious is still young, and she can learn it, I'll be bound for it; it cannot, after all, be so very difficult, for I see every day that people manage it one way or another."

"Well," answered Fairy Bonbon, as she dismissed him, "I will see what I can do. I must tell you before-hand, however, that Gracious will have much to suffer, and she will find it very bitter."

"Very possible, gracious Madam Bonbon," replied

he. "I also have gone through many bitter things, and have not gained very much after all, so have the kindness still to make a queen of her; I ask nothing."

With these words he took leave.

Meanwhile Fairy Grumble-do had provided for almost all the fourteen princes. She had sent some of them out into the wide world to seek their fortunes, whereby they had at last succeeded in obtaining kingdoms, and the rest she had wedded to rich princesses, so that at least they were safe from want. For little Prince Chaffinch, as yet, however, she had done nothing; so she came one day to court in her usual agreeable humour, and found papa and mamma caressing and fondling their child.

"Ha," said she, "that is a properly spoiled young gentleman, who will never be good for anything all his days. I lay any wager he does not know A from B. Repeat me your yesterday's lesson, sir, at once, and if you miss a single word, you shall have a proper whipping."

Chaffinch immediately repeated his lesson, which, as usual, he had learnt perfectly, and went through his examination in a style which was quite wonderful for his age. The king and queen did not dare to let their gratification at this appear, for fear thereby of redoubling Madam Grumble-do's ill-humour, for she now maintained that the instruction given to the prince was not worth a farthing; that it was far too difficult and too learned for him.

She then turned to the king and queen: "Pray, what is the reason of your never having asked me to do anything for him yet? It is just your way. I have been worried into providing for all your other simpletons—they are the most stupid kings reigning; but that one, of whom something might perhaps be made, is to be spoilt by you, just because he is your nest-quackel. But I will not allow it any longer. He shall go out, and directly too. He is a fine youth, and it would be a shame to leave him any longer with you. I will not have to reproach myself with that; folks know that I am your friend, and they shall not have to say that I encourage you in your follies. Now, let us have no words about it; let us consider together what is best to be done, for I am not at all obstinate; I am always willing to listen to good advice."

The king and queen said very politely that she must decide on that, for she knew very well that her will was theirs.

"Well then," replied Fairy Grumble-do, "he must travel; travelling gives a young man a proper finish."

"Very true," said both king and queen with one voice. "But," continued the queen, "consider that the outfit of the other princes very much exhausted our coffers, and that just at present we have not the means wherewith to send out Chaffinch in a style befitting his rank. It would be very unpleasant for folks to say, 'That is the son of a king, and he travels like a poor student.'"

"So, that's your vanity, is it?" growled the fairy; "truly vanity is vastly becoming to people who have fourteen children. You say the other youths have cost you so much; then, I did nothing for them, I suppose; you leave all that out of your calculation. Pray, what did they cost you? Just their bits of meals when they were at home, and a couple of boxes full of clothes when they went on their travels. Who found all the rest? Not you, truly; it was I; but you are a pair of ungrateful creatures, so you are."

"Kind madam," answered the queen, "my husband has set down all the expenses in the account-book; you can convince yourself."

"A pretty thing, indeed," rejoined Fairy Grumble-do. "Pray, how long has it been in fashion for a king to keep a debtor-and-creditor ledger like a tailor? That sounds vastly regal, truly. What is the use of all the good counsels I have given you, if this is the way you conduct yourselves. Shame on you! However, I will not worry myself, but I will put an end to the thing at once. The youth is as giddy as a butterfly, and wherever he goes he will be telling everybody 'I am a prince and my father is a king.' Is it not so, eh?"

"Dearest madam godmamma," interposed Prince Chaffinch, "I will say nothing but what you desire me to say."

"Wait till you are asked, Master Pert!" rejoined she; "you shall say nothing at all, and I'll take care to prevent you from opening your self-sufficient beak. Only wait a moment!"

As she blustered out this, she touched him with her wand, and transformed him into the little bird which to this day bears his name. The king and queen wished to embrace him, but there was no doing that any longer now he had become so small; they could only set him on their fingers. They had scarcely time to kiss him even, for he flew off, in obedience to the fairy, who pronounced

85

these terrible words : " Fly where thou canst ; do what thou must."

The tears of the king and queen, it is true, did move Fairy Grumble-do a little, but she would not let that be seen, and merely said, " That is just like you ; you are served quite rightly," and then she seated herself in her post-chaise, which was drawn by seven magpies and seven cocks, who made a shocking noise ; and off she drove in a very ill-humour to the assembly of the fairies, which was held that very day.

By chance she was seated next to the kind fairy Bonbon, and as the mouth is prompt to speak about that of which the heart is full, she related to the latter all the trouble she had had in providing suitably for the fourteen princes ; during which narration she did not fail to give it well to the king and queen, just as if they were present. At last she asked her colleague if she happened to have a kingdom or a princess to bestow on Prince Chaffinch.

Fairy Bonbon, notoriously the best-hearted creature in the world, who was quite averse to this incessant scolding, told her that she would willingly undertake to find one, but only on condition that Fairy Grumble-do should not interfere in it, and permit her first to put the young prince to the proof.

"Do what you please," resumed the latter, speaking more through her nose than ever—"do what you please, so that I hear no more about the matter."

She then renounced all her fairy rights over Prince Chaffinch, and then drew up a formal contract, which they both signed with their own hands in presence of the lawyer and of competent witnesses.

Bonbon, who soon perceived that her two protegé's were well suited to each other, resolved to look still closer into the matter, in order to proceed the more securely, and to make Gracious truly happy. But she was much pressed for time as the day of her departure was irrevocably fixed, and was rapidly approaching. She had therefore to devise some means by which the two might have an opportunity of working out their own destiny by faith and truth. The first thing she did, therefore, was to catch Chaffinch, whose natural sprightliness caused him to delight greatly in flying about, to shut him up in a cage, and bring him to her castle.

As soon as the young enchanted prince beheld Gracious he was very joyful, flapped his wings, and tried with all his strength to get out of the cage and fly to her. He was delighted, however, when she said to him, "Good morrow, my little bird; dear, how beautiful you are!" Yet he felt grieved at the same time that he could only answer her by his twittering, but he did that as agreeably as he could, and made every demonstration of tenderness that a bird could. This greatly touched Gracious, though she did not in the least suspect the truth; and she said, quite unreservedly to Bonbon, that she had always been particularly fond of chaffinches; at which the kind fairy smiled, and made her a present of the enchanted prince, on condition of her taking care of him as of the apple of her eye. This Gracious willingly promised, and did so too with the greatest satisfaction.

When the day came for the fairy to depart, she said to Gracious, "Take great care of the chaffinch, and never let him out of the cage; for were he to fly away, I should be extremely displeased."

She then entered her carriage, which was made of silver-paper. Her castle, her garden, her domestics and her horses, all went off through the air with her, and Gracious now remained alone and sorrowful in her little house of porcelain, which assuredly was very pretty; but what avails prettiness when one is sad? The garden was constantly full of cherries, gooseberries, oranges, and, in short, of all imaginable fruits, always ripe and well-flavoured; the oven, of biscuits, tea-cakes, and macaroons; the store-room, of sweetmeats and confectionery of all kinds: and all these good things might well have consoled her, but she could not enjoy them, for the little chaffinch slept unbrokenly in his cage. She visited him every five minutes, but still he did not wake, and she mentally reproached the fairy with having robbed her of such sweet consolation. At last, after trying vainly every means of awaking him, she resolved to examine him closer, to see if she could not discover the fairy's secret.

It is true she did not arrive at this resolution without that uneasiness and self-reproach which one always feels when acting contrary to an express command. She even opened the cage several times, and then shut it again suddenly; but at last she blamed herself for her timidity, summoned courage, and took the bird in her pretty little hand. No sooner was he out of the cage than he flew out and perched on the window-frame, which most unfortunately she had not closed, so little had she thought on what might occur to her. Embarrassed and alarmed, she endeavoured to catch him again.

The chaffinch flew into the garden, and she jumped out of the window, which fortunately was on the ground-floor; but such was her anxiety that she would have sprung out, had it been on the fourth story. Calling him by the prettiest and tenderest names, she sought to entice him, but whenever she fancied she would certainly catch him, off he flew, from the garden to the field, and on towards a great forest, which filled her with despair, for she knew perfectly well how useless it would be to hunt after a chaffinch in a forest; when suddenly, the bird, of which she had never lost sight, turned into the prince as she had seen him when she was a child.

"What! is it you, Prince Chaffinch," exclaimed she,—"and you fly me?"

"Yes, it is I, lovely Gracious," replied he; "but a supernatural force obliges me to keep far from thee; I desire to approach thee, and cannot."

They now indeed perceived that they were always at least four paces distant from each other. Gracious, enraptured at again seeing the prince, forgot how disobedient she had been to the fairy, and her fears grew calm, in proportion as love took possession of her heart.

As neither of them dared return to the little dwelling which they had left, nor indeed did they know the way back, they went into the wood, gathered nuts, and asked each other a hundred questions as to what had occurred since they last met. They then rejoiced at their good fortune in being again together, and refreshed themselves with the hope of now remaining near each other. At last they saw a peasant's hut, and went to it to request shelter for the night, that they might resolve on what they should do the next day.

The prince, when they got very near to it, said to Gracious, "Wait here under this great tree, whilst I go and reconnoitre the house and its inhabitants."

When he got there, he found a woman who was sweeping before her door, and of her he inquired if she would receive him and Gracious for the night into her house.

The old woman answered: "You seem to me to be two disobedient children, who have run away from your parents, and do not deserve to meet with compassion."

Chaffinch was, to say the truth, a little embarrassed by this remark, but he said all sorts of flattering things to her, and offered to labour for her; in short, he spoke like a lover willing to make any sacrifice for his beloved, for he began to fear that Gracious would have to pass the night in the wood, exposed to the wolves, of which he had heard such terrible stories.

Whilst he was trying to persuade the hard-hearted old woman, it happened that the giant Koloquintius, the king, or to speak more accurately, the tyrant of the whole district, who was hunting in the wood, rode past the very spot where Gracious was waiting. He thought her surprisingly charming, and was a good deal astonished that she did not think him equally so, nor appear to be enchanted at seeing him. Without saying a word to her, he desired one of his suite to lift up the little maiden and place her under his arm, which being done, he set spurs to his horse, and galloped off to his capital city.

The cries and lamentations of Gracious did not move him in the least, and she now—when it was too late— repented of her disobedience. Her cries disturbed Prince Chaffinch and the old woman in their conversation; the former ran towards the spot where he had left Gracious; but who can describe his grief, when he saw her under the giant's arm! Had he been there at

92

the right moment, he would have endeavoured at the risk of his life to prevent that deed of violence, but now he had nothing to do but to follow her. But night overtook him, he lost sight of her, and quite exhausted, he sat down to give free course to his grief and tears.

As he sat, he perceived, close to him, a little light, like that of a glow-worm. At first he paid no attention to it, but the light grew larger and larger, and at last changed into a female clothed in a brown garment, who said to him : " Console thyself, Chaffinch, do not give way to despair; take this flask, which is made of a gourd, and this shepherd's pouch; thou wilt find them always filled with whatever thou desirest to eat and drink. Take also this hazel-rod, and when thou hast need of me, put it under thy left foot and call me; I will always come to thy assistance. This little dog is commanded never to leave thee, thou may'st want him. Farewell, Chaffinch. I am the kind Bonbon."

Chaffinch was already greatly moved by these gifts, but when he heard the name which Gracious had so often pronounced, he sank at the fairy's feet, embraced her knees, and cried: " Ah, beneficent lady, Gracious has been carried off, how is it possible that your Highness did not hasten to deliver her ? "

"I know what has befallen her," replied Bonbon,—
"but she was disobedient, I want not to know anything
about her; thou alone must aid her."

At these words, the light and the fairy disappeared,
and Chaffinch sat in such darkness that he could not
see his hand when he held it before his eyes. He was
however, much comforted by thinking that he could
now be of assistance to Gracious, though fear and anxiety
still tormented him greatly, and his new friend, the
little dog, was unable by all its caresses to divert him.

At last, the longed-for day dawned, and he was
now able to continue his wanderings. Towards evening
he arrived at the chief city, where he found everybody
talking only of Gracious' beauty, and of Koloquintius'
passion for her. It was said that the giant was very
shortly to marry her, and that he had already commenced
building a palace for the new queen. This news cut
little Chaffinch to the heart.

When the people with whom he was speaking, saw
his shepherd's pouch, they said, "This is a handsome
little shepherd, why should he not tend the king's
sheep? His majesty is in want of a shepherd, and
would no doubt confer that high office upon him."

The desire of being near Gracious determined

Chaffinch to take this hint. He therefore presented himself before Koloquintius, who regarded him attentively : as he only asked for courteous treatment, and required no wages, the king appointed him to be his own private shepherd. His new office did not, however, bring him into the vicinity of Gracious, so that he did not gain much thereby. He only learned that Koloquintius was very melancholy because Gracious did not respond to his love, and this comforted him a little.

Some days after, as he was following his sheep, he saw a state carriage, attended by twelve negroes on horseback, with drawn swords, quit the palace, and in this carriage sat Gracious. Little Chaffinch heroically threw himself in the way of the horses, held his shepherd's staff before them, and thundered out with his feeble voice, "Wretches ! whither go you ?"

When Gracious saw her Chaffinch in such great peril, she fainted, and he also lost his senses. When he came to himself, he seized his hazel wand,—instantly the good Bonbon stood beside him.

"Ah, kind lady !" said he, " Gracious is lost, perhaps already dead !"

" No," replied the Fairy, " Koloquintius is only sending her to the tower because he is furious at her coldness to him, and her fidelity to thee. Consider how thou may'st get thither also; think for thyself. I will assist thee; only I cannot change thee into a bird, because thou hast already been one; at all events Gracious will have much to suffer, for the tower is a terrible prison, but it serves her quite right,—why was she disobedient?"

Thereupon she vanished.

The prince, in great distress, conducted (that is, his little dog did it for him) the king's sheep along the road which the carriage that conveyed Gracious had taken, and he shortly came within sight of the terrible tower, which stood in the midst of a great plain, and had neither windows nor doors, only a small aperture at the top; it could only be entered by a subterranean passage, the entrance to which was concealed in a neighbouring mountain, which it was necessary to point out to those who were unacquainted with it. Prince Chaffinch was very glad that he had received such a clever little dog from the fairy, for it did all his business for him, whilst he kept his eyes constantly fixed on the tower. The more he considered, the more he was convinced of the impossibility of getting into it; but love, which conquers all difficulties, at last inspired him with a plan.

96

After he had lamented a thousand times that he could not again be a bird, he besought the good fairy Bonbon, to change him into a paper kite. She granted his request, and conferred on his little dog the power of effecting the transformation; he barked three times, took the hazel-rod in his mouth, and touched the prince with it, who now became a paper kite, with power to resume his own form as occasion might require. Then, by the aid of his faithful dog, the prince succeeded in first reaching the top of the tower, and then getting within it to Gracious.

It was no small delight to her to hear the assurances of his love, nor was it a less one to him to hear the same from her, and gratefully did he express his acknowledgments—for, in spite of his altered form, he still retained his speech. The pleasures of this conversation would have caused him to forget altogether that he could not remain for ever in the tower, and that he must feed his flock, if the little dog, more faithful to duty than he, had not pulled the string to which he was fastened, just at the right moment.

Chaffinch no sooner reached the ground, than he resumed his own figure, and drove the flock back again to the royal sheepfold; but his whole thought was on the pleasure of flying to his dear Gracious, which caused him to be greatly vexed whenever the wind blew too strongly for him to be able to ascend, and Gracious shared in his grief.

Thus they went on for some time; but as there are always to be found people who interfere in what does not concern them, others who want to know everything, and still more, others who are always striving to show themselves very obliging to the great and rich; it was soon observed by some of these, that the kite very often descended from the dark tower. Koloquintius was informed of it; he instantly went thither, in order to punish the audacious persons who dared to convey letters in this manner to Gracious, for it never struck him that the kite could serve for any other purpose. Chaffinch and Gracious were just in the most interesting conversation, when they were disturbed from it by the vehemence with which the faithful dog pulled back the prince, for Koloquintius ran up to him, exclaiming vehemently: "Where is the shepherd, where is the shepherd? I must kill him, because he has not informed me of what is going on here."

The dog, fearing that Koloquintius might take the string out of his mouth, and so get the prince into his own hands, let the kite fly, which was carried far away by the wind, which happened to be very high, and catching up the gourd flask, and the shepherd's pouch, ran off to his master, whom he loved very much, and who now had resumed his own figure. Favoured by the approaching night, they concealed themselves in the mountains, whilst Koloquintius, foaming with rage, was obliged to drive his sheep home himself. In order that no one should approach little Gracious, he caused his whole army to draw up on the plain, and commanded them to watch day and night, that no one whatsoever should approach the tower.

Prince Chaffinch beheld all this from the high mountain where he and the dog had placed themselves, and again appealed to Bonbon for assistance. She immediately appeared, but when he begged her to give him an army, wherewith to combat that of Koloquintius, she vanished without saying a word, and only left him a rod, and a great bag of sugar-plums. When one is sad, and one's heart is heavy, one is not much inclined to take a joke; and at first Chaffinch thought she meant to make a jest of him; but when he reflected how kindly she had always acted towards him, his confidence in her returned, and he took the bag of sugar-plums under his arm, and the rod in his right hand, and accompanied by his faithful dog, advanced valiantly to meet the foe. As he came nearer to them, he remarked that they grew gradually less and less, and that their lines contracted; and when he got so near that they could hear him speak, he perceived, to his no small astonishment, that all these formidable soldiers, and moustached grenadiers, had shrunk into children of four years old, so that he cried aloud to them:— "Yield this moment, or you shall all be whipped."

Then the whole army began to cry, and ran away, pursued by the dog, who soon threw them into complete disorder. To as many as he could catch, Chaffinch gave sugar-plums, whereupon they immediately swore to obey him.

Encouraged by their example, the others soon returned, and they one and all submitted to Chaffinch; so that Koloquintius was now left without an army to defend him, whilst the prince had a formidable one; for as soon as they submitted voluntarily to him, they all recovered their former size and strength.

By this time Koloquintius arrived; but he no sooner saw Prince Chaffinch than he likewise lost his giant form and strength, and became not merely a little child like the others, but a very little dwarf, with crooked legs. The prince caused a dragoon's cap, and a gay-coloured garment, with hanging sleeves, to be made for him, and destined him to be train-bearer to Gracious, and to attend upon her in her apartments.

After this great victory the first care of Chaffinch was to hasten to the dark tower, in order to set his beloved free. After so many sufferings and sorrows, her joy at finding herself again free was indescribable. As they reached the city, Fairy Bonbon and Fairy Grumble-do also arrived there from opposite directions. The two lovers now expressed to them their warmest gratitude, and requested them to decide their fate. Fairy Grumble-do replied :—

"I assure you I have never troubled my head about you; I should have been a fool indeed to concern myself with such light ware. You are nothing to me, for the rest of your blessed family give me quite enough to do without you. Such a parcel of relations as belong to Prince Chaffinch, never did king's son, in all the wide world, possess before; a pretty brood truly."

"Dear madam and sister," interposed Fairy Bonbon, in the gentlest manner, "you know our agreement; only have the kindness to cause the king and queen, and the worthy coal-man, to come hither, and I will undertake the rest."

"So," rejoined Madam Grumble-do, "I am to be wedding coach-man—am I?"

"Oh! not so, dear madam and sister," answered Bonbon; "you have only to say if it is not agreeable to you, and I will go myself."

"A pretty errand—a dog's errand," snarled Madam Grumble-do, who nevertheless ordered her car to turn into a coach, and to bring thither the desired guests. Whilst Bonbon, Gracious, and Chaffinch, were caressing each other, Fairy Grumble-do met the Court-dwarf, Kolo-

quintius, who came in her way just at the right moment,
—for every one was welcome to her so that she had
some one to scold,—and she gave it him prettily on the
text of his vanity and self-love.

"Now you are punished," said she, "and nobody
pities you; but, on the contrary, you are the laughing-
stock of all your former subjects; that, however, you
have always been, though formerly they ridiculed you
secretly, and in whispers; now, however, they do it
loudly, and in the market-place; it will do you a deal
of good."

So she continued to abuse him till the arrival of the
king and queen, when she let him go and turned to them.

"You need not trouble yourselves to thank me for
anything; it was not I who sent for you, and indeed I
am very sorry you are come, for now there will be no
getting rid of you again.   Good counsel would be
thrown away upon you now, you irrational creatures. "

She then perceived the old coal-man, and exclaimed:—
" A pretty father-in-law that, for a prince."

The coal-man was not the sort of person to take such
an address pleasantly, and would soon have given her a
rough answer, but that the good Fairy Bonbon came up
and begged the company to walk into the house.   But

Fairy Grumble-do did not like that neither; the general joy made her peevish.

Gracious embraced her dear father a thousand times, who all this while had not suffered any privation, for Bonbon had made him a present of the porcelain house in which she had often received the king and queen. These fondled their little Chaffinch, and willingly consented to his marriage with Gracious, when proposed to them by Bonbon. The subjects of Koloquintius were absolved from the oath they had sworn to him, and acknowledged Prince Chaffinch as their lawful monarch. Thus did the pretty prince obtain a fine kingdom and a charming wife.

Chaffinch and Gracious long governed in peace and happiness, and had a great many dear children, who also became kings and queens, for a good and pretty daughter makes not alone her own happiness, but also that of her parents, and her husband.

THE WOLF AND THE NIGHTINGALE.

[Swedish.]

———◆———

IN ancient times, when matters went on in the world very differently from what they now do, there reigned a king in Scotland who had the loveliest queen that ever graced a throne. Her beauty and amiability were such, that her praise was sung by every minstrel and tale-teller, and they called her the Scottish phœnix. This fair queen bore to her husband two children, a son and a daughter, and then died in the prime of her youth.

The king mourned for her many years, and could not forget her; he even said that he would never marry again. But human resolutions are unstable, and can never be depended on; and after the lapse of years, when the children were already grown up, he took to himself a second wife. The new queen was an evil-disposed woman, and made indeed a stepmother to the king's children. Yet the prince and princess were mirrors of grace and loveliness, and this was the cause of their stepmother's hatred of them; for the people, who loved the memory of the former queen, were constantly praising the young people, but never said anything about her; and whenever she appeared in public with the young princess, they always applauded and welcomed the latter, exclaiming, " She is good and fair like her mother." This roused her jealousy; she was full of spite towards them, and pondered how she might play them some evil trick; but she concealed the malignity of her heart under the mask of friendliness, for she dared not let the king perceive that she was ill-disposed towards them, and the nation would have stoned her and torn her in pieces if she had done them any harm.

The princess, who was called Aurora, was now fifteen years of age, blooming as a rose, and the fairest princess far and near. Many kings' sons, princes and counts, courted her and sought her hand; but she replied to them all, " I prefer my merry and unfettered girlhood to any lover," and thereupon they had nothing to do but to return from whence they came.

At last, however, the right one came. He was a prince from the East, a handsome and majestic man, and to him she was betrothed with the consent and approbation of the king and of her stepmother. Already the bridal wreath was twined; musicians were hired for the dance, and the whole nation rejoiced at the approaching nuptials of the fair Princess Aurora. But far other thoughts were in the queen's heart, and with threatening gestures she said to herself, "I will hire musicians who shall play a very different tune, and those feet shall dance elsewhere than in the bridal chamber. For," continued she, "this throws me quite in the shade, and my sun must set before this Aurora; especially now that she is going to have such a stately man for her husband, and will give descendants to her father, for I am childless. The nation, too, delights in her, and receives her with acclamation, but takes no note of me. Yet I am the queen: yes, I am the queen, and soon all shall know that it is I who am queen, and not Aurora."

And she meditated day and night how she might ruin the princess and her brother; but not one of her wicked plans succeeded, for they were too well guarded by their attendants, who valued them like the apple of their eye, and never left them day nor night, because of the dear love they bore to their mother, the departed queen.

At length the bridal day arrived, and the queen having no more time to lose, bethought herself of the most wicked art she knew, and approaching the young people in the most friendly way possible, begged them to go with her into the rose-garden, where she would show them a wonderfully beauteous flower which had just opened. Willingly they went with her, for the garden was close to the palace, and no one suspected any evil, for it was only mid-day, and the king and the grandees of the land were all assembled in the great hall of the palace where the nuptials were to be solemnised.

The queen led her step-children to the furthermost corner of the garden where grew her flowers, till they came beneath a dark yew tree, where she pretended to have something particular to show to them. Then she murmured to herself some words in a low tone, broke off a branch from the tree, and with it gave some strokes on the backs of the prince and princess. Immediately they were transformed. The prince, in the shape of a raging wolf, sprang over the wall and ran into the forest; and the princess as a grey bird, called a nightingale, flew into a tree and sang a melancholy air.

THE WOLF AND THE NIGHTINGALE.

So well did the queen play her part, that no one suspected anything. She ran shrieking to the castle, and with rent clothes and dishevelled hair sank on the steps of the hall, acting as if some great disaster had befallen her, and by the king's command her women carried her to her chamber. A full quarter of an hour passed ere she came to herself. Then she assumed an attitude of grief, wept, and exclaimed, "Ah, poor Aurora, what a bridal day for thee! Ah, unfortunate prince!"

After repeatedly exclaiming in this manner, she at length related that a band of robbers had suddenly burst into the garden, and had forcibly torn the royal children from her arms, and carried them off; that they had struck herself to the ground and left her half dead; and she then showed a swelling on her forehead, to produce which she had purposely hit her head against a tree. They all believed her words, and the king commanded all the great lords, and counts, and knights, and squires, to mount their horses and pursue the robbers. They traversed the forest in all directions, and visited every cave, and rock, and mountain, for at least three miles round the palace, but they could not find a trace of either the robbers or the prince and princess. The king, however, could not rest, and caused further search and enquiries to be made, for weeks and months; and he sent messengers into all the countries he could think of; but all was in vain, and at length it was as if the prince and princess had never been in existence, so entirely had they disappeared.

The old king, however, thought that the robbers had been tempted by the fine jewels that the prince and princess wore on the wedding day, and that they had stripped them of those and then murdered them, and buried their bodies in some secret place: this so grieved him that he shortly after died. On his deathbed, as he had no children, he bestowed his kingdom on his wife, and besought his subjects to be true and obedient to her as they had been to him. They gave their promise, and acknowledged her as queen, more out of love for him than for her.

Thus four years passed away, when, in the second year after the king's death, the queen began to govern with great rigour; and with the treasures the king had left behind him, she hired foreign soldiers whom she brought over the sea to guard her and to keep watch over the palace; for she knew that she was not beloved by her subjects, and she said, "That they should now do out of fear what they would not do for love."

110

THE WOLF AND THE NIGHTINGALE.

And so it came to pass, that from day to day she became more hated by every one, but nobody durst show his hate, for the slightest whisper against her was punished with death. Nevertheless, the murmurs and whispers still went on; and it was commonly said among the people, that the queen had a hand in the children's disappearance; for, in truth, there were plenty of persons who, on account of her sharp eyes and her affected love for the children, suspected her of evil practices against them. These murmurs, so far from dying away, went on increasing; but the queen cared not for them, and thought "they will remain the brutes into which I have transformed them, and no one will deprive me of the crown." However, things turned out otherwise than she expected.

Meanwhile the poor royal children led a sorry life. The prince had fled to the forest as a grey wolf, and was obliged to conduct himself like a wolf, and howl like one too, and by day to wander about in desolate places, and to prowl about at night like a thief; for wolfish fear had also sprung up in his heart. And also, he was obliged to live like other wolves, on all sorts of prey—on wild animals and birds, and in the dreary winter-time he was often obliged to content himself with a mouse, and live on very short commons, and with chattering teeth, to make his bed amongst the hard cold stones. And this certainly was very different from the princely mode of life to which he had been accustomed previous to his being driven into this wild savage misery.

He had, however, one peculiarity, which was, that he only destroyed and devoured animals, and never desired to take human blood. Yet there was *one* after whose blood he did thirst, and that was the wicked woman who had transformed him; but she took very good care never to go where she might be within reach of that wolf's teeth. It must not, however, be supposed that the prince, who was now a wolf, still preserved human reason. No; all had grown dark within him, and under the form of the beast as which he was condemned to scour the forest, he had also very little more than brute understanding. It is true, a dim instinct often drew him towards the royal residence and its gardens, as though he had cause to expect that he should find prey there; but he had no clear remembrance of the past: how indeed should it have lasted under a wolf's skin? At those moments when he felt the impulse, he was always also seized with unusual fierce-

112

ness; but as soon as he came within a thousand paces
of the spot, a cold shudder passed through him and
compelled him to retire. This was the effect of the
queen's magic art, which enabled her to keep him
banished from her to just that distance, and no further.

She, however, did all in her power to destroy him,
and caused her attendants to hunt very frequently in
the forest which surrounded the castle, thinking that it
was most probable that he was still there. On this
account, twice in almost every week, she caused noisy
hunts and battues after wolves and foxes to be held
there; and, as a pretext for these, she kept a great many
pretty deer there, of which our royal wolf did not fail
to devour as many as he could catch. He, however,
always contrived to escape the danger, although the
dogs often had their claws in the hair of his back, and
the hunters aimed many a shot at him. He concealed
himself for the moment, and when the noise ceased and
the bugles no longer resounded, he returned to the
thicket, which was close to the castle, and lay in the
sunny spots where, as a boy and youth, he had often
played. Still he knew nothing of the past, but it was
a mysterious love that drew him thither.

The Princess Aurora as we have said had flown up

into a tree, being transformed into a nightingale. But her soul had not become dark beneath its light feathery garb, like the prince's within the wolf's hide; and she knew much more than he, both of her own self and of men, only she was deprived of the power of speech. But she sang all the more sweetly in her solitude, and often so beautifully, that the beasts skipped and leaped with delight, and the birds gathered round her, and the trees and flowers rustled and bent their heads. I think the very stones might have danced had they but had the power to love, but their hearts were too cold. Men would soon have remarked the little bird, and much talk would have arisen about her, but some secret power withheld them from entering the wood, so that they never heard the nightingale sing.

I have already related how the queen persecuted the poor royal wolf with hunts and battues, so that he was the innocent cause of great trouble and inconvenience to the whole wolvine family. As great evil too befel the little birds, and in those days of tyranny, it was a great misfortune to be born either a thrush, a linnet, or a nightingale, in the neighbourhood of the castle. For the queen, after the death of the king had thrown all the power into her own hands, suddenly pretended to

114

have an illness of so peculiar a kind, that not only were the cries, cawing, and chattering of birds of prey insupportable to her, but even the sweetest twittering and warbling of the merry little birds affected her unpleasantly; and in order to make people believe this, she fainted on two occasions when she heard them sing.

This, however, was only a deception; her wicked aim was to kill the little nightingale, if by chance it should still frequent those groves and gardens. She knew full well that the little bird could not approach within a hundred paces of the castle, for she had cast her witch-spell upon her, as well as upon her brother. Under the pretext of this nervous sensibility to tender and delicate sounds, war was waged, not only against the pretty little royal nightingale, but against all the warblers in the vicinity. They were all proscribed and outlawed, and the queen's foresters and gamekeepers received the strictest orders to wage war against every feathered creature, and not to spare even the robin : no, nor the wren, at whom no sportsman ever before fired shot.

This terrible hatred of the queen's was a misfortune for the whole feathered race, not only for those which lived at large in the woods and groves, but even for those which were kept in the court-yards and houses. No feathered creature was to be found in the capital city, nor in the vicinity of the royal residence; for the people thought to pay court to the queen, and to win her favour, by imitating her caprices. There was a destruction of the feathered tribe, like another slaughter of the innocents. How many thousand canaries, goldfinches, linnets, and nightingales; nay, even how many parrots and cocka-toos, from the East and West Indies, had their necks wrung! Discordant, or melodious throats, the chat-tering, and the silent, were all menaced with one fate; it became a crime to be born either a goose, or a turkey, or a hen; and the common domestic fowls grew as scarce as Chinese golden pheasants. If the queen had waged such war against the feathered race for another ten years, they would have quite died out of the country. Indeed, not only were all the birds murdered, but scarcely did a human being now take a walk in the wood, for fear of being suspected of going thither in hopes to hear the song of a bird.

And thus it was, that no one ever heard the wondrous song of the little nightingale, except here and there a solitary sportsman, and these never spoke of it, lest they should be punished by the queen for not having shot it. And indeed, to the honour of the foresters it must be

said, that most of them followed their own good disposition, and seldom shot any little bird, but they were
obliged to fire through the forest till it rang again.
And this prevented any singing, and indeed many birds
withdrew from it altogether, on account of the incessant
noise, and never returned. The little nightingale,
however, whom heaven especially protected, so that she
escaped all the plots against her life, could not forsake
the green forest behind the castle, where, in her childhood, she had played, and skipped about, so that
although she flew away as soon as the bugles sounded,
and the halloos and hurrahs echoed through the wood,
she always returned again. And although her little
songs, as coming from a sad heart, were, for the most
part, melancholy and plaintive, still it was pleasing to
her to live so amongst the green trees, and gay flowers,
and to sing something sweet to the moon and stars;
and she was unhappy only during a few months in the
year. This was the season when autumn approached,
and she was obliged to go with the other nightingales
into foreign climes until the return of spring.

The little feathered princess confined herself then
mostly to the trees and meadows where she had sported
as a child; or in later years, with companions of her

own age, had twined wreaths and garlands; or in the happiest days of her life, had wandered in those solitudes with her beloved. Her favourite haunt was a spot where grew a thick green oak, which spread over a murmuring rivulet, and which served as a covert for the soft whispers of their love. In this place she often saw the wolf, who was also led thither by a dim feeling of the past, but she knew not that it was her unfortunate brother. Yet she grew attached to him, because he so often lay down and listened to her song as though he understood it; and she often pitied him for being a harsh and wild wolf, that could not flutter from bough to bough, like herself and other little birds. But now I must also tell of a man, who, in that solitary forest, was often a listener to the little nightingale. This man was the eastern prince, her destined bridegroom when she was yet a princess.

Whilst the old king yet lived, he loved this prince beyond all other men, because of his virtues and valour, and on his death-bed had recommended him to the queen as her counsellor and helper in all difficulties and dangers, and especially as a brave and experienced warrior. On this account, after the king's death, he had remained about the queen, solely for love of the departed. But he soon perceived that the queen hated him, and was even plotting against his life, so he suddenly withdrew from her court, and left the country. She, however, caused him to be pursued as a traitor and a fugitive, and sent forth a decree, proclaiming him an outlaw, by which every one was empowered to slay him, and bring his head, on which a high price was set, to the royal castle. But he escaped to his father's land, which lay many hundred miles to the east of the queen's palace, and there dwelt with him. Still in his heart, he found no rest, and his grief for his vanished princess never subsided. A wonderful thing also came upon him, for once every year he disappeared, without any one being able to discover whither he went. He then saddled his horse, clad himself in obscure-looking armour, and rode off so that no one could trace his path. He felt himself impelled to enter the country of the queen who had outlawed him, and to visit that forest wherein the princess had disappeared. This powerful impulse seized him annually, just before the time when the princess had vanished, and he rode through wild, desolate, and remote places, until he reached the well-known spots, where he had once wandered with his betrothed. The green oak by the rivulet, was also his favourite place. There he passed fourteen nights in tears, and prayers, and lamentations for his beloved; by day, however, he concealed himself in the neighbouring thicket. There he had often seen and heard the little nightingale, and taken delight in her wonderful, and almost bird-surpassing song.

Yet they knew nought of each other; and although the little bird always felt sadness, and longing in her heart, when the knight had ridden away, still she knew not wherefore, and her deep and languishing Tin! Tin! still resounded in his heart when he had returned to his father-land. It was, however, with him, as with most other men who love, or do something mysterious, which puzzles all around them, he was not conscious of his own secret. That he was impelled each year to ride stealthily away he knew full well—but wherefore he was so impelled, he knew not at all.

Now a long time had passed since the death of the king, and it was already the sixth year since the royal children had disappeared, and the queen lived in splendour and enjoyments, and caused the beasts to be hunted, and the birds to be shot, and was no less harsh and cruel to her subjects than to the wild inhabitants of the woods. She fancied herself almost omnipotent, and thought her good fortune and power would have no end. Still, ever since that day, she had never entered the forest, a secret terror had always withheld her. She, however, did not allow herself to dwell upon it, nor did she perceive that a magic spell was the real cause.

Now it came to pass that she had appointed a grand festival and banquet, to which were invited all the princes and princesses of the kingdom, and all the nobles and all the principal officials. In the afternoon a grand wolf hunt was to take place in the forest, at which the princes intreated her to be present. She hesitated a long while under all kinds of pretences, but at last she allowed herself to be persuaded. She, however, placed herself in a very high chariot, and bade three of her bravest warriors, completely armed, to seat themselves beside her. She also commanded several hundred armed outriders to keep before and behind and by the side of the chariot, and a long train of carriages, full of lords and ladies, followed. The wolf was never out of her thoughts, but she said to herself: "Let the wolf come; nay, let a hundred wolves even come, this brave company will soon make an end of them." Thus does providence blind even the most far-seeing and cunning when they are ripe for punishment; for it had been foretold to her by other masters of her godless art, that she must beware of the sixth year. But of that she thought not then.

And it was a fair and cheerful spring day, and they went out into the forests with trumpets and horns, and the steeds neighed and the arms clashed, and the naked swords and spears glittered in the sun; but the queen outshone them all in her most splendid attire and all her jewels, as she sat enthroned in her high chariot. Already the chase had commenced with loud huzzas and hurrahs, and the clanging horns of the hunters and the baying of the dogs. Then a lion rushed before them followed by a boar; but they did not fear, and every man stood firm at his post, and they struck down the monsters. But ere long came a still more dreadful beast, which filled them all with alarm. A tremendous wolf rushed from the thicket upon the green plain, and howled so awfully, that hunters, dogs, and riders, all took flight. The wolf ran like an arrow from a bow; nay, he did not run, but flew between the men and horses, and not one of these remembered that he was armed with a bow, and a spear, and a sword, so dreadful was the aspect of the monster, and so terrifically did he open his foaming jaws. The queen, who saw him making towards her chariot, shrieked "Help! help!" The women screamed and fainted, many a man cowardly did the same. No one thought of obstructing the wolf's course, and with one spring, he threw himself on the chariot, tore from it the proud woman, and dyed his teeth and jaws in her blood. All the rest had fled, or stood at bay.

And oh, wonder! when they endeavoured to rally their courage in order to attack, the wolf was no more to be seen, but where he had just stood appeared the form of a handsome and armed young man! The men were astonished at the magic change, but some brandished their weapons as though they would attack him as a second monster. Then suddenly an ancient lord came forward from among them, the chancellor of the kingdom, and forbade them, crying aloud, "By my grey hairs I charge you, men, hold off! You know not whom you would strike;" and before they could collect their thoughts he lay prostrate on the ground before the young man and kissed his knees and hands, saying, "Welcome, thou noble blossom of a noble sire, who again art risen in thy beauty! And rejoice, oh nation; the son of thy lawful king is returned, and he is now your king!"

At these words many hastened round and recognised the prince, and hailed him as their lord, and then the rest followed their example. They were full of terror, and astonishment, and joy, all at once, and thought no more of the demolished queen nor of the wolf; for that the prince had been the wolf they had no idea.

The young king desired them all to follow him to his father's castle; he also stopped the chase, and the horns and trumpets which just before had disturbed the woods, now resounded before him to celebrate his happy return. And when again he was within, and

124

looked down from his father's turrets, tears filled his
eyes, and he wept both in joy and sorrow; for he
remembered now all his trouble and thought of the
bitter past, which lay upon him like a heavy dream.
Then suddenly all grew clear in his mind, and he was
able to relate to the chancellor and the nobles of the
kingdom what had befallen him, and that only by the
heart's blood of the old wicked witch, who was called
his stepmother and their queen, could he be restored to
his own form. The report of this astonishing wonder
immediately circulated through the city and amongst
the whole nation; and they all rejoiced that their
beloved king's son was restored to them, and that the
queen, whom they hated, had been torn in pieces
by the fangs of the wolf which she herself had
created.

But as the prince gradually came to himself, and
bethought himself of all that had occurred, it lay heavy on
his heart where his beloved sister, the Princess Aurora,
might be, and whether she also were concealed within
the skin of some animal, or feathery covering. Then
he remembered her melancholy bridal day. And he
enquired of every one about her; but all were silent, for
none could give him any information. Then he again

became sad and full of care, but this care and sadness were soon changed into joy.

For when all the noise of the wolf-chase took place, the poor prince from the East was just then lying concealed in his thicket, and the charming little nightingale was silent, and hidden amongst the green leaves of her oak. But a mysterious sensation shot through her little heart as soon as the thirsty fangs of the wolf, her brother, were bathed in the queen's blood.

Now when the chase was over, and the forest again was still, and the sun had set, the prince came out of his dark recess, and leant sadly against the stem of the green oak, wetting the grass with his tears, as was his nightly custom; and his heart seemed more than usually oppressed with sorrow. The little bird in the branches, however, began to sing to him, as was her wont, and he fancied that she sang differently from before, and with more enigmatical significance, and almost in a human voice. And a shudder came over him, and in great agitation he exclaimed, looking up amongst the branches:—"Little bird, little bird, tell me, canst thou speak?"

And the little nightingale answered yes, just as human beings are wont to answer, and wondered at

herself that she was able to speak, and for joy she
began to weep, and for a long time was silent. Then
again she opened her little beak, and related to the
man, in an audible human voice, the whole history of
her transformation, and that of her brother, and by
what a miracle he had again become a man. For in a
moment all had become clear in her mind, as if a spirit
had whispered it all to her.

The man exulted in his heart when he heard her
tale, and he reflected much within him, and revolved
many a plan; and the little bird frolicked and flew con-
fidingly around him; yet although she now knew her
own history, and what had occurred so well, she knew
not in the least who he was. And he enticed the
little bird, and caressed it, and fondled it, and intreated
it to come with him, and he would place it in a garden
where bloomed eternal spring, and where no falcon ever
entered, and no one ever fired a shot. That would be
far pleasanter than to flutter about in wild thickets,
and have to tremble at the thought of winter, and of
hunters and birds of prey. But the little bird would
hear nothing of it, and praised freedom and her green oak,
and twittered, and sang, and fluttered round the man, who
took no heed, for he seemed plunged in other thoughts.

But see what were his thoughts! For before the little bird was aware, the man had caught her by her little feet, and hastily made off, threw himself on his horse, and flew full gallop as if pursued by a tempest to an inn which he knew in the city, not far from the castle, took there a solitary chamber, and shut himself up in it with his little bird. When the little bird saw him take out the key, and give other signs of its being her prison, she began to weep bitterly, and to implore him to let her fly; for she felt quite oppressed and wretched in the closed room, and could not but think of her green trees, and her cherished liberty. But the man took no notice of her tears and supplications, and would not let her fly.

Then the little bird grew angry, and began to transform herself into various shapes, in order to terrify the man, that he might open the doors and windows, and be glad that she should fly away. So she became in succession a tiger and lion, an otter, a snake, a scorpion, a tarantula, and at last a frightful dragon, which flew upon the man with poisonous tongue. But none of these frightened him in the least, but he kept his determination, and the little bird had all her trouble for nothing, and was obliged to become a bird again.

And the man stood in deep thought, for something he had read in ancient tales came into his mind. So he drew a knife from his pocket, and cut a gash in the little finger of his left hand, where the heart's blood flows most vigorously. And he smeared the blood on the little head and body of the bird, which he had no sooner done than the miracle was completed.

That very moment the little bird became a most lovely maiden, and the prince lay at her feet and kissed her hand, respectfully and submissively. The nightingale had now become the Princess Aurora, and recognised in the man her bridegroom, the prince from the land of the East. She was quite as young and beautiful as she was six years before, at the time of her transformation. For it is a peculiarity of transformations that the years during which persons are transformed do not add to their age, but a thousand years do not count for more than a second.

It is easy to imagine the joy of the pair; for when two loving hearts which have remained faithful to each other, meet again, after a long time, that is truly the greatest joy on earth. But they did not linger long together, but caused the king to be informed that two foreign princes from a distant land had arrived at his court, and requested his royal hospitality. Then the king went out to welcome them, and recognised his beloved sister Aurora, and his dear friend the prince from the land of the East, and was overjoyed; and the nation rejoiced with him, that all was restored as before, and that the kingdom no longer belonged to strangers.

After a few days he set the royal crown upon his head, and began to govern in his father's stead. He celebrated his sister's nuptials with the greatest magnificence, and there was dancing and feasting and knightly games. She and the prince also received from him a noble establishment both of land and attendants, so that they were able to live almost like kings. Aurora had, however, begged her brother to give her the wood, wherein as a bird she had fluttered through so many cheerful, and also sorrowful days, and this he willingly granted her. She built there a stately royal castle by the stream where she had so often sat and sung, and the thick green oak came into the centre of the palace-garden, and flourished yet many a year after her, so that her posterity still played beneath its shadow. She, however, caused a command to be issued that the wood should to all times be left in its natural majesty; she also gave peace to all little singing-birds, and forbade,

130

in the strongest manner, traps or snares to be set within those sacred precincts, or that the little creatures should be molested in any way. And her brother reigned as a great and pious king, and she and her brave husband lived in happy love till they arrived at a snow-white age, and saw their children's children around them, till at length, accompanied by the blessing of God and men, they sank softly to sleep. It has been a custom ever since, amongst their children and descendants, that the eldest prince of their house should be christened Rossignol, and the eldest princess Philomela; for she desired to establish a pious recollection through all times of the marvellous misfortune that befel her when she was transformed into a nightingale. For Rossignol means, in fact, Rose-bird—the nightingales sing chiefly in the rose season—and Philomela, friend of song. The word nightingale means, however, songstress of the night, and this is the best of all.

THE ENCHANTED CROW.

[Polish.]

———◆———

N a royal palace dwelt, once upon a time, three fair sisters, all equally young and pretty; the youngest, however, although not at all more beautiful than the two elder, was the best and most amiable of them all.

About half a mile distant from the palace, stood another lordly dwelling, but which had then fallen into decay, although it still could boast of a beautiful garden. In this garden the youngest princess took great pleasure to wander.

Once as she was walking up and down between the lime trees, a black crow hopped from under a rose-bush. The poor bird was all mutilated and bloody, and the princess was moved with compassion for him. The

132

crow no sooner perceived this than he broke out into
the following discourse :—

" No black crow am I by birth, but an unhappy
prince, suffering under a malediction, and doomed to
pass my years in this miserable condition. If thou wilt,
oh youthful princess, thou canst rescue me. But to do
so, thou must resolve to be ever my companion, to
forsake thy sisters, and to live in this castle. There is
a habitable chamber in it, wherein stands a golden bed ;
in that chamber thou must live in solitude. But forget
not, that whatsoever thou mayest see and hear by night,
thou must let no cry of fear escape thee; for if thou
shouldst utter but one single moan my tortures will be
doubled."

The kind-hearted princess did forsake her father
and sisters, and hastened to the castle ; and there dwelt
in the chamber which contained the golden bed. She
was so full of anxious thought that she could not sleep.
As midnight drew near she heard, to her no small
terror, some one creeping in. The door opened wide,
and a whole band of evil spirits entered the chamber.
They kindled a great fire on the hearth, and placed
over it a large cauldron, full of boiling water. With
great noise and loud cries they approached the bed,

133

tore from it the trembling maiden, and dragged her to the cauldron.

She was almost dead from fear, but she uttered no sound. Then suddenly the cock crew, and all vanished. The crow immediately appeared, and hopped joyfully about the room, and thanked the princess for her courageous behaviour, for the sufferings of the unhappy bird were already lessened.

One of her elder sisters, who had much curiosity in her disposition, having heard of this, came to visit the princess in her ruined castle. She besought her so earnestly, that the kind-hearted maiden at length permitted her to pass one night beside her, in the golden bed. When the evil spirits appeared as usual about midnight, the elder sister shrieked aloud from fear, and immediately the cry of a bird in pain was heard.

The young sister from that time never received the visits of either of her sisters. Thus did she live; solitary by day, and suffering by night the most terrible alarm from the evil spirits; but the crow came daily to her, and thanked her for her endurance, assuring her that his dreadful sufferings were greatly mitigated.

134

THE ENCHANTED CROW.

Thus had passed two years, when the crow came to her, and thus addressed her :—

"In one year more I shall be delivered from the punishment to which I am condemned; for then seven years will have passed over my head. But before I can re-assume my real form, and gain possession of my treasures, thou must go out into the wide world, and become a servant."

Obedient to the will of her betrothed, the young princess served for a whole year as a maid, and notwithstanding her youth and beauty, she escaped all the snares laid for her by the ill-disposed.

One evening while she was spinning flax, and her white hands were wearied with work, she heard a rustling, and an exclamation of joy. A handsome young man entered her presence, knelt before her, and kissed the little weary white hands.

"It is I," cried he, "I am the prince, whom thou, by thy goodness, whilst I wandered in the form of a black crow, didst deliver from the most dreadful tortures. Return with me now to my castle, there will we live together in happiness."

They went together to the castle where she had

135

undergone so much terror. The palace was, however, no longer recognisable, it was so improved and adorned, and in it did they dwell together for a hundred happy and joyous years.

THE DRAGON-GIANT AND HIS STONE-STEED.

[Russian.]

NOT one amongst the numerous wives of Vladimir the Great was comparable in beauty to the Bulgarian Princess Milolika. Her eyes resembled those of the falcon; the fur of the sable was not more glossy than her eyebrows, and her breast was whiter than snow.

She had been carried off by robbers of the Volga, from the vicinity of Boogord, the capital of her native country, and on account of her rare beauty they deemed her worthy to be a wife of the great monarch. They therefore conducted her to Kiev, the residence of the mighty Vladimir, and presented her to him. Vladimir, a good judge of female charms, the moment he beheld her, was enchanted by the surpassing beauty of the Bulgarian princess, and in a short time his love for her became so great that he made her his consort, and dismissed all his other wives. The proud heart of the king's daughter was touched by this proof of his affection, and she rewarded his tenderness with reciprocal and true love.

The life of Vladimir was now one of great happiness. His conquests had procured him riches in superfluity; a long period of peace had augmented the prosperity of his country; his subjects loved him as their father; and the tenderness of Milolika made earth seem to him as heaven.

One day as in company with his consort and his Bojars, he sat in the golden chamber by his oaken table, holding a festival in memory of a victory over the Greeks, the sound of a warrior's horn was heard at a distance. The rejoicings in the lofty hall suddenly ceased. The monarch and the Bojars cast their eyes to the ground, full of thought and heaviness. Swâtorad alone, the spirited Voivode of Kiev, started up from the table, and leaving his goblet undrained, approached the great monarch. "Thou art," spake he, as he bent low before him, "thou art our father and our lord, thou art the child of renown: wherefore sinks thy head? Why does the sound of the warrior's horn make thy heart heavy? Even if it be a hostile knight who now

154

appears before the capital, hast thou not enough brave heroes to confront any foe? Away then! Send forth thy heralds to demand who dares to defy the country of the Russians?"

Vladimir looked friendly upon the gallant Swâtorad, and thus replied to his address: "I thank thee for thy zeal, good Swâtorad; but my anxiety does not arise from fear. I have defeated hosts, made myself master of fortified cities, and overthrown kings: how should I know fear? But it was my desire henceforth to preserve to my subjects the blessing of peace, and that alone is the cause that this challenge to combat makes me sorrowful. If however it must be so, I will defend my country and myself. Go and send heralds to demand who dares to come forth against Kiev, to challenge Vladimir to battle?"

The brave Swâtorad immediately sent forth two heralds, who sprang upon their horses and rushed to the open plain, where they at once beheld a monstrous tent, before which a horse of unusual size was grazing. As soon as the horse perceived them, he stamped upon the ground, and cried aloud in a human voice: "Awake powerful son of the dragon, Tugarin awake! Kiev sends heralds to thee."

This marvel considerably astounded the heralds, and their amazement was increased when they beheld issuing from the tent a giant of the most monstrous kind, beneath whose footsteps the earth resounded. Yet they did not lose their composure, but discharged their commission as beseemed them well. "Who art thou?" cried they, after they had courteously bent before him. "Who art thou, bold youth from a foreign land? What is thy name, and how stands thy report in thy fatherland? Art thou a Czar, or a Czarewitsch? A king or a king's son? We are sent by the invincible prince of Kiev, the son of renown, by Vladimir, to ask thee why thou darest to advance against Kiev?—how thou darest to challenge him to combat?"

The questions displeased the giant, and he fell into fierce wrath. Lightning flashed from his eyes, his nose sent forth sparks, and he addressed the heralds in a voice of thunder: "Contemptible wights, how dare ye to put such questions to me? The herald's staff alone protects you from my fury. Return, and tell your prince that I am come to fetch his head, in order to carry it to the great king, Trewul, of Bulgaria, who is wrath with him, for the abduction of his sister Milolika. Tell him, that nought can save him; neither the

156

summit of the mountain, nor the darkness of the forest, and that he cannot redeem his head by gold, nor by silver, by jewels, nor by pearls. What I am called, and what my report is in my country, it needs not that you should know; sufficient, that I show you what I can perform." At these words, he grasped an enormous stone, which lay near the tent, and flung it with such force into the air, that it resembled a little speck.

Full of terror, the heralds returned to Kiev, and presenting themselves before the monarch, related what they had seen and heard. When Milolika heard that the horse had called the stranger knight Tugarin, Son of the Dragon, she grew pale, and a stream of tears bedewed her cheeks. "Ah," cried she, "beloved husband, we are lost! Nought can save us, but our flight to the sacred Bug. Tugarin is an invincible enchanter. His magic power ceases only on the shores of the Bug. Thither let us fly." *

Vladimir endeavoured to re-assure his consort. He represented to her that the brave warriors, and the walls of the impregnable Kiev, would afford them sufficient protection; but Milolika was not to be comforted.

* The river Bug was especially held sacred by the Slavonians, and its waters possessed the power to destroy all kinds of magic.

157

"Thou knowest not, beloved husband," said she, sobbing and crying, "how dangerous is this giant, Tugarin, to me and my family, and how bitterly he must hate thee, since he was my betrothed, and awaited my hand." Vladimir besought Milolika to explain to him this enigma, and she related the following :—

"I am the daughter of the Bulgarian king, Bogoris, and of the princess Kuridana. My birth-place is the city Shikotin, where my parents were wont to pass the summer months. As this city lies on the banks of the Volga, it offers great facilities for fishing, a diversion to which my mother was extremely partial.

"Once, when my father was fighting against a neighbouring nation, my mother endeavoured to while away her grief at his absence by her accustomed diversion, and caused the nets to be spread in the Volga. The fish were very plentiful, and a great number of barks and boats covered the river, amongst which, the vessel in which my mother was embarked, was distinguishable by its magnificence and elegance. Surrounded by her ladies, and her body-guard, Kuridana stood in the centre of the vessel, and beheld with pleasure the spectacle of the fishery, when suddenly a mountain, that was situated on the other side of the river, burst

158

with a tremendous crash. Every eye was directed to the spot, and they saw issue from the aperture, a man of rude, and terrific aspect, seated on a car of shining steel drawn by two winged horses. He directed his course towards the river, and when he reached the water, the steel car rolled over the waves, as if they had been firm land. When it was perceived that he was bending his way to my mother's bark, heralds were dispatched in a boat, to inquire why he presumed to approach the princess without permission. But the fierce being, who was a powerful and malignant enchanter, did not permit the unfortunate heralds to discharge their commission. As they began to speak, he blew upon their boat, overset it, and all who were in it were buried beneath the waves. At this melancholy sight, my mother's attendants seized their bows, and discharged a shower of arrows against the intruder; but in vain, for the arrows rebounded from him, and fell shivered into the water.

" The greatest amazement now seized all present, for they became petrified when the magician with a single word, bound every boat, with its crew, so that they stood motionless, whilst he, with outstretched arms, hastened towards my mother, and endeavoured to remove her into his car. But some unseen power crippled all his efforts. Each time he endeavoured to seize Kuridana, his arms sank powerless, and he was, at length, obliged to desist from the vain enterprise. He then sprang into the bark, cast himself on his knees before her, and in the most moving, and earnest expressions, besought her love. He promised her all the treasures of the world, and the highest earthly happiness, if she would reward his vehement love with reciprocal affection, or only lay aside the talisman which she wore upon her breast. This talisman, which now preserved her, she had received at her birth from a beneficent enchantress, and as she well knew its force, she had drawn it out of the case where she usually concealed it, and held it before his eyes.

"Then the evil one trembled so violently, that at last, as if stricken by lightning, he fell to the ground, and not until Kuridana had again enclosed the talisman, did he recover from his insensibility. He then sprang up, and mounted his steel car, uttering the most fearful threats, 'Think not,' cried he, foaming with shame and rage, 'think not to escape my hands; I will possess thee, and will force Bogoris himself, by the most dreadful devastation of his country, to yield thee to me. Behold, I swear by Tschernobog,* that I will either slay, or gain possession of thee. Thou shalt see me soon again.' With these words he disappeared.

"Kuridana then left the spot, and not believing herself secure in Shikotin, retired to the strong city of Boogord, where she awaited, in great anxiety, the result of this alarming adventure.

"The very next morning, appeared on the plain before the capital city, a dreadful two-headed monster, of that dragon species which, in the language of my country, is called Sylant. It devoured herbs, and flocks, and men, and devastated the surrounding country with its poisonous breath. In a short time, the region round Boogord became a desert, and many brave warriors, who sought to free their country of this demon, fell victims to their patriotism and valour. The Sylant appeared each morning before the walls, and bellowed out with a fearful voice,: 'Bogoris, give me Kuridana, or I will make thy country a desert!'

"No sooner did my father hear of the misfortune which menaced his people, and his beloved Kuridana, than he left his career of victory, and hastened to the capital.

* Tschernobog was the evil spirit of the Slavonians, and no one could swear more solemnly, than by Tschernobog.

What were his feelings when he beheld the misery which the monster had spread over his land! But greater bitterness still awaited him, for when the first tempest of joy and grief, which his return had excited in the hearts of all, and especially in that of Kuridana, had subsided, this noble-minded princess proposed herself as a willing sacrifice for the king, and the good Bulgarians. 'No!' cried Bogoris, 'sooner will I perish, than lose thee. I will combat the Dragon. Perhaps the Gods will grant me victory, and if I am vanquished in the fight, at least I shall die for thee, and for my country.' The most generous dispute now arose between the magnanimous pair, and finally they agreed to appeal to the decision of the magnates of the empire, who should decide the dispute.

"The king assembled them, and when they had heard Kuridana's resolution, they loaded her with panegyrics, and expressions of gratitude. 'Thy magnanimous sacrifice alone, Kuridana,' said the eldest of the assembly, an aged man, of a hundred years, 'can rescue us and Bulgaria. For, supposing that Bogoris were to fight with the Sylant, and fall, would not our misfortune be greater still? No, Prince! thou must preserve thyself for thy people, in order to heal

162

the wounds which the Dragon has inflicted. Kuridana alone can save us.' All the magnates coincided with the old man, and Bogoris was in despair.

"It was morning, and the dreadful words : 'Bogoris, give me thy wife !' at that moment resounded round the palace. Kuridana courageously arose, embraced her speechless husband, and bade him an eternal farewell.

"At the words '*for ever*,' Bogoris sank senseless on the ground. Manly as his heart had been up to that hour, it could not endure separation from the beloved Kuridana. The high-minded wife bedewed him with her tears, but at length, turning to the nobles, who stood round her weeping, she said : ' Lead me where you will. I am prepared to endure everything for my husband and my country.' They now reverentially supported her trembling steps, and conducted her as rapidly as her weak state permitted, to the front of the city.

"Meanwhile the altars smoked with incense, and both priests and people supplicated for the deliverance of their noble princess.

" Shortly after the magnates had left the palace with Kuridana, Bogoris came to himself, and when he perceived that he was alone, he guessed his misfortune, and his despair knew no bounds. He drew his sword, and was in the act of piercing his breast with it, in order not to survive Kuridana, when a matron of beautiful and majestic aspect stood before him, staid his hand, and thus addressed him:

" ' What, Bogoris! Dost thou despair ?—Be tranquil; the Sylant has no power to harm Kuridana. The talisman which she wears on her breast, will, at all times, and under all circumstances, mock his power. I am the enchantress Dobrada, the protectress of thy wife, she who, as thou knewest, hung the talisman around her immediately on her birth. But it is not now requisite that I should reveal to thee the causes which induced me to provide her with that shield against danger. Enough, that I foresaw at her birth that she would have much to fear from the love of a powerful sorcerer, called Sarragur. And because I am ever willing to do all the good I can, I hung around her this talisman, which protects her from his utmost power, and will now defend her from the Sylant, who is no other than Sarragur himself. For, when he perceived that I was opposed to his passion, and had taken Kuridana under my protection, he sought to avenge himself on me, by every kind of secret mischief, so that I was at length obliged to chastise him. By my superior

164

power, I enclosed him within a mountain by the Volga, and bound his fate by the most awful spell, which even Tschernobog respects, to a golden fish, which I sank in the depths of the Volga. By this spell, Sarragur was to remain in his subterranean prison until some mortal should draw up the golden fish; and should he ever thus obtain his freedom, he could then never transform himself into an evil and noxious animal, except on the condition that he should never again resume his own form, and should perish shortly after the transformation. It chanced that a sturgeon swallowed the golden fish, and this sturgeon was caught on the very day when Kuridana was diverting herself with the fishery. Sarragur thus became free, and the first use he made of his freedom was to endeavour to carry off Kuridana, whom he still loved with unabated passion.

" ' When this attempt was baffled by the power of the talisman, and still more, when he perceived Kuridana's aversion for him, he became furious, and transformed himself into the Sylant, although he knew what must be the consequences. Madman, his hour is come, and thou, Bogoris, art destined to destroy him. Receive from my hands the sword of the renowned Egyptian king, Sesostris. It possesses

165

the wonderful power of destroying every spell, and with it thou wilt overpower the sorcerer, though he should summon all the powers of hell to succour him. Only, mark what I am now about to say. In order to extirpate Sarragur, and every remembrance of him from the earth, thou must cut off both the heads of the Sylant by one stroke. If thou succeed not in doing this, and hewest off but one head, the sorcerer, it is true, will lose his life, but he will escape to his cavern, where, before he expires, he will lay an egg, in which will be enclosed all his magic power, and from the head hewn off, will arise a horse of stone, which shall receive life at the moment the bad spirits shall have hatched the egg, and from this egg will issue the giant Tugarin, who, one day, will be formidable to thy children. For, not only will he inherit from his father the entire power to work evil, whereby so much misery has befallen thee and thy land, but he will also love thy daughter as fiercely as Sarragur loves thy wife. Thy son Trewul will refuse him his sister's hand, and then he will desolate the country, until Milolika's hand is promised to him. He also is to be conquered by no other weapon than the sword of the wise Sesostris, and a knight who shall live without having been born, is destined to slay him. After

166

thy victory over the Sylant, hang up the sword in thy armoury amongst the other swords there, and at the appointed time fate will give it into the hands destined wield it. Of that which I have now told thee, reveal not a word, except to thy wife, and she may hereafter repeat it to her daughter.'

"Having uttered these words, Dobrada shrouded herself in a rose-coloured cloud, and disappeared. Heavenly perfumes filled the chamber, and Bogoris felt that all sorrow had vanished from his soul. Hastily he vaulted on his horse, and rushed to deliver his wife and his country from the fell sorcerer.

"When he reached the plain, he beheld the efforts of the Sylant to grasp Kuridana, and how he was impeded by the talisman, from coming close to her. Bogoris immediately unsheathed his sword, and flew upon the monster. When the Sylant perceived his antagonist, he sent forth fire streams from both his jaws, which, however, were rendered innocuous by the sword of Sesostris. In order to bring the combat to a speedy conclusion, Bogoris aimed a powerful stroke at the heads of the monster, which would assuredly have separated both from the trunk, and so have extirpated the sorcerer and all remembrance of him from the earth, if the

167

Sylant, at the very moment the stroke fell, had not soared into the air. By this movement, he saved one

head. The other rolled on the ground, and immediately became stone. Awfully bellowing, the impure being flew to his cavern. Bogoris pursued, but in vain; the Sylant disappeared in the mountain by the Volga, which immediately closed on him.

"My father regretted that he had not succeeded in entirely annihilating the sorcerer and all his brood; but joy at having delivered his beloved wife and his

168

country, soon prevailed over sorrow. He committed the future to the Gods, and after he had revealed to my mother the predictions of the good enchantress, he hung up the sword of Sesostris in his armoury.

" My parents passed the remainder of their lives in uninterrupted peace and content. When I was grown up, my mother related to me her history, and at the same time revealed to me what awaited me through the giant Tugarin. She then hung round me the talisman which she had received from Dobrada. Shortly after this both my parents died. After their death I lived several years with my brother in undisturbed tranquillity, till one day the report arose of a wonderful phenomenon of nature, which was to be seen in the vicinity of the capital. The king, my brother, went thither, and I accompanied him. They showed us a stone which daily increased in size, and was assuming the form of an enormous horse. Everybody marvelled at this sport of Nature, as they called it; but I remembered Dobrada's predictions, and doubted not that the hour of Tugarin's birth, and of my misfortunes, was arrived. Whilst I was still thinking on it, we were alarmed by an earthquake. The neighbouring Sylant Mount,—for from the time the Sylant had escaped thither, it had borne that name,—opened, and a giant of monstrous size stepped forth. He strode across the Volga, and went straight to the stone horse. The moment he laid his hand on it, it became animated. The giant sprang upon it, and dashed towards me. He tried to seize me, but quickly drew back his robber hands, as if they had been burnt. The power of the talisman withstood him. He then turned towards my brother, and cried out in dreadful tones :—'Hear, Trewul! I see that thy sister cannot be carried off by force, and therefore I require of thee to persuade her to give me her hand voluntarily. I give thee three days for consideration, and when they are expired, I either receive Milolika from thy hands, or I make thy country desolate.' After these terrible words he departed on his colossal steed, with the rapidity of lightning.

"We returned heavy-hearted to the city, where my brother immediately assembled the council, and laid before it the giant's demand, and his threats. The counsellors were unanimously of opinion, that, as the princess was averse to giving her hand to the giant, an army must be sent against him, of sufficient force to set his menaces at nought. Ten thousand archers, and two thousand horsemen, in armour, were hastily collected, and on the dawn of the third day, were drawn out on the plain before the city, to await the giant. Tugarin soon appeared, and the Bulgarians at once discharged their arrows and darts at him, but they proved as powerless against him as formerly against his father. They rebounded from him as from a rock. At this attack, the giant broke forth with mingled rage and scorn:—'What,' bellowed he, 'does Trewul send troops against me? Must I then become his enemy? Woe to the helpless being!' And without further delay, he seized the horsemen and archers by the dozen, and swallowed them a dozen at a time, till not a man was left.

" He then began to lay waste and destroy everything round the city. Men and cattle were all engulfed in the monster's insatiable maw. He shattered the dwellings of the inhabitants with his gigantic fists. Whole forests were uprooted by him, and the hoofs of his enormous horse trod down fields and meadows. At length my brother, in order to put a stop to the universal misery, resolved to sacrifice me. With bitter tears he announced to me that he knew no other means of saving himself and his country from destruction, than to promise my hand to the giant. I replied to him only by my tears, and he reluctantly sent an embassy to invite Tugarin to Boogord. He came. Proudly he advanced to the gate where Trewul and the nobles of the land awaited him. I was in despair. At length I bethought me of a means of escape. I agreed to bestow my hand on the giant, on condition that, through some beneficent power, he should first obtain the form and stature of an ordinary man. I trusted that this would not easily be done, and in the mean time I might be able to effect my escape. Tugarin, blinded by his love for me, did not hesitate to accept the condition, and swore by Tschernobog, that he would not require me to be delivered to him until my requisition was satisfied. He established himself in Boogord, and served my brother with great zeal. I soon found an opportunity of making my escape, and wandering a whole day without food, was at last taken by the robbers of the Volga, and brought to thy court.

"You will now, my beloved husband," said Milolika, as she concluded her narration, " easily comprehend the danger which threatens you. Tugarin must hate thee, since thou art my husband. His power is great, and no one can vanquish him, except the knight who came unborn into the world, and no weapon can slay him, but the sword of the wise Sesostris.

172

Thou and all thy brave heroes are powerless against him. Therefore, dear husband, let us flee. On the banks of the sacred Bug we shall be safe; no magic can operate there."

This narration made the deepest impression on the heart of the prince; he could not, however, resolve to abandon his country in the hour of need, and besides, to fly before a single warrior, great as he might be, seemed still not a very honourable proceeding. "What!" exclaimed he, "shall the monarch before whom the East trembles, whose courage the whole world admires, shall he shrink in the moment of danger,—shall he, with all his might, flee before a single foe? No: sooner a hundred times will I die the most cruel death!" But with all this how was he to comfort Milolika? How was he to withstand the dreadful giant, seeing that he had not, unborn, beheld the light, neither did he possess the sword of the Egyptian king Sesostris? These difficulties weighed upon his soul. The first, however, he soon disposed of. He bethought himself that the lime with which the walls of Kiev were constructed, had been tempered with water from the sacred Bug, and consequently would prevent the giant from entering the city. This sufficed to tranquillise Milolika, who no longer insisted on flight, as she perceived that her beloved Vladimir was just as secure in Kiev, as he would be on the shores of the Bug. As far as she herself was concerned, the giant could avail nothing, since the power of the talisman would shield her from every danger. But still the thought of the combat with this giant, greatly disturbed the prince. "Where," said he, "is the unborn mortal who is destined, with the sword of Sesostris, to destroy the fell Tugarin?"

Lo! suddenly a knight of bold and noble aspect, armed with a costly sword, and cased in shining armour, but without shield or lance, rode at full speed into the court of the palace. He sprang from his spirited steed, and gave him to his lusty squire. Then he proudly advanced up the steps, to the golden chamber of the great monarch, and addressed Vladimir as follows :—" My name is Dobrünä Mikilitsch, and I come to serve thee."

"Thou art welcome," replied Vladimir, "but how is it possible that thou hast escaped the giant Tugarin, who holds the road to Kiev in blockade?"

"Tugarin!" rejoined the knight, "*I* fear him!— already would I have laid his great head at thy feet, but that I desired to achieve that deed in thy presence."

174

The monarch marvelled at the boldness of the stranger-youth, and inquired if he seriously intended to combat the giant.

"Assuredly," said Dobrünä, "and with that object am I come to Kiev."

"But knowest thou not, that none can vanquish the giant, except only a knight who came into the world unborn?"

"I know it," replied Dobrünä, "and that knight am I!"

"Hast thou, then, the sword of Sesostris?"

"Behold it," said Dobrünä, as he drew the sword from its scabbard, "and if thou wilt permit me, mighty prince, to relate to thee my history, thou wilt know that it is I who am appointed by destiny to rid the earth of the monster Tugarin."

The monarch joyfully granted him permission, and Dobrünä thus commenced:—

"It is true that I had both a father and a mother, but not the less did I behold the light of the world without going through the process of being born. Shortly before my mother would have brought me forth, she was slain by robbers, during a journey she was making with my father, to visit a relation. My father being

175

also killed, I must doubtless have perished, if the beneficent enchantress Dobrada, who was just then passing by, had not rescued me, and taken me under her protection. She carried me to the beautiful island, in the ocean, where she usually dwells, and brought me up with the greatest care. She nourished me with the milk of a lioness, bathed me several times a day in the waves of the ocean, and inured me by day and night to labour and privation. This mode of education rendered my body so strong, that in my tenth year, I was already able to tear up the strongest trees by the root. Six ancient men instructed me in all the six-and-twenty known languages, and in arms, wherein I made such progress, that in my fifteenth year I was able to parry at once all the six swords of my teachers. Dobrada recompensed me for my diligence with the shining armour I now wear, which possesses the virtue of protecting my body from every danger.

" Shortly after that time, the enchantress whom I loved and honoured as a mother, thus addressed me :— ' Dobrünä Mikilitsch, thy education is completed, and it is time that in foreign lands thou shouldst by knightly deeds acquire renown and honour. Go forth : thou art destined for great things. It is not permitted to

176

me to reveal all the future to thee; but thus much thou mayst know: thou wilt obtain possession of the wondrous sword of the wise Sesostris of Egypt. As soon as thou approachest it, the sword thou now wearest will fall of itself to the earth, and that of Sesostris will become agitated. Take possession of it in peace, for thou wilt require it, for a great service thou must render to him in whose armoury thou wilt find it; for with it thou wilt destroy a mighty sorcerer and giant, who has worked him much woe. Whatever else thou mayst require during thy travels,' continued she, 'this ring will supply. Thou hast but to turn it three times on thy finger, in order to see every reasonable wish fulfilled.'

"She then bade me enter a boat into which she followed me. The boat shot through the waves like an arrow, and I presently sank into a profound sleep. How long our journey was I know not; for when I awoke I found myself alone on a vast plain, not far from a large city. But Dobrada could not have long quitted me, for the heavenly perfumes which ordinarily surrounded her, yet floated round me, and far in the eastern horizon I saw the rose-coloured cloud which always shrouded her. My soul was now filled with sadness at the thought that

I was now separated from the wise and kind Dobrada, whom I loved as my mother.

"At length I regained my composure. I wished that I had a horse and squire that I might ride into the city that lay near me, and as at the same time I accidentally turned on my finger three times the ring, whose virtue I scarcely recollected, I saw at once before me a squire with two horses, of which I selected the finest and the most richly adorned for myself, and left the other for my squire; and thus I rode into the city.

"At the gate I was informed that the city was called Boogord, and was the capital of the Bulgarian empire. Trewul reigned in Boogord, and the giant Tugarin was at his court. The king had been obliged to promise him the hand of his sister, in order to avert the total ruin of his country, which the giant had devastated until Trewul had acceded to his desire. When I appeared in the king's presence, I made a very favourable impression on him, and he not only received me into his service, but made me keeper of the armoury, the first dignity at the Bulgarian court.

"From the first moment that Tugarin beheld me, he manifested the bitterest hate towards me; and when I heard what evil he had brought on Trewul and his land, I doubted not that he was the sorcerer and giant I was destined to overthrow. But the sword of Sesostris was still wanting to me. It was however not long before this invaluable weapon came into my possession.

"I entered the royal armoury in order to inspect the weapons entrusted to my care, and I had scarcely crossed the threshold when the sword I wore fell to the ground, and amongst the numerous others that hung there, I observed one moving to and fro. I could not doubt that this was the wonderful sword of the Egyptian king with which I was to slay the giant. I took possession of it with the greater confidence, from the knowledge that by its aid I should rid Trewul of so dangerous an enemy to himself and his family. I girded it upon me, and hung mine in its place.

"From that moment the giant avoided me, knowing most likely by his magic art that I was in possession of the sword that was to be fatal to him, and ere long he disappeared from Boogord, telling the king he was going in search of Milolika.

"I immediately took leave of the king, and set out in pursuit of the giant. I gained information on my way that he had gone to Kiev, where Milolika resided as thy wife. I hastened after him, and am come, as I see, at the right moment to prevent misfortune. I now await thy permission, mighty prince, to engage in combat thy enemy and mine."

As he concluded Dobrünä bent one knee before the monarch, who rose from his seat, and taking the golden chain from his own neck, threw it round the knight's with the following words: "Let this mark of my favour prove to thee, Dobrünä Mikilitsch, how greatly I rejoice to have so brave a knight in my service. To-morrow thou shalt engage the giant, and I doubt not that thou wilt conquer." He then commanded that an apartment should be prepared for him in the palace, and all due honour be paid to him. Dobrünä returned thanks to the monarch for the favours shown him, and took leave in order to repose after his journey, and to gather strength for the approaching fight.

In the mean time the heralds by Vladimir's command went round the city, and summoned the people to assemble on the walls the following morning, to witness the combat between the knight and the sorcerer, and the priests offered up solemn sacrifices to implore blessings on Kiev and the knight against the malignant sorcerer and the powers which aided him.

THE DRAGON-GIANT.

Scarcely had the purple-tinted Simzerla * spread her glowing mantle over the sky, and decked the path of the great light of the world with her thousand coloured rays, before the vast population of Kiev impatiently thronged to the walls in order not to delay the grand spectacle. The monarch attended by his consort and all the magnates of the empire, ascended a tribunal which had been hastily erected over the principal gate of the city for this great event.

The clangor of trumpets and horns at length announced the arrival of the knight. Ten thousand corsletted warriors rode with uplifted lances before him, and drew up in two lines before the gate. After them, on a richly caparisoned charger, rode the knight in his shining armour, bearing in his hand the precious sword of Sesostris. The people welcomed him with a cry of joy, and the warriors clashed their arms as he appeared before the gate. With noble bearing and knightly aspect he turned his horse and saluted the monarch by thrice lowering his sword. "Great ruler of Russia," he began, "at thy command I go forth to fight the sorcerer and giant Tugarin, who has presumed to challenge thee to combat." "Go forth," replied

---

* Simzerla was the Aurora of the Slavonians.

Vladimir, "go forth, valiant youth, and fight in my name the vile sorcerer: may the Gods give thee victory!" Dobrünä then dashed at full speed through the lines of warriors to the white tent, followed by the acclamations and the blessings of the spectators.

The giant, who had been awakened by the unusual noise of the trumpets and horns, and the joyful cries of the people, had already mounted his horse, and was in the act of riding towards the city to ascertain the cause, when he beheld the knight approaching. When he recognised in him the dreaded keeper of the Bulgarian monarch's armoury, who was in possession of the wonderful sword, he set up a fearful yell. Foaming with rage he rushed with outspread arms against the knight to grasp him; but Dobrünä laughed at his impotent fury, and in order better to overcome him, he first touched with his sword the enchanted horse, which immediately crumbled into dust. He then caused the magic-destroying weapon of the wise Sesostris to gleam over the head of the sorcerer, who, by the sudden crumbling of his horse, had fallen to the earth. Tugarin's destruction seemed inevitable, and the beholders from the walls already shouted forth their plaudits to the victor, when at once all the powers

THE DRAGON GIANT.   P. 183.

of hell broke forth to aid their beloved son. A stream of fire crackled between the combatants, fiery serpents hissed around the knight, and a thick cloud of smoke enveloped the giant. But short was this infernal display. Dobrünä touched the stream with his sword, made a few strokes with it in the air, and the fiery flood and the hissing serpents vanished. He then approached the smoke which concealed the giant, but scarcely had he thrust his sword into it, when like the enchantments that also disappeared. The giant was seen outstretched on the ground, and heard to roar with terror. No sooner did he perceive that the smoke which concealed him had vanished, than he sprang up and rushed, as if in madness, on the knight. Dobrünä awaited him unmoved, and as the giant stretched forth his monstrous hands for the second time to seize him, he cut them both off with a single stroke. The second stroke of that wondrous sword, wielded by the strong hand of the knight, severed the vile head from the shoulders. The colossus fell, and the earth shook beneath his weight.

Then the people lifted up a cry of joy. A hundred thousand voices shouted, "Long live our monarch, and the conqueror of the giant, Dobrünä Mikilitsch!"

The knight, who had dismounted to raise the fallen

183

enemy's head on the point of his sword in sign of victory, was about to remount in order to give the monarch an account of his combat, when he beheld him coming towards him, accompanied by his consort and the magnates of the empire. The courteous knight hastened forward and laid the giant's head at his feet. The great prince embraced him in presence of the assembled people, and placed on his finger a gold ring, whilst Milolika hung around him a gold-embroidered scarf. Dobrünä bent his knee and thanked the royal pair in graceful and courteous words for these marks of favour. They then all returned full of joy to the city, where the festivities and rejoicings in honour of the knight lasted many weeks.

Vladimir also despatched messengers to his brother-in-law, Trewul, to inform him of his marriage with the beautiful Milolika, and the overthrow of their common enemy, the giant Tugarin. Dobrünä however remained at the court of Vladimir, and performed many more great and valiant deeds, which procured him great fame and honour, and rendered great service to the monarch, and he became the most beloved and most esteemed, both by prince and people, of all the knights in Vladimir's court.

184

THE STORY OF SIVA AND MADHAVA.

[Sanskrit.]

———◆———

THERE still exists a town famed for its splendour and richness, called Ratnapura. In it there once dwelt two rogues, Siva and Madhava, who, with the help of their confederates, contrived to make both rich and poor of that place victims to their cunning and rapacity.

Once these two individuals met together to consult. "This town," they said, "has so entirely been laid under contribution by us, that we can have no reasonable hopes of any further success; let us, therefore, go to Ujjayini, and settle ourselves down there. The house-priest of the king, Sankar'aswarni by name, is considered a very rich man, and if, by some contrivance, we could possess ourselves of his treasures, it would be easy to curry favour with the charming and lovely

women of the Malavese. The Brahmins, without ex-
ception, call him avaricious and miserly, for, though so
rich that he measures his treasures by the bushel, he
begrudges every offering to their altars, and it is only
on compulsion he gives a portion of the dues. It is
also well known that he has a remarkably beautiful
daughter, whom, if we once are able to gain his confidence, one of us must receive as a wife from his own
hands."

After this, these two rogues, Siva and Madhava,
having first matured their plans and resolved upon the
parts each individually was to play, took their departure from the city of Ratnapura and soon arrived at
Ujjayini.

Madhava, disguised as a Rajput, remained with his
followers in a small village outside the city; but Siva,
more versed in all the arts of deceit, entered the town
alone, garbed in the habit of a devout penitent. He
built a cell on an elevated place on the banks of the
Sipra, from whence he could be well observed, and here
he laid on the ground a deer-skin, a pot wherein to
collect alms, some darbha-grass, and some clay.

At the first dawn of morning he rubbed his whole
body over with clay; he then entered the river, and

remained with his head for a considerable time under the water; leaving the bath, he steadfastly fixed his gaze on the sun, then, holding in his hand some kusa-grass, he knelt before the image of a god, murmuring his prayers; he then plucked holy flowers, which he sacrificed to Siva, and when his offering was concluded he again began to pray, and remained long lost in deepest devotion.

On the following day, in order to gather alms, he wandered through the town, mute, as if dumb, leaning on a staff, and his only raiment consisting of the small skin of a black gazelle. After having made his collections at the houses of the Brahmins, he divided the gifts received into three parts; the first he gave to the crows, the second to the first person he met, and with the third he fed himself; then slowly counting the beads of his rosary, with constant and fervent prayers, he returned to his cell. The nights he devoted, apparently, to deepest meditation, and to the solution of great religious and philosophical questions.

Thus, by daily repeating these deceptions, he impressed on the inhabitants so great an idea of his sanctity that he was universally revered; and, when he passed, the people of Ujjayini reverentially bowed and knelt before him, exclaiming, "This is, indeed, a holy man!"

Meanwhile, his friend Madhava had, through his spies, received intelligence of all these doings, and now, magnificently dressed like a Rajput he also entered the city. He took up his abode in an adjacent temple, and went to the banks of the Sipra to bathe in the river. After having performed his ablutions, Madhava saw Siva, who, lost in prayer, knelt before the image of the god. The former then, along with his retinue, prostrated himself in reverence before the holy man; and addressing the people around him, said, "There lives not on earth a more devout penitent; more than once in my travels have I seen him, when, as here, he has been visiting the sacred rivers and the holy places of pilgrimage."

Though Siva had well observed and heard his companion, no feature betrayed the fact; immoveably as before, he continued in his devotion. Madhava soon after returned to his dwelling.

In the depth of night in a lonely place they again met, where, after having well feasted, they consulted together upon their next proceedings at the dawn of morning Siva returned to his cell, and Madhava commanded one of his companions at an early hour of the day as follows:

THE STORY OF SIVA AND MADHAVA.

"Take these two robes of honour and present them to Sankar'aswarni, the house-priest of the king, and address him thus :—' A Rajput named Madhava, treacherously assaulted, and by his nearest relations driven from his empire, has, with the vast treasures of his father, taken refuge in these realms, and is anxious to present himself before the king and offer him the faithful and gratuitous services of himself and his brave followers. He has therefore sent me to thee, thou ocean of fame, to beg thy permission to visit him.'" As Madhava had commanded him, the follower, holding the robes of honour in his hands, waited at the house of the priest. Watching a favourable opportunity when the priest was alone, he presented himself before him, laid the presents at his feet, and delivered Madhava's message. The priest, full of dignity, received them condescendingly, and longing for some of the treasures to which the messenger had made no slight allusions, he graciously acquiesced in the demand.

Madhava consequently went the following day at a proper hour to visit the priest, accompanied by his followers, dressed like courtiers, in magnificent robes, and with silver spears in their hands. A messenger was sent in advance to announce them, and the priest

receiving them at the entrance of his house, most reverentially saluted them, and gave them the very best
welcome. Madhava after having passed a short time
in pleasant conversation, and made a favourable impression on the priest, returned to his own dwelling.

The following day he again sent two robes of honour,
and then presented himself to the priest, saying: "We
are anxious as early as possible to enter the service of
the king, for time hangs heavily on our hands; let our
sole recompense be the honour of attending him, for
we have sufficient treasures for all our wants."

When the priest had heard this, hoping to extract
large sums from him, he granted his request, and
immediately went to the king, who, out of esteem
and love for his religious adviser, at once permitted
the introduction of the Rajput at court.

On the following day the priest formally introduced
Madhava and his followers to the king, who graciously,
and with honours received them, and at once appointed
the former to fill a high station in the household, for he
was greatly pleased with his appearance, which in everything resembled that of a high-born Rajput. Thus was
Madhava fairly installed at court, but every night he
went secretly to Siva, to consult with him about their

190

plans. Once the avaricious priest said to Madhava, who with his rich presents had shown him marked attention: "Come and live in my house," and as he pressed him very much, Madhava and his followers removed to the spacious dwelling of the priest.

Madhava had procured a great quantity of ornaments and trinkets set with false stones, wondrously well imitated; these he had inclosed in a jewel-box, which, slightly opening it that the priest might learn its contents, he begged him to deposit in his treasury. By this artifice he entirely won his confidence, and being thus secure, he feigned illness, and by abstaining for several days from taking any food, at last grew so thin and emaciated, that he had every appearance of being in a very alarming state of health. A few more days thus passed away, and the illness seemed to make rapid progress, when in a faint voice he thus addressed the priest, who was sitting at the side of his bed: "The malady which is devouring my strength and energies seems a retribution from the Gods for some of the sins my flesh has committed; bring therefore to me, O wise and pious man, some distinguished Brahmin to whom I may bequeath my treasures to insure my salvation here and there; for what man, even of ordinary

191

wisdom would, when life is ebbing, set value on gold or jewels !"

Whereupon the priest answered : " I will do as thou wishest."

Out of gratitude, Madhava knelt down and kissed his feet. But whatever Brahmin the priest brought to the sick man, not one pleased him; he said an inward voice told him that their life was not pure enough, their favour with Brahma not sufficient. When this had been several times repeated, with the same result, one of the rogues, who was standing by, suggested in a low tone of voice, " As not one of all these Brahmins seems worthy of the benefits intended to be conferred; the holy priest, Siva, so celebrated for his sanctity, who dwells on the shores of the Sipra, might be sent for: perhaps he might find favour with our master."

Madhava when appealed to, sighed heavily, and as if unable in his agony to articulate, bowed his head by way of consent. The priest forthwith rose and went to Siva, whom he found absorbed in deepest meditation. After having walked round him without being observed, he at last placed himself on the ground facing him. The impostor having finished his long-protracted prayers, raised his eyes, when the priest reverentially saluted him, and said : " Most holy man, if thou wouldst permit me, I have a petition to make to thee; there lives at my house a very rich Rajput, by name, Madhava, born in the south, and lately arrived from thence. He is dying, and wishes for some holy individual to whom he may give his riches; if it should please thee, I think it is for thee he intends all his treasures, which consist in ornaments and jewels of inestimable value."

Siva having attentively listened to this, thoughtfully and slowly answered : " Brahmin, how should I, whose whole earthly striving and longing is after immortal reward; whose only aspiration is heaven, there to have my prayers and my privations recognised and approved; whose meagre maintenance is derived from alms of the charitable; how should I feel any wish or desire for earthly possessions ?"

Whereupon the king's priest answered : " Say not so, noble and pious man ! Well you know the pleasure of the God towards the Brahmin-priest, who in his own person is able to offer hospitality to the Gods and to man; who within his own house can welcome and relieve the devout pilgrim; who with rich contributions can assist in the embellishments of their temples and

193

the splendour of their service, and who by taking a wife can extend his sphere of utility and philanthropy. Only by the possession of treasures these things are achievable, therefore it is laudable in man to strive after wealth. The father of a family is the best of Brahmins."

To which Siva answered : " Whence should I take a wife ? My poverty prevents my alliance with any great family."

When the priest heard this he thought the treasures already his own, and having found a favourable opportunity, he said to him : " I have an unmarried daughter, her name is Vinyasvamini ; she is most beautiful ; her I will give thee to wife. The treasure that will be thine through the generosity of Madhava, I will guard and preserve for thee ; choose, therefore, the pleasures and the bliss of the married state."

Siva attentively and with inward pleasure listened to the words of the priest, in which he saw their deep-laid scheme and their anxious wishes brought into fulfilment, and with diffidence he answered : " Brahmin, if by so doing I shall be able to please you and gain your favour, I consent to it ; and as regards the treasure, to you I leave the whole and sole control and management thereof,

194

as neither my understanding nor inclination lies in that direction."

Rejoiced at this answer of Siva, the priest forthwith took him into his house, assigned him a suite of apartments there, and announced to Madhava his arrival and what he had done, for which the latter warmly thanked him. Next the priest gave his unhappy daughter in marriage to Siva, thus sacrificing her to his avarice; and on the third day after the nuptials he led the bridegroom to Madhava, who now assumed a faintness as if in the last gasp of dissolution. After a pause, apparently rallying all his strength, he said: "In deepest humiliation I salute thee, most holy man, and beg of thee to accept, as I am dying and shall have no use for it, all that I possess of earthly wealth." He then had the artfully imitated jewels brought from the priest's treasury, and according to the sacred rites and customs on such occasions, had them presented to Siva. The latter, in accepting them, handed them over to the priest without even looking at them, saying, " Of such things I understand nothing, but you know their value."

" I will take care of them, as agreed between us," answered the priest; and again deposited the supposed treasure in its former place of security. Siva, after

195

having in solemn words pronounced his blessing over Madhava, returned to the apartments of his wife.

The following day Madhava seemed already greatly recovered, and ascribed this wonderful change to the influence of his gift and the holiness of the man on whom he had bestowed it. In warmest terms, he thanked the priest for his kind interference, and assured him of his everlasting gratitude. With Siva he now openly allied himself, praising him every where, and declaring that through his great powers alone his life had been preserved.

After the lapse of a few days Siva said to the priest, " It is not right that I thus should continue to live in thy house where I must be of vast expense to thee; thou hadst better give me a sum, if only corresponding with half the value of the gems, which you consider so precious."

The priest, who in reality priced these jewels and ornaments at an inestimable sum, a sum capable of purchasing an empire, was very glad to assent to such a proposition; and with the idea of giving something like the twentieth part of their value, he gave him all the money he possessed. He then had documents drawn out, in which on both sides the exchange of the properties was legally secured, for fear that Siva in the course of time might repent of his bargain. They then separated, Siva and his wife living in greatest joy and happiness, and soon they were joined by Madhava, with whom the former now divided the treasures of the priest.

After some years the priest wanted money to make some purchase, and taking a part of the ornaments, he went to a goldsmith who had a stand in the market to offer them for sale. This man, who was a great judge, after narrowly examining them, cried out, full of astonishment—" The man who has manufactured these must indeed be a great artisan; for though of no intrinsic value, they are the finest and most wonderful imitations that ever were worked out of such materials; for these stones are nothing but glass, and the setting nothing but gilt metal."

Having heard this, the priest, breathless though full of despair, ran back to his house, fetched the contents of the whole casket, and, unwilling to believe, went from one merchant to the other to have his treasure examined; but in every instance the answer was the same—" Only glass and brass !" The priest, as if he had been struck by lightning, fell senseless on the ground, and had to be carried home; but early the following morning having recovered, he ran to Siva and said to him, "Take back thy jewels, and return me my money."

This the other refused, alleging that the greater part of it had already been expended, and the rest he had so invested as to be most useful for his wife and children.

Thus disputing they both went before the king, on whom Madhava at the time was in attendance. The priest in the following words made the king acquainted with his case: " Behold, my gracious king, these ornaments; they are all artfully manufactured out of valueless metal, coloured pieces of glass and crystal. Without knowing this, and believing them real, I have given Siva my whole fortune in exchange for them, and he already has spent it."

To which Siva answered: " From my very childhood, mighty king, have I lived in holy seclusion and devotion; from this seclusion the father of my wife drew me forth, pressed and entreated me to accept the gift of honour, with the value of which I was wholly ignorant; but he assured me he was aware of its great pecuniary worth, and he would guarantee it to me. On my accepting it, without even giving it a look, I handed it over to him: he afterwards voluntarily purchased it from me, giving me his own price, and in proof of this I adduce this contract in his own handwriting: now, mighty ruler, judge between us; I have in truth laid the case fairly before you."

Siva having thus concluded his defence, Madhava addressed himself to the priest, saying: "Speak not derogatorily of this holy man, now your son. Whatever the cause of your grievance, he is innocent, as you yourself are good and upright; but I also owe an explanation to my liege and master. In what way can I have committed myself?—neither from you nor him have I taken or accepted the least benefit. The fortune my father left me I had for years given into the custody of an old and tried friend of our house; removing it from thence I presented it, under the circumstances your majesty is aware of, to this Brahmin. But if they had not been real gems, but only worthless metal and glass as this worthy priest intimates, by what means was my restoration to health so wonderfully wrought? That I gave it with pure and honest intention, witness for me the all but miracle by which I was saved!"

Thus spoke Madhava without changing a feature; but the king and his ministers laughed, and testified the good opinion they entertained for him. They then

199

pronounced the following judgment:—" Neither Siva nor Madhava are in the least to blame, they are wholly innocent."

In sorrow and shame the priest went his way, robbed of his whole fortune, and punished for his avarice and the heartless manner in which he had sacrificed his daughter; though fortunately for her and no thanks to her father, she found in Siva a good and affectionate husband.

The two rogues altered their mode of life: thenceforward they walked in the path of virtue and welldoing; and favoured by the king, whom they faithfully served, they lived many years honoured, respected, and happy in Ujjayini.

THE GOBLIN BIRD.

[Betschuanian, South Africa.]

WO brothers one day set out from their father's hut, to seek their fortune. The name of the elder one was Maszilo, the younger one was called Mazziloniane. After a few days' journeying they reached a plain, from which branched two roads ; the one led eastwards, the other westwards. The first road was covered with the footmarks of cattle, the other with the footmarks of dogs. Maszilo followed the latter road, his brother went in the opposite direction.

After some days travelling Mazziloniane passed a hill which formerly had been inhabited, and felt not a little astonished at beholding a great quantity of earthen vessels, all of which were placed upside down. In the hope of finding some treasure concealed under them, he removed several, until he came to one of immense

o

size.   Mazziloniane, gathering all his strength, gave it a violent push, but the vessel remained immoveable. The young traveller now doubled his exertions, but in vain.   Twice he was obliged to fasten the girdle round his loins, which through his exertions had burst; the vessel seemed as if rooted to the ground.   But all at once, as if by magic, it was upset by a slight touch, and revealed to the youthful and trembling Mazziloniane, a hideous and deformed giant.

"Why dost thou disturb me?" demanded the monster, in a voice of thunder.

Mazziloniane, having recovered from his first fright, observed with horror that one of the legs of the giant was as thick as the stem of a large tree, whilst the other was of an ordinary size.

"As a well-merited punishment for thy temerity in disturbing me, thou shalt henceforth carry me about;" and so saying the monster jumped on the shoulders of the unfortunate youth, who, unable to support such a weight, fell prostrate on the ground. Recovering himself with difficulty, he endeavoured to advance a few steps, and again he fell to the earth, his strength now wholly failing him. But the sight of an eland, which was swiftly passing by, presented to his mind the means of delivery.

"Dear father," said he, with trembling voice, to the abortion, "release me for a moment; the reason why I cannot carry you is that I have nothing wherewith to fasten you to my back; give me a few moments to kill the eland which has just passed by, and out of its hide I will cut some thongs for that purpose."

His demand was granted, and with the dogs that had accompanied him he disappeared from the plain.

After he had run a considerable distance he took refuge in a cavern. But the thick-legged monster, tired of waiting, soon followed, and wherever he discovered a footmark of the youth, he in a mocking voice cried out :—

"The pretty little footmark of my dear child, the pretty little footmark of Mazziloniane."

The youth heard him approaching, and felt the ground tremble under his steps. Seized with despair he left the cavern, and calling his dogs, he set them on the enemy; stroking and encouraging them, he said—

"On! my brave dogs, kill him, devour him, but leave his thick leg for me."

The dogs obeyed the command of their master, and soon there was nothing left but the deformed and shapeless leg, which now he fearlessly approached, and with his axe cut into pieces, and, O wonder! out of it came a herd of most beautiful cows, one of them being as white as the driven snow; overjoyed he drove the cattle before him, taking the road leading to his father's hut.

Meanwhile the other brother having got possession of a great number of dogs, he also returned towards his home, and they both now met on the same place where they so shortly before had separated. The

204

younger embracing the elder brother, offered him part of his herd, saying to him : " As fortune has favoured me most, take what you like, but you must leave me the white cow, for to no one else can she ever belong."

But Maszilo seemed to have placed his every desire upon this very animal; regardless of all the rest, he begged and intreated his brother to give up to him the possession thereof; but in vain were his prayers. Having journeyed together for two days, on the third day they came to a spring—" Let us tarry here," said Maszilo, I am faint and exhausted with thirst; let us dig a deep hole, and convey the water into it, that it may get cool and fresh."

When they had dug the well, Maszilo went in search of a great flat stone, and with it covered the hole to protect the water from being heated by the rays of the sun ; after the water had been sufficiently cooled, Maszilo drank first. His brother was now going to do the same, but the moment he bent himself over the well, Maszilo suddenly taking him by the hair, forced his head under the water, and held it there until he was suffocated ; he then pushed the corpse into the hole, and covered it over with the stone.

With drooping head, though now sole master of the herd, the murderer proceeded on his journey, but hardly had he advanced a few steps, when a little bird perched on the horn of the white cow, and in a mournful tune sang: "Tsiri! tsiri! Maszilo killed Mazziloniane to get possession of the white cow which the murdered brother so much loved."

Enraged, he killed the bird with a stone, but hardly had he sufficiently recovered himself to proceed on his journey, when the bird again came flying, placed itself on the same spot, and repeated the same words; Maszilo again killed him with a stone, and then crushed him with his heavy staff; but within a few minutes the bird reappeared for the third time, again perching on the horn of the cow, and repeating the same words.

" Ah, Demon !" cried Maszilo, choking with rage, " I will try a more effectual way to silence thee;" whereupon he threw his staff at the hated little bird, who in such doleful tunes had stirred up and upbraided his conscience-stricken soul: he again killed it, and then lighting a fire, in it he burnt the bird to ashes, which he scattered in the winds.

Now convinced that the goblin-bird would return no more, Maszilo, full of pride and hardiness, returned to

THE GOBLIN BIRD

P. 207.

his father's dwelling. On his arrival there, he was surrounded by all the villagers, who, full of curiosity,
gathered around him, in admiration of the rich flock,
and praised his good fortune, but the first impulse of
their curiosity satiated, they almost with one voice
inquired " Where is Mazziloniane ?"

" I know not ; we went different ways," answered he.

Many of his relations now surrounded the white
cow, and exclaimed : " Oh how beautiful she is ! what
fine hair ! what a pure colour ! happy the man that
owns such a treasure ! "

Suddenly, their exclamations were changed into deep
silence, for upon one of the horns of the much-admired
animal appeared a little bird, singing in most melancholy
strains, " Tsiri ! tsiri ! Maszilo killed Mazziloniane, to
get possession of the white cow which the murdered
brother so much loved."

" What ! has Maszilo killed his brother ?" all exclaimed, and, full of horror, turned away from the
murderer, unable to account to themselves for the
emotion he inspired, and the strangeness of the dis-
closure. Infuriated, they drove Maszilo from their
home, into the desert : in the confusion this occasioned,
the little bird flew to the murdered man's sister, and

whispered in her ear, "I am the soul of Mazziloniane; Maszilo has killed me; my body lies in a well near the desert, go bury it—" and then the bird flew back into the desert, evermore to be the companion of the murderer.

THE SHEPHERD AND THE SERPENT.

[German, Traditional.]

———◆———

N a peaceful, pleasantly situated little village, there once lived a poor shepherd youth.

Near the village was a valley, a lonely retired spot, whither the youth always guided his flock; and it seemed as though he had selected that quiet valley for his favourite retreat. He never took his noon-day meal, nor lay down to repose in the cool shade, except in that beloved place. Thither was he ever drawn by an irresistible longing.

The place itself was simple enough—a rugged block of stone, beneath which murmured a little rivulet, and a wild cherry-tree which overshadowed the stone with its leafy branches, were all that was to be seen there; but the youth felt happy when he spread his meal

209

upon that stone, and drank from that streamlet.
When, after having partaken of his meal, he stretched
himself to rest upon the stone, he would fancy he heard
a mysterious singing, and sometimes a sighing too,
beneath it; he would then listen and watch, but
would finally slumber and dream. His spirit seemed
to be ever wrapped in mysterious unearthly happiness. On going forth with his flocks in the morning,
and returning home with them in the evening, this
unaccountable longing seemed always to take possession of him. He liked not to accompany the throng
of merry village youths and maidens who went about
singing and frolicking on festive evenings, but preferred to walk alone, silent and even melancholy. But
when the fair morning dawned again, and he went
forth with his lambs over heath and meadow, his spirit
grew ever more serene as he drew nearer to the beloved
stone and to the shade of the dear cherry-tree. It
often happened, too, that whilst he rested there and
played upon his flute, a silver-white serpent came out
from under the stone, and after wreathing herself
caressingly at his feet, would then erect herself and
gaze upon the shepherd, until two big tears would roll
from her eyes, and then she softly slid back again:

on these occasions a still more peculiar and strange feeling filled the shepherd's heart.

At length he altogether ceased to associate with the merry band of youths and maidens; their mirthsome noise was unpleasant to him; whilst, on the contrary, the still solitude became more and more dear to him.

One lovely Sunday in the spring time—it was Trinity Sunday, which the peasants call "Golden Sunday," and which they always keep with especial festivity— when the youth of the village were to have a merry dance beneath the linden-trees, the pensive shepherd boy, drawn by that inexpressible longing, directed his steps at mid-day to the lonely valley of the stone and cherry-tree. He gazed serenely upon the dear spot, and then sat down and listened musingly to the rustling of the leaves and the mysterious sounds under the stone, when suddenly a bright light shone before his eyes, a pang of terror shot through his heart, and looking up he saw a beauteous form arrayed in white like an angel, standing before him with a soft expression and folded hands, whilst with transported senses he heard a sweet voice thus address him: "O youth, fear not, but hear the supplication of an unhappy maiden, and do not drive me from thee, nor flee from my misfortune. I am a noble princess, and have immense treasures of pearls and gold; but for many hundred years I have languished under enchantment, have been banished beneath this stone, and am doomed to glide about in the form of a serpent. In that shape I have often gazed on thee and conceived the hope that thou mayest release me. Thou art still pure in heart as a child. Only once throughout the whole year, this very hour on Golden Sunday, am I permitted to wander on the earth in my own form; and if I then find a youth with a pure heart, I may implore him for my deliverance. Release me then, thou beloved one! release me, I implore thee by all that is holy!"— The maiden sank at the shepherd's feet, which she clasped as she looked up to him weeping. The heart of the youth heaved with transport; he raised the angelic maiden and faltered out: "Oh say only what I must do to free thee, thou fair beloved one!"

"Return hither to-morrow at the same hour," replied she, "and when I appear before thee in my serpent form, and wind myself around thee, and thrice kiss thee, do not, oh! do not shudder, else must I again languish enchanted here for another century!" She vanished, and again a soft sighing and singing issued from beneath the stone.

212

THE SHEPHERD AND THE SERPENT.

On the following day, at the hour of noon, the shepherd, not without fear in his heart, waited at the appointed place, and supplicated Heaven for strength and constancy at the trying moment of the serpent's kiss. Already the silver-white serpent glided from beneath the stone, approached the youth, twined herself round his body, and raised her serpent head, with its bright eyes, to kiss him. He remained steady, and endured the three kisses. A mighty crash was then heard, and dreadful thunders rolled around the youth, who had fallen senseless on the ground. A magic change passed over him, and when he was restored to his senses, he found himself lying on white cushions of silk, in a richly-adorned chamber, with the beautiful maiden kneeling by his couch, holding his hand to her heart. "Oh, thanks be to Heaven!" exclaimed she, when he opened his eyes; "receive my thanks, beloved youth, for my deliverance, and take as thy reward my fair lands, and this palace with all its rich treasures, and take me too as thy faithful wife: thou shalt henceforth be happy, and have plenitude of joy!"

And the shepherd was happy and joyful; that longing of his heart which had so often drawn him towards the stone, was gloriously satisfied. He dwelt, remote

213

from the world, in the bosom of happiness, with his fair spouse; and he never wished himself back on earth, nor amongst his lambs again. But in the village there was great lamentation for the shepherd who had so suddenly vanished: they sought him in the valley, and by the stone under the cherry-tree, whither he had last gone, but neither the shepherd, nor the stone, nor the cherry-tree were to be found any longer; and no human eye ever again beheld any trace of either.

THE EXPEDITIOUS FROG.

[Wendian.]

FOX came one day at full speed to a pond to drink. A frog who was sitting there, began to croak at him. Then, said the fox, "Be off with you, or I'll swallow you."

The frog, however, replied: "Don't give yourself such airs; I am swifter than you!"

At this the fox laughed; but as the frog persisted in boasting of his swiftness, the fox said at length: "Now, then, we will both run to the next town, and we shall see which can go the faster."

Then the fox turned round, and as he did so, the frog leapt up into his bushy tail. Off went the fox, and when he reached the gate of the city, he turned round again to see if he could spy the frog coming after him. As he did so, the frog hopped out of his tail on the ground. The fox, after looking all about without being able to see the frog, turned round once more in order to enter the city.

Then the frog called out to him: "So! you are come at last? I am just going back again, for I really thought you meant not to come at all."

EASTWARD OF THE SUN, AND WESTWARD OF THE MOON.

———•———

IN days of yore there lived a poor charcoal-burner who had many children. His poverty was so great, that he knew not how to feed them from day to day, and they had scarcely any clothes to cover them. Nevertheless all the children were very beautiful, but the youngest daughter was the most beautiful of them all.

Now it happened on a Thursday evening, late in the autumn, that a terrible storm came on. It was dark as pitch, the rain came down in torrents, and the wind blew till the windows cracked again. The whole family sat round the hearth, busy with their different occupations ; suddenly some one gave three loud knocks at the window; the man went out to see whom it could be, and when he got outside the door, he saw standing by it, a great white bear.

P

"Good evening to you!" said the bear.

"Good evening!" said the man.

"I have called," said the bear, "to say that if you will give me your youngest daughter in marriage, I will make you as rich as you now are poor."

The man thought that would not be amiss, but he considered that he must first consult his daughter on the subject; so he stepped in, and told her that a great white bear was outside the door, who had promised to make him as rich as he was now poor, provided he would give him his youngest daughter in marriage. The maiden, however, said "No," and would hear nothing at all about the matter; so the man went out again, spoke very civilly to the bear, and told him to call again next Thursday evening, and in the mean time he would try what could be done. During the week they tried to persuade the maiden, and told her all kinds of fine things as to the riches they were to have, and how well she herself would be provided for, till at last she consented. So she washed the two or three things she had, dressed herself as well as she could, and made herself ready for the journey.

When the bear returned the following Thursday evening, all was ready : the maiden took her bundle in

EASTWARD OF THE SUN AND WESTWARD OF THE MOON.   P. 219.

her hand, seated herself on his back, and off they went. When they had gone a good way, the bear asked her: "Do you feel sad?"

No, that she did not in the least.

"Mind you hold fast by my shaggy coat," said the bear, "and then there will be nothing to fear."

Thus she rode on the bear's back far far away—indeed nobody can say precisely how far it was—and at last they arrived at a great rock. The bear knocked, and a door opened, through which they entered a large castle, in which were a great many rooms, all lighted with lamps, and glittering with gold and silver: there was also a grand saloon, and in the saloon stood a table covered with the most costly viands. The bear then gave her a silver bell, which he told her to ring when she wanted anything, and it would immediately be brought to her. Now after she had eaten and drunk, and towards evening grew tired, and wished to go to bed, she rang her bell, and immediately a door opened into a chamber, where there was as beautiful a bed as she could wish for, ready prepared for her; the pillows were covered with silk, and the curtains fringed with gold, and all her toilette utensils were of silver and gold. As soon, however, as she had extinguished the light, and lay down in her bed, some one came and lay down by her side, and this happened every night; but she could never see who it was, as the person never came till after the light was put out, and always went away before day-break.

Thus she lived for some time, contented and happy, till at length she felt so great a desire to see her parents, and brothers and sisters, that she grew quite dull and melancholy. Then the bear asked her one day why she was always so still and thoughtful.

"Ah!" replied she, "I feel so lonely here in the castle, for I so much wish to see my parents, and brothers and sisters, once more."

"That you can easily do," said the bear, "but you must promise me that you will never converse with your mother alone, but only when all the others are present; for she will try to take you by the hand and lead you into another room, in order to speak to you alone, but do not consent to it, for if you do, she will make both you and me unhappy."

The maiden said she would be very careful to do as he desired her.

The following Sunday the bear came to her, and said she might now begin her journey to her parents.

She seated herself on his back, and they commenced their journey. After they had travelled a very long time, they came to a great white castle, and she saw her sisters going in and out, and all was so beautiful and grand, it was quite a pleasure to behold it.

"That is where your parents dwell," said the bear, "now do not forget what I have said to you, or you will make yourself and me very miserable."

She would not forget, repeated the maiden, and she entered the castle; the bear, however, went back again. When her parents saw their daughter, they were more delighted than it is possible to express. They could not thank her enough for what she had done for them, and they told how wonderfully comfortable they were now, and inquired how matters went with her. Oh, she also was very happy, returned the maiden, she had everything she could desire. What else she told them, I do not exactly know, but I believe it was no every-day tale that she told them. In the afternoon, when they had dined, it happened exactly as the bear had foretold; the mother wanted to talk with her daughter in private, but the maiden remembered what the bear had said, and would not go with her, but said : "Oh, we can say what we have got to say, quite as well here."

Now, how it happened, I cannot tell, but all I know is, that her mother persuaded her at last, and then she got the whole history from her. The maiden related how some one came into her bed every night, but that she had never seen who it was, and that made her so uneasy, and the day seemed very long to her, because she was always alone.

"Who knows !" said the mother, "surely it must be some wizard who sleeps by you ; but if you will take my advice, when he is fast asleep, get up and strike a light, and see who it is; but be careful not to let any grease drop upon him."

In the evening the bear came to fetch the maiden home. When they had gone a good way he asked her if it had not happened as he had told her.

"Yes," she could not deny that it had.

"Have you listened to your mother's counsel ?" said the bear ; "if you have, you have ruined yourself and me, and our friendship is at an end."

"No," she had not done so, replied she.

Now when they had got home, and the maiden had gone to bed, the same happened as usual, some one

222

came and lay down by her. During the night, however, when she heard that he was asleep, she rose and kindled a light, and then she saw lying in her bed the handsomest prince that can be imagined, and she immediately loved him so well, that she could not refrain from kissing him that very moment. But as she did this, she accidentally let three drops of oil fall from her lamp, upon his shirt, and thereupon he awoke.

"What have you done?" cried he, as he opened his eyes; " now you have made yourself and me unhappy for ever. If you had but held out for a year, I should have been delivered; for I have a step-mother who has enchanted me, so that by day I am a bear, but at night I become a man again. But all is over for us both, for I must now leave you, and return to her. She dwells in a castle which lies *eastward of the Sun,* and *westward of the Moon,* and there I shall be obliged to marry a princess who has a nose three ells long."

The maiden then began to weep and bemoan herself; but it was too late, the prince was obliged to go. She asked him if she might not accompany him.

" No," said he, " that must not be."

" Can you not then tell me the road that I may find

you?" inquired she; "for I suppose I may be allowed that."

"Yes, that you are right welcome to do," said he; "but there is no road that leads to it; for the castle lies eastward of the Sun, and westward of the Moon, and you will never get there."

In the morning when she awoke, the prince and the castle had both vanished, and she found herself lying on the bare earth, in a thick dark forest, and she was dressed in her old clothes, and near her lay the same bundle that she had brought with her from her former home. When she had rubbed her eyes till she was quite awake, and had cried till she could cry no longer, she began her journey, and wandered for many a long day, till at last she came to a great mountain. At the foot of the mountain sat an old woman, playing with a golden apple; the maiden asked her if she could tell her the way to where the prince lived with his step-mother, in a castle which was situated eastward of the Sun, and westward of the Moon, and who was to marry a princess who had a nose three ells long.

"How come you to know him?" asked the woman. "Can you be the maiden whom he wished to marry?"

"Yes," she replied, "she was that maiden."

" So ! then you are the chosen one ! " resumed the woman; "ah ! my child," continued she, " I would willingly help you, but I myself know nothing more of the castle than that it lies eastward of the Sun, and westward of the Moon, and that you are almost certain never to get there ; I will, however, lend you my horse, and you may ride on him to my next neighbour ; perhaps she may be able to tell you the way thither, but when you have reached her, just give the horse a pat under the left ear, and bid him go home again; and now take this golden apple, for perhaps you may find a use for it."

The maiden mounted the horse, and rode for a long, long, time ; and at last arrived at another mountain, where sat an old woman with a golden reel. The maiden asked her if she could tell her the way to the castle, which lay eastward of the Sun, and west-ward of the Moon. This old woman, however, said just like the other, that she knew nothing more about the castle than that it lay eastward of the Sun, and westward of the Moon, "and you are almost sure never to find it," added she, " but I will lend you my horse to ride upon to my next neighbour, and perhaps she may tell you the way ; when you get there, however, just give the horse a pat under his left ear, and tell him to go home; now take this reel, for perhaps you may find some use for it."

The maiden seated herself on the horse, and rode for many days and weeks; at last she again arrived at a mountain where an old woman sat spinning with a golden distaff. The maiden now again inquired about the prince, and the castle which was situated eastward of the Sun, and westward of the Moon.

" Are you she whom the prince wished to marry ? " asked the woman.

" Yes," replied the maiden.

But this old woman knew no more about the castle than the two others.

"Eastward of the Sun, and westward of the Moon, lies the castle, and you are almost certain never to get there. But I will lend you my horse, and you may ride upon him to the East Wind; perhaps he may be able to tell you the way, but when you get to him, give the horse a pat under the left ear, and bid him go home, and now take this golden distaff, you will probably have occasion for it."

She rode now a very long time, and at last arrived where the East Wind dwelt, and asked him if he could not tell her how to get to the prince who lived in the castle which lay eastward of the Sun, and westward of the Moon.

"Truly, I have often heard tell of the prince, and of the castle too," said the East Wind, "but I cannot tell you the way, for I have never blown so far; but I will carry you to my brother, the West Wind; perhaps he may know, for he is much stronger than I am. You have only to seat yourself on my back, and I will bear you thither."

The maiden seated herself on his back, and off they went. When they reached the West Wind, the East Wind told him that he had brought a maiden who was to marry the prince who dwelt in the castle that lay eastward of the Sun, and westward of the Moon, and asked if he could tell the way thither.

" No," answered the West Wind. " I have never blown so far. But," said he, addressing the maiden, " you may seat yourself on my back, and I will carry you to the South Wind; he may be able to tell you, for he is much stronger than I, and blows and blusters every where."

So the maiden seated herself on his back, and when they had reached the South Wind, the West

Wind asked him if he did not know the way to the castle which lay eastward of the Sun, and westward of the Moon, for the maiden whom he had brought with him, said he, was to marry the prince who dwelt there.

"I have blown pretty far, and pretty strong in my time," said the South Wind, " but I never went so far as that. If, however, you desire it," said he to the maiden, " I will carry you to my brother, the North Wind, who is the eldest and strongest of us all, and if he cannot tell you the way, you may rest assured you will never find it."

The maiden seated herself on his back, and off they went at such a rate that the plain heaved again.

In a very short time they reached the North Wind; but he was so wild and turbulent that long before they got up to him, he blew, I know not how much snow and ice, in their faces.

"What do you want?" cried he, in a voice that made their skin creep.

"Oh, you must not be so rough with us," said the South Wind; "for here am I, your own brother, and this is the maiden who is to marry the prince who dwells in the castle which lies eastward of the Sun, and westward of the Moon, and she is very desirous to ask you if you cannot give her some information about it."

"Yes, I know full well where it lies," said the North Wind; "I wafted an aspen leaf thither, once; but I was so fatigued that I could not blow for many a long day afterwards. If, however, you are resolved to go," said he to the maiden, "and are not afraid, I will take you on my back and try whether I can waft you so far."

"Yes," said the maiden, "there I must and will go, by all possible means, and I will not be frightened either, let it be as bad as it may."

"In that case you must pass the night here," said the North Wind; "for we must have the whole day before us, if we are to go there."

Early the next morning the North Wind awakened her, got himself into breath, and grew so large and strong, that it was terrible to behold; and off they dashed through the air, as if the world were coming to an end. Then arose such an awful storm, that whole villages and forests were overturned, and as they passed over the ocean, the ships sank by hundreds. On they went still over the water, so far as no one would believe, but the North Wind became weaker and weaker, and so weak did he become, that he could scarcely blow any more, and he sank lower and lower, and at last got so low, that the waves flowed over his heels.

"Are you frightened?" inquired he of the maiden.

"No, not in the least," said she.

Now they were only a very little way from land, and the North Wind had scarcely any strength remaining, to enable him to reach the shore under the windows of the castle that lay eastward of the Sun, and westward of the Moon. When he did get there, however, he was so weary and faint, that he was obliged to rest many days before he could return home.

In the morning the maiden seated herself under the windows of the castle, and played with her golden apple, and the first person who saw her, was the long-nosed princess whom the prince was to marry.

"What do you ask for your golden apple?" inquired the princess, as she opened her window.

"It is not to be had for gold nor for gain;" said the maiden.

"If you will not part with it for gold nor for gain, what will you take for it?" demanded the princess: "I will give whatever you ask."

"Well, then, if you will let me pass a night by the prince's side, you shall have it," said the maiden.

"Oh! that you are quite welcome to do," said the princess, and took the golden apple.

But when at night the maiden came into the prince's chamber, he was fast asleep; she called to him and shook him, and cried and moaned, but she could not awaken him, and as soon as the morning dawned, the princess with the long nose came and drove her out of the room.

That day the maiden again placed herself under the castle windows, and unwound the yarn from the golden reel, and the long-nosed princess spoke to her as on the day before. She asked her what she would take for the reel, but the maiden said it was not to be had for gold nor gain, but that if she might pass another night beside the prince, the princess should have it. She agreed, and took the golden reel. But when the maiden entered the chamber the prince was fast asleep; and, let her call and shake him, and weep and wail as she might, she could not rouse him; and when the morning dawned, the princess with the long nose again came and drove her away.

This day the maiden seated herself as before with

her golden distaff and span. When the princess saw the distaff, she wanted that also, and opened the window, and asked what she would sell it for. The maiden replied as before, neither for gold nor gain; but if the princess would let her pass another night with the prince, she should have it. Yes, she was very welcome, said the princess, and took the distaff. Now it happened that some persons who slept close to the prince's apartment, had heard the lamentations and melancholy cries of the maiden during the two nights, and that morning they told the prince of it. So in the evening when the princess brought the drink which the prince was accustomed to take before he went to bed, he pretended to drink it, but in reality he poured it on the ground behind him, for he suspected strongly that the princess had mixed a sleeping potion with it. Now when the maiden went into his room that night, he was wide awake, and was overjoyed at seeing her, and he made her tell him all that had happened to her, and how she had contrived to get to the castle. When she had related all he said:—

"You are come just at the right moment; for to morrow is to be my wedding with the princess; but I want nothing of her and her long nose, for you are the only one I will wed. I shall therefore say, that I want to know what my bride is fit for, and I shall require her to wash the three spots of oil out of my shirt. This she will willingly undertake to do, but I know that she will not succeed ; for the spots were made by your hand, and can only be washed out again by Christian hands, and not by the hands of such a pack of sorcerers as she belongs to. I shall, however, say, that I will have no other bride than she who can succeed, and when they have all tried and failed, I shall call you, and desire you to try." So the night passed happily away, and on the bridal day the prince said :—

" I should like vastly to see what my bride is fit for."

" That is no more than fair," said the step-mother.

" I have such a beautiful shirt," said the prince, " that I should like to wear it on my bridal day, but there are spots of grease on it, and I would willingly have them washed out ; I have in consequence resolved to wed none but her who is able to wash them out."

Truly, that was no such mighty matter, thought the women, and immediately set to work ; and the princess with the long nose began to wash away as fast as she could. But the longer she washed, the larger and darker grew the spots.

"Oh! you do not know much about the matter," said the old sorceress, her mother: "give it to me."

But when she got hold of the shirt, it grew darker still, and the more she washed and rubbed, the larger grew the spots. Now the other witches of the establishment all tried their hands on the shirt, and the longer they washed the worse it grew, and at last the whole shirt looked as if it had been put up the chimney.

"Ah! you are all good for nothing," cried the prince; "there sits a poor beggar wench under the windows; I'll lay any wager she knows more about washing than all of you put together. Come hither, wench!" cried he; and when she came, he asked her:—

"Can you wash that shirt clean?"

"I don't know," said the maiden; "but I think I can."

So the maiden took the shirt, and under her hands it soon became as white as the falling snow.

"Ah, I will have thee for my bride!" cried the prince, and when the old sorceress heard that, she fell into such a tremendous rage, that it killed her; and I think that the princess with the long nose, and the whole pack of witches, must have expired also, for I have never heard of them since. Then the prince and his bride set free all the Christians who were confined in the castle; and they took as much gold and silver as they could carry away, and went far away from the castle that lies eastward of the Sun, and westward of the Moon. But how they contrived to get away, and whither they went, I do not know; if, however, they are what I take them for, they are at no very great distance from here.

THE LITTLE MAN IN GREY.

[Upper Lusatia.]

MINER, a blacksmith, and a nun were travelling together through the wide world. One day they were bewildered in a dark forest, and were so wearied with wandering that they thought themselves right fortunate when they saw, at a distance, a building wherein they hoped to find shelter. They went up to it, and found that it was an ancient castle, which, although half in ruins, still was in condition to afford a habitation for such distressed pilgrims as they. They resolved therefore to enter, and held a council how they might best establish themselves in it, and they very soon agreed that it would be best that one of them should always remain at home whilst the other two went out in search of provisions. They then cast lots who should first stay behind, and the lot fell on the nun.

236

So when the miner and the blacksmith were gone out into the forest, she prepared the food, and when noon arrived, and her companions did not return, she ate her share of the provisions. As soon as she had finished her meal a little man, clad in grey, came to the door, and shivering, said: " Oh, I am so cold!"

Then the nun said to him: " Come to the fire and warm thyself."

The little man did as the nun desired him, but presently after he exclaimed: " Oh, how hungry I am !"

Then the nun said to him : " There is food by the fire ; eat some of it."

The little man fell upon the food, and in a very short time devoured it all. When the nun saw what he had done she was very angry, and scolded him for not having left any food for her companions. Upon this the little man flew into a great passion, seized the nun, beat her, and threw her from one wall to the other. He then quitted the castle and went his way, leaving the nun on the floor. Towards evening the two companions returned home very hungry, and when they found no food they reproached the nun bitterly, and would not believe her when she told them what had happened.

The following day the miner proposed to keep watch in the castle, and said he would take good care that no one should have to go to bed fasting. So the two others went into the forest, and the miner looked after the cooking, ate his share, and put the rest by on the oven. The little grey clad man came as before, but how terrified was the miner when he perceived that this time the little man had two heads. He shivered as on the preceding day, saying : " Oh, how cold I am !"

Much frightened, the miner pointed to the hearth. Then the little man said : " Oh, how hungry I am !"

" There is food on the oven," said the miner; " eat some."

Then the little man fell to with both his heads, and soon ate it all up, and licked the plates clean. When the miner reproached him for eating all up, he got for his pains just the same treatment as the nun. The little man beat him black and blue, and flung him against the walls till they cracked ; the poor miner lost both sight and hearing, and at last the little man left him lying there, and went his way.

When the blacksmith and the nun returned hungry in the evening, and found no supper, the blacksmith fell into a great rage with the miner, and declared that when his turn should come next day to watch, the castle, no one should want a supper. The next day, at meal time, the little man appeared again but this time he had three heads. He complained of

cold, and was bidden by the blacksmith to sit by the hearth. When he said he was hungry, the blacksmith gave him a portion of the food. The little man soon dispatched that, and looked greedily round with his six eyes, asking for more food, and when the blacksmith hesitated to give it him, he tried to treat him as he had done the nun and the miner; the blacksmith, however, was no coward, and seizing a great smith's hammer, he rushed on the little man, and struck off two of his heads, so that he made off as fast as he could with his remaining head. But the blacksmith chased him through the forest along many a pathway, till at last he suddenly disappeared through an iron door. The blacksmith was thus obliged to give up the pursuit, but promised himself not to rest until, with the aid of his two companions, he should have brought the matter to a satisfactory conclusion.

Meantime the nun and the miner had returned home. The smith set their supper before them as he had undertaken to do, and then related his adventure, showing them the two heads he had cut off, with their staring glazed eyes. They then all three resolved to free themselves altogether, if possible, from the little grey man, and the very next day they set to work. They searched a long time before they could find the iron door through which he had disappeared the preceding day, and great toil did it cost them before they were able to break it open. They then found themselves in a great vaulted chamber wherein sat a beautiful maiden at a table, working. She started up, and threw herself at their feet, thanking them as her deliverers, and told them that she was the daughter of a king, and had been confined there by a powerful sorcerer. Yesterday afternoon she had suddenly felt that the spell was loosened, and from that moment she had hourly expected her freedom, but that besides herself there was the daughter of another king confined in the same place. They then went in search of the other king's daughter and set her at liberty also. She thanked them joyfully in like manner, and said that she also had felt since yesterday afternoon that the spell was unbound. The two royal maidens now informed their liberators that in concealed caves of the castle great treasures were hoarded, which were guarded by a terrible dog. They went in search of them and at length came upon the dog, whom the blacksmith slew with his hammer, although he endeavoured to defend himself.

The treasure consisted of whole tons of gold and silver, and a handsome young man sat beside them as if to guard them. He came to meet them and thanked them for setting him free. He was the son of a king, but had been transformed by a sorcerer into the three-headed little man and banished to that castle. By the loss of two of his heads the spell was taken off the two royal maidens, and when the blacksmith slew the terrible dog he himself was delivered from it. For that service the whole of the treasure should be theirs.

The treasure was then divided, and it was a long time before they could complete the distribution. The two princesses, however, out of gratitude to their deliverers, married the miner and the blacksmith, and the handsome prince married the nun; and so they passed the rest of their lives in peace and joy.

RED, WHITE, AND BLACK.

[Normandy.]

———◆———

THE eldest son of a mighty monarch was once walking alone in a field, which, as it was the depth of winter, happened to be covered with snow. He perceived a raven flying by, and shot him. The bird fell dead on the ground and the snow was sprinkled with his blood. The glossy black of his plumage, the dazzling white of the snow, and the red blood, formed a combination of colours which delighted the eyes of the prince. The impression did not pass away from his memory; the colours seemed perpetually to float before his eyes, and at length he conceived in his heart an intense desire to possess a wife who should be as rosy as that blood, as white as that snow, and have hair as black as the plumage of that raven.

One day as he sat profoundly musing on the object of his desires, a voice said to him :—"My prince, go travel into Marvel-land, and there in the centre of an immense forest you will find an apple-tree, bearing larger and fairer fruit than you have ever yet beheld; pluck three of the apples, but forbear to open them until you shall be again at home; they will present you with a bride exactly such as you covet."

Marvel-land was very remote from the prince's home, and very difficult of access, but nothing could deter him from undertaking the journey. He started forthwith, travelled over land and sea, and searched the forest with the utmost diligence, till at length he found the tree. He broke off three fine apples, and as, in the first transports of his joy, he could not resist the curiosity which urged him, he opened one of them on the spot. A lovely maiden came out of it so enchantingly fair, and so exactly corresponding to the image he had formed, that he was lost in admiration. But the maiden, so far from being well disposed towards him, gazed on him with looks of scorn, and bitterly reproaching him for having carried her off, vanished from his sight.

This great disappointment might naturally have reduced him to despair; but as he was of a disposition

244

to be easily consoled, he soon comforted himself with the trust that the two remaining apples would give him compensation for his loss. Full of this sweet hope, he resolved not to open them until he should reach his own country. But even the saddest experience does not always suffice to enable us to resist temptation. The prince's impatience was stronger than his reason, and a second time he yielded to his desire of opening one of the remaining apples.

He was at that time on the sea, and as there is very little amusement to be had during a voyage on that element, perhaps very few persons would have acted otherwise than he did. He persuaded himself that if he caused the whole of the deck to be covered with an awning, the fair one could not escape him. He there-fore opened the second apple, and as before, a maiden of unequalled beauty stood before him; she manifested the same displeasure as the former one, and notwith-standing the precautions he had taken, disappeared in like manner. But even these two experiences barely sufficed to render the prince prudent.

At length however he reached his native country, and on opening the remaining apple, a third maiden as lovely as the others, but far more gentle, appeared.

245

He immediately married her, and they were the happiest couple in the world.

After a time he was obliged to go out to war against a neighbouring potentate, and thus to quit his beloved. The queen-mother, in whose power the young bride now found herself, had never approved the marriage. She caused her daughter-in-law to be murdered in a barbarous manner, flung the corpse into the moat that surrounded the castle, and to complete her guilty deed, she substituted for the unhappy queen a person who was entirely devoted to herself.

When the prince returned he was greatly astonished to find a wife so different from the one he had left. But the queen his mother assured him confidently that the person she presented to him was his wife. She did not attempt to deny the great alteration in her appearance, but she ascribed the transformation to the effect of magic.

In truth, the mode by which the prince had obtained his wife did give some appearance of probability to the queen's assertion, and at all events, whether from softness of disposition, or absence of distrust, the prince believed what he was told. But all was unavailing to make him forget his first passion. Night and day he

246

mused upon the past, and would pass whole hours leaning against the window of his palace.

One day as he was thus musing in deep melancholy, he perceived in the castle moat a fish whose shining scales were red, white, and black. He was so struck by the sight that he never withdrew his eyes from the fish. The old queen, who considered this extraordinary attention to the fish as a consequence of his early passion, resolved to destroy every object that might tend to recall it to his memory. She therefore commanded the false princess to feign the most vehement longing to eat the very fish which had so attracted her husband's attention. He could not deny a request which in the opinion of all others was so innocent. The fish was caught, served at the table of the supposed princess, and the prince relapsed into his usual melancholy.

Not very long after he was comforted by the appearance of a tree which was red, white, and black. The tree was of an unknown genus, no one had planted it, nor sown any seed; it had suddenly grown up on the spot where the scales of the fish had been thrown away.

This fair tree gave the prince great pleasure and the queen equal displeasure; she at once resolved on its destruction in spite of the sad prince's remonstrances. It was uprooted and burnt; but from its ashes suddenly arose a magnificent palace constructed of red rubies, white pearls, and black ebony. The three colours which the prince so loved, produced now an enchanting effect. Long did he endeavour in vain to enter that fair palace; the gates remained fast closed, and at last he contented himself with incessantly contemplating it, and passed day after day in this occupation which recalled to him the object of his wishes.

His constancy was at last rewarded; the gates flew open; he entered the palace, and after traversing numerous apartments, he found in a small chamber his first wife whom he had so tenderly loved, and whose memory was so dear to him. She reproached him for having by his yielding disposition caused her so much suffering, but at the same time testified the vivid joy which she felt as she perceived that he was so deserving of the forgiveness she bestowed on him.

The happiness of the re-united pair was not again disturbed, and they lived together perfectly satisfied with their destiny.

THE TWELVE LOST PRINCESSES AND THE WIZARD KING.

[African.]

———◆———

NCE upon a time there lived a king who had twelve daughters, whom he loved so tenderly that he could not bear that they should be out of his presence, except when he was sleeping in the afternoon, and then they always took a walk. On one occasion, it happened that whilst the king was enjoying his afternoon's nap, the princesses went out as usual, but they did not return home. This threw all the inhabitants of the country into the greatest trouble and affliction, but the king was still more grieved than any of his subjects. He sent messengers to every corner of his kingdom, and into all the foreign lands he had ever heard mentioned, causing search to be made for his daughters; but no tidings could he get of them.

R   249

So, after a time, it became quite clear to everybody that they had been carried off by some wizard. The report of this soon spread from city to city, and from country to country, till at last it reached the ears of another king, who lived far, far away, and this king happened to have twelve sons. When the twelve princes heard the marvellous tale about the twelve princesses, they begged their father to permit them to travel in search of the missing royal maidens. The old king, however, for a long time would not hear of any such thing, for he feared that he might never see his sons again; but they threw themselves at his feet, and besought him so long and earnestly that at last he yielded, and gave them leave to set out on their travels. He caused a vessel to be equipped for them, and gave the charge of it to one of his courtiers, called Commander Rod. Long, long did they sail, and whenever they touched on the coast of any country, they made every inquiry about the princesses, but could not discover the least trace of them.

They had nearly completed the seventh year since they first set sail, when a violent storm arose. It blew such a gale that they thought they never should reach the shore; but on the third day the tempest subsided, and suddenly it became quite calm. All on board were now so fatigued by the hard work they had done during the tempest that they all went to sleep at once, excepting only the youngest prince, who became very restless, and could not sleep at all. Now whilst he was pacing the deck, the vessel neared an island, and on the shore was a little dog running backwards and forwards, and howling and barking towards the ship as if it wanted to be taken on board. The king's son whistled to it, and tried to entice it to him, but it seemed afraid to leave the shore, and only barked and howled louder still. The prince thought it would be a sin to leave the poor dog to perish, for he supposed it had escaped there from some ship that had foundered during the storm. He therefore set to work to lower the boat, and after having rowed to the shore, he went towards the little dog, but whenever he was about to lay hold of it, it sprang from him, and so lured him onward, till at last he found himself unexpectedly in the court of a great and magnificent castle, when the little dog suddenly changed into a beautiful princess.

The prince then noticed, sitting on the beach, a man so gigantic and frightful that he was quite alarmed. "You have no cause for uneasiness," said the man; but when the prince heard his voice he was more frightened still.

" I know very well what you want ; you are one of the twelve princes who are in search of the twelve lost princesses. I know also where they are. They are beside my master, each sitting on her own chair, and combing the hair of one of his heads, for he has twelve. You have now been sailing about for seven years, and you have to sail for seven years more before you will find them. As to what concerns yourself, individually, you should be welcome to remain here and marry my daughter, but you must first kill my master, for he is very harsh to us, and we have long been quite tired of him : and when he is dead I shall be king in his place. Try now if you can wield this sword," said the wizard, for such he was.

The prince tried to grasp a rusty sword which hung against the wall, but could not stir it from the spot.

" Well, then you must take a draught out of this flask," said the wizard.

The prince did so, and was then able to unhang the sword from the wall ; after a second draught he could raise it, and the third enabled him to wield it with as much ease as his own.

252

"When you return on board the vessel," said the wizard prince, "you must conceal the sword in your hammock, so that Commander Rod may not see it. He cannot wield it, I know, but he will hate you on that account, and try to kill you. When seven more years all but three days shall have passed away," he continued, "the same that has befallen you now will again occur: a violent gale will arise, with storm and hail, and when it is over, all will be again fatigued, and lie down in their hammocks. You must then take the sword, and row to land. You will arrive at a castle guarded by wolves, bears, and lions, but you need not fear them; they will crawl at your feet. As soon as you enter the castle, you will see the giant sitting in a splendidly adorned chamber, and a princess will be seated on her own chair, beside one of his twelve heads. As soon as you see him you must with all speed cut off one head after the other, before he awakes, for should he do that, he will eat you alive."

The prince returned to the ship with the sword, and did not forget what the wizard had told him. The others were still lying sound asleep, so he concealed the sword in his hammock without Commander Rod or any of the others perceiving it. A breeze now sprang up, and the prince awakened the crew, and told them that with such a fair wind they must no longer lie sleeping there. Time wore on, and the prince was for ever thinking of the adventure that awaited him, and much doubted that it would have a fortunate issue.

At last, when seven years all but three days were over, everything happened just as the wizard had foretold. A fierce tempest arose, and lasted three days, and when it was over the whole crew were fatigued, and lay down to sleep in their hammocks. The youngest prince, however, then rowed to the shore, and there he found the castle, guarded by wolves, bears, and lions, who all crawled at his feet, so that he entered without opposition. In one of the apartments sat the king, asleep, and the twelve princesses sat each on her chair, employed as the wizard had said. The prince made signs to them that they should retire; they however pointed to the wizard, and signed to him in return that he had better quickly withdraw. But he tried to make them understand, by looks and gestures, that he was come to deliver them, and when, at length, they understood his design, they stole softly away one after the other. Then the prince rushed on the wizard king, and cut off his heads, so that the blood flowed like

254

a great river, and when he had convinced himself that the wizard was dead, he rowed back to the vessel, and again concealed the sword. He thought he had now done enough unaided, and as he could not carry the giant's corpse out of the castle without assistance, he resolved that the others should help him. He therefore awakened them, and told them it was a shame that they should lie sleeping there, whilst he had found the princesses, and delivered them out of the wizard's power. They all laughed at him, and said he must have been asleep too, and had only dreamt that he had become such a hero; for it was far more likely that one of themselves should deliver the princesses than such a youth as he.

Then the prince told them all that had happened, so they consented to row to the land, and when they beheld the river of blood, and the wizard's castle, and his twelve heads lying there, and saw also the twelve princesses, they were convinced that he had spoken the truth, and so assisted him in throwing the heads and the corpse of the wizard into the sea. They were now all right merry and pleased, but none were better pleased than the princesses to be delivered from the task of sitting all day beside the giant, combing his twelve heads.

The princes and princesses, after they had collected as much of the gold and silver, and as many of the costly articles in the castle as they could carry, returned to the vessel, and again set sail. They had not gone far, however, when the princesses recollected that, in their joy, they had omitted to bring away with them their golden crowns, which were in a great chest, and these they very much desired to have with them. As no one else seemed inclined to go back for them, the youngest of the king's sons said: "Since I have already dared to do so much, I may as well also fetch the golden crowns, if you will take in the sails and wait my return."

Yes, they were willing to do that; they would lower the sails and wait till he returned. But the prince was no sooner out of sight of the vessel than Commander Rod, who wished to play the principal part, and to marry the youngest princess, said: "It was no use for us to stay here waiting for the prince, who, we may be sure, will not come back; besides," added he, "you know full well that the king has given to me full power to sail when and where I think proper;" then he insisted further that they should all say that it was he who had set the princesses free: and if any one of them should dare to say otherwise it should cost him his life. The princes were afraid to contradict him, so they sailed away. Meanwhile the younger prince had rowed to the shore, and soon found in the castle the chest containing the golden crowns, and after a great deal of trouble and fatigue, for it was very heavy, he succeeded in heaving it into the boat. But when he got out into the open sea, the ship was no longer in sight. He looked north, south, east, and west, but no trace could he discover of it, and he quickly guessed what had occurred. He knew that to row after it would be quite useless, so he had only to turn back and row again to the shore. It is true that he was rather alarmed at the idea of passing the night all alone in the castle, but there was no avoiding it; so he screwed up his courage as well as he could, locked all the gates and doors, and lay down to sleep in a bed which he found ready prepared in one of the apartments. But he felt very uneasy, and became much more terrified, on presently hearing in the roof over his head, and along the walls, a creaking and cracking, as if the castle were about to split asunder; and then came a great rustling close to his bed, like a whole haystack falling down. How-

ever, he was in some degree comforted when he immediately after the noise heard a voice bidding him not to
be alarmed.

> " Fear not, fear not, thy friend I am ;
>   I am the wondrous bird called Dam.
>   When thou 'rt in trouble call on me :
>   I shall be near to succour thee,"

said the voice, and then added : " As soon as you wake
to-morrow morning, you must go directly to the
Stabur*, and fetch me four bushels of rye for my
breakfast ; I must have a good meal, otherwise I can
do nothing for you."

When the prince awoke in the morning, he saw by
his bed-side a terribly large bird, who had a feather at
the back of his head as long as a half-grown fir tree.
The prince immediately went to the Stabur and brought
thence four bushels of rye, as the wondrous bird Dam
had commanded, who, as soon as he had taken his
breakfast, desired the prince to hang the chest containing the golden crowns on one side of his neck, and as
much gold and silver as would balance it on the other,

---

* A building used as a kind of store-room or larder, and supported on
short pillars or posts, so as not to allow it to touch the ground.

THE TWELVE LOST PRINCESSES AND THE WIZARD KING.   P 259.

and then to get upon his back and hold fast by the long feather. The prince obeyed and off they went, whizzing through the air at such a rate, that in a very short time they found themselves exactly above the ship. The prince then wished to go on board, that he might get the sword which the wizard had given him.

But the wondrous bird Dam told him that he must not do so: "Commander Rod," added he, "will not discover it; but if you go on board he will try to kill you, for he very much wishes to marry the youngest princess; but make yourself easy about her, for every night she places a drawn sword on the bed by her side."

At last they reached the castle of the wizard prince, who gave the young prince a hearty welcome. He seemed as if he could not make enough of him, for having killed his sovereign, in whose stead he was now king. He would willingly have given his daughter and half his kingdom to the young prince, but that the latter was so much in love with the youngest of the twelve princesses, that he could think of no one but her, and he was all impatience to be off again.

The wizard, however, besought him to have a little patience, and told him that the princesses were doomed to sail about still for twice seven years before they could return home. As to the youngest princess, the wizard said exactly the same as the wondrous bird Dam: "You may be quite at ease concerning her," said he, "for she always carries a drawn sword to bed with her. And if you do not believe me, you may go on board when they next sail past this place, to convince yourself; and, at the same time, bring me the sword I lent you, for I must positively have it back."

Now after seven years' more wandering, the princes and princesses were again sailing past the island ; a terrible storm came on as before, and after it was over the king's son went on board and found them all fast asleep as on the former occasions ; but by each of the princes a princess also lay asleep. Only the youngest princess slept alone, with a naked sword beside her; and on the floor, in front of the bed, lay Commander Rod, also sound asleep. The king's son took the sword from his hammock, and rowed to the island, without any one having perceived that he had been on board.

The prince, however, grew more and more impatient, always wishing to set out again.

At length, when the second seven years were completed all but three weeks, the wizard said to him : " Now you may prepare for your voyage, since you are determined not to remain with us. I will lend you an iron boat that will go of itself on the water, by your merely saying to it: 'Boat, go forwards.' In the boat you will find a boat-hook, which you must lift up a little when you see the ship right before you. Such a fresh breeze will then spring up, that the ship's crew will forget to look after you. As soon as you get near the ship, raise the boat-hook a little higher, and then a storm will arise that will give them other work to do than spying after you. When you shall have passed the ship, raise the boat-hook for the third time, but you must be careful each time to lay it down again, else there will be such a tempest, that you, as well as the others, will perish. On reaching the shore, you need take no further trouble about the boat than to turn it upside down, shove it into the sea, and say: 'Boat, go home again.'"

When the prince was departing, he received from the wizard so much gold and silver, together with other treasures, and clothes and linen which the princess had made for him during his long stay in the island, that he was a great deal richer than any of his brothers.

He had no sooner seated himself in the boat and said, "Boat, go forwards," than on it went, and when he came in sight of the ship, he raised the boat-hook, and a breeze sprang up, so that the crew forgot to look after him; and on nearing the vessel he did the same, when such a storm and gale arose, that the ship was covered with the white spray, and the waves broke over the deck, so that the crew had no leisure to remark him. At last when he had passed the ship, he raised the boat-hook the third time, and the crew found enough to do to make them quite forget him. He reached the land long before the ship, and, after taking his property out of the boat, he turned it over, shoved it into the sea, saying, "Boat, go home," and away it went.

He now disguised himself as a sailor, and went to the wretched hovel of an old woman, to whom he said he was a poor shipwrecked sailor, the only one of the crew who had escaped drowning; and he begged shelter in her hut for himself and the things he had saved from the wreck.

"Ah, heaven help me," replied the woman, "I can give no one shelter. I have not even a bed for myself, let alone any one else."

Oh! that did not signify, said the sailor, so that he had but a roof over his head, it was all one to him what he lay upon; therefore she would not surely refuse him the shelter of her roof, since he was content to take things as he found them.

In the evening, he brought his things to the cottage, and the old woman, who did not at all dislike to have something new to talk about, began inquiring who he was, where he had been, and whither he was going; what were the things he had brought with him; on what business he was travelling, and whether he had heard anything of the twelve princesses who had disappeared so many years ago, with so many other questions, that it would be tiresome to repeat them.

But the sailor replied that he felt so ill, and had such a terrible headache from the fatigues he had undergone during the storm, that he could not accurately recollect anything that had passed; but that after he should have had a few' days repose, and recovered from his labours, she should hear all.

The next day, however, the old woman renewed her questions, but the sailor pretended still to have such a terrible headache, that he could not rightly remember anything; though he did let a word or two drop, as by accident, which showed that he did know something about the princesses.

Off ran the old woman to tell this news to all the gossips in the neighbourhood, who hurried one after the other to the hut, to hear all about the princesses; and to ask whether the sailor had seen them, if they were soon coming, and a hundred other questions.

Still the sailor had such a terrible headache, that he could not answer their questions. Thus much, however, he did say: that if the princesses were not wrecked during that fierce storm, they would certainly arrive in fourteen days, or even sooner. He had certainly seen them alive, but they might have since perished.

One of the gossips went forthwith to the royal residence, and related all that she had heard; and when the king heard it, he desired that the sailor should be brought to him.

The sailor replied, " I have no clothes in which I can appear before the king."

But he was told that he must go, for the king must and would see him, whatever appearance he might make, for he was the first person who had ever brought any news of the princesses. So he entered the king's presence, when he was asked if he had really seen the princesses.

" Yes," said the sailor, " but I know not if they still

live, for when I saw them, it was during such a fierce storm, that we were wrecked. But if they did not then go to the bottom, they may be here in about fourteen days, or perhaps sooner."

When the king heard this, he was almost frantic with joy, and at the appointed time for the arrival of the princesses, he went down to the shore in state to meet them; and great was the rejoicing through the land, when at last the ship sailed into port, with the princes, and princesses, and Commander Rod. The eleven elder princesses were in high spirits and good humour; but the youngest, whom Commander Rod was anxious to marry, was very sad and wept incessantly, for which the king chid her, and asked her why she was not happy and cheerful, like her sisters. She had no cause, thought he, to be sad, now she was delivered from the wizard, and had such a fine man as Commander Rod for her lover. The Princess however durst not tell the truth, for Commander Rod had told the king that it was himself who had liberated the princesses, and had threatened to kill any one who should say otherwise.

Now, one day while the princesses were making their wedding clothes, a man in a coarse sailor's jacket, with a pedlar's pack on his back, came and asked them if they would not like to buy some fine things for their wedding, for he had some costly articles of gold and silver.

"Yes," said they, "very possibly they might," and they looked very attentively at the ornaments, and still

more so at him, for they could not help fancying that they had seen both him and the goods before.

At last the youngest princess said, that he who had such costly articles, might perhaps have others still more suitable to them.

266

" Very possibly," returned the pedlar.

But her sisters bade her be quiet, and remember Commander Rod's threat.

Shortly after, when the princesses were sitting at the window, the king's son came again in his coarse sailor jacket, carrying the chest with the golden crowns.

On entering the hall, he opened the chest, and now when the princesses recognised each her own golden crown, the youngest princess said :—" To me it seems only fair and just, that he who suffers for us, should receive the reward to which he is entitled ; our deliverer is not Commander Rod, but he who has now brought us our golden crowns, is also he who destroyed the wizard."

Then the king's son threw off his jacket, and stood there far more splendidly attired than any of the rest.

The king now caused Commander Rod to be put to death for his perfidy, and gave his daughter in marriage to the young prince.

The rejoicings in the royal residence were very great, and each prince took his princess away to a different realm, so that the tale was told and talked about in no less than twelve distinct kingdoms.

THE STUDY OF MAGIC UNDER DIFFICULTIES.

[Italian.]

———◆———

N the island of Sicily, and in the fair and famous city of Messina, dwelt a man, Lactantius by name, who was a great proficient in two different arts. By day, and ostensibly to his fellow-citizens, he carried on the trade of a tailor; but by night, and secretly, he studied the art of necromancy. One evening, when he had locked himself in his room, and was occupied with all kinds of magic works, as ill luck would have it, a young man, one of his apprentices, came to the door. Dionysius, such was his name, had returned to fetch from the chamber of Lactantius something which he had forgotten. When he perceived that the door was closed, but at the same time heard a noise within, he crept gently up, peeped through the keyhole, and witnessed his master's magic doings. Such delight did this give the young man, that from that moment he thought of nothing but how he might secretly learn his master's art. Needle, thimble, and shears thenceforth were little troubled by him; he cared alone to learn that which no one cared to teach him, and so from having been an industrious, attentive, useful workman, he became careless, idle, and inattentive. Lactantius perceiving this change in his apprentice, discharged him from his service, and sent him back to his father, who was much grieved in consequence.

The father having repeatedly lectured his son, with tears besought him to attend to his duty, and taking him back to the tailor, earnestly begged him to receive his son once again, desiring him, should he again neglect his business, to punish him severely.

Lactantius, out of kindness to the poor man, was soon persuaded; he again received his pupil, and instructed him carefully every day in cutting out and sewing. As, however, Dionysius would absolutely learn nothing, his master gave him many a sound caning, so that the poor apprentice, who received more blows than bread, was always black and blue, all of which he bore with the greatest patience, so insensible had he become to everything through the engrossing desire to learn that secret art which he night after night watched his master carry on, as he stood peeping through the keyhole.

Lactantius, who took him for the stupid lout he appeared to be, at last gave himself no further trouble to conceal his witchcraft from him, thinking that as he could not even learn the business of tailoring, which is so easy, he would far less comprehend witchcraft, which is really a puzzling art. He therefore no longer made a secret of his practices to Dionysius, who now thought himself the most fortunate of men, and who although others considered him such a blockhead, in a very short time became such a proficient in the magic art, that he understood more of it than his master.

One day, as the father was passing by Lactantius' house, not seeing his son in the shop, he entered, and found that, instead of working with the other apprentices, he was cleaning the house, and in short, performing all the offices of a housemaid.

This so disturbed the good man, that he took his son home with him, and thus lectured him: " Thou knowest, Dionysius, how much I have expended on thee, in the hope that thou wouldst learn a useful business, whereby one day to support thyself and me; but, alas! I have sown my seed on the waters, for thou refusest to learn anything. Truly this will be my death, for I am so poor I know not how to support myself, nor have I any means of providing for thee. Therefore, I beseech thee, my son, learn to support thyself in any respectable way thou canst."

Having said this, the old man began to weep, when Dionysius, moved by his distress, replied: "Dear father, I thank you a thousand times, and from my heart, for all the trouble and anxiety you have had on my account: but I beg you will not think, because I did not learn tailoring, as you wished me, that I have therefore passed the time in idleness. On the contrary, by night-watching and unwearied efforts, I have learned an art which I hope hereafter to exercise so efficaciously that you and I shall live all our days in peace and joy. That you may not imagine that I say this merely to satisfy you for the moment, I will at once give you a proof of what I affirm.

"To-morrow, by means of my secret art, I will transform myself into a fine horse; saddle and bridle me, and lead me to the market, and sell me. When you shall have made your bargain, go quietly home, your pocket full of money, and you shall find me here again in the same form which I now bear. Judge therefore whether or not I have learned something useful, since in so short a time I can earn for you the necessaries of life. Take especial heed, however, when you sell me, not to part with my bridle; this, come what will, you must carefully retain, else I shall not be able to return, and perhaps you may never see me again."

The next morning Dionysius stripped himself in presence of his father, and after anointing himself with a certain ointment, he murmured some words, whereupon, to the inexpressible astonishment of the good old man, in the place of his son, a fine powerful horse suddenly appeared, which he immediately harnessed as his son had instructed him, and led him to the market. As soon as the merchants and horse-dealers saw him, they gathered round him, quite delighted with the beauty of the horse, the action of whose limbs and whole body was so perfect, and who showed such a fleetness and fire, that it was quite surprising. All inquired if the horse were for sale, to which the old man replied in the affirmative.

By accident, Lactantius was in the market, and as soon as he saw the horse, and had narrowly examined him, he at once discovered that it was a magic horse. He therefore withdrew unperceived from the crowd, and hastened home, disguised himself as a merchant, and provided with an ample sum of money, returned to the market, where he found the man still with his horse. He approached the animal, and after attentively observing him, recognised in him his apprentice, Dionysius. He then asked the old man if he would sell him, and they soon concluded a bargain. Lactantius paid him two hundred gold pieces; but as he took him by the bridle to lead him away, the old man objected, saying that he had sold the horse but not the bridle, which he must have back again. Lactantius however contrived to talk him over, so that he obtained the bridle as well as the horse, which he led home, and fastening him to the stall, gave him for breakfast and supper so many hundred blows, that the poor beast became nothing but skin and bones, and excited the compassion of all who beheld him.

Lactantius had two daughters, who, when they saw their father's barbarity, went daily into the stable to do what they could for the poor horse. They caressed him, patted him, and treated him with all possible kindness, and one day went so far as to lead him by

the halter to drink at the stream. The moment, however, the horse found himself by the water, he threw
himself into it, and transforming himself into a little
fish, he disappeared in the waves.

At this extraordinary occurrence the maidens stood
speechless with astonishment, and returning home, gave
way to the deepest sorrow. Some time after Lactantius
returned, and went into the stable to administer a little
further chastisement to his horse, when to his great
astonishment he found him gone. Very indignant
thereat, he went to his daughters, and beheld them in
tears. Without inquiring the cause, for he knew full
well the cause of their trouble, he said to them : " My
children, fear nothing, only tell me what has become of
the horse, in order that I may at once take measures
concerning him."

The poor maidens composed themselves on hearing
these words, and related to him what had happened.
When the father had heard the story, he hastened to the
river, transformed himself into a large fish, dashed
into the water, and as fast as his fins could carry him
pursued the little fish, intending to swallow him.

When the latter beheld the voracious fish, with its
terrible teeth, he was dreadfully alarmed at the thought

of being swallowed by him, and approaching the bank of the river, he left the water, and in the form of a beautiful ruby, set in gold, he threw himself unseen into the little basket which the king's daughter, who happened just then to be amusing herself with picking up little pebbles on the sand, carried on her arm.

As soon as the princess, who was called Violante, returned home, she took her treasures out of the little basket, and perceived the ring shining amongst the pebbles. Quite delighted, she placed it on her finger, and could not desist from contemplating it.

At night, when the princess had retired to her sleeping apartment, the ring suddenly changed into a handsome young man. He laid his hand on the princess's mouth, who was about to scream aloud, then threw himself at her feet and besought her forgiveness. He assured her he was not there with any disrespectful purpose, but only to implore her assistance, and then told her his misfortune, and the persecutions he had to endure.

Violante, somewhat re-assured by the bright light of the lamp which burned in her chamber, as also by the words of the young man, whom she found very hand-some and attractive, felt compassion for him, and said :

275

"Young man, thou art very bold in entering a place where thy presence was not desired. But in consideration of thy misfortune, I will forgive thee. Thy narration has awakened all my compassion, and I will show thee that I am not made of marble, nor have a heart of adamant. I am even resolved, so far as my honour will permit, to give thee my entire protection."

The young man humbly returned thanks, and, when day dawned, again transformed himself into the ring, which the princess placed amongst her most costly jewels.

It happened just about that time, that the king fell dangerously ill, and all his physicians declared his disease was incurable.

This came to the ears of Lactantius, who thereupon disguised himself as a physician, went to the royal palace, and being introduced to the king, inquired carefully respecting his symptoms, felt his pulse, examined his countenance, and said: "Your majesty's disease is no doubt an obstinate one, and very dangerous; but take courage: in a short time I will restore you to health, for I possess a remedy by which I can in a few days cure the severest and most dangerous illness that exists."

"Master physician," replied the king, "if you restore

me to health, I promise to reward you so richly that you shall be content for the rest of your life."

"My sovereign," rejoined the physician, "I desire neither rank, honours, nor riches, but only request your majesty will grant me one favour."

The king readily promised this, on condition that he should require nothing that was impossible.

"I ask nothing more of your majesty than a ruby set in gold, which is now in the possession of the princess your daughter."

When the king heard this modest request, he sent for his daughter, and in presence of the physician, desired her to fetch her whole stock of jewels. The princess obeyed, leaving out, however, the precious ring. But when the physician had thoroughly examined them, he said the ruby he wished for was not amongst them.

Violante, who valued her ruby above all the rest, affirmed that she had no other jewels than those now before them; whereupon the king said to the physician: "Retire now, and return to-morrow; I will undertake that my daughter shall give me the ring."

When the physician was gone, the king called Violante, and inquired in the gentlest manner, where was the beautiful ruby which the physician wished for; saying that if she would give it to him, she should have in its place a still more beautiful and precious one. But she positively denied having it in her possession.

She no sooner returned to her apartment, than she locked herself in, and began to weep bitterly at the thought of losing her poor ruby, which she bathed with her tears, and kissed with the utmost tenderness.

When the ruby felt the hot tears that fell from the princess's eyes, and heard her deep sighs, it assumed the human form, and said to her: " Princess, on whom my life hangs, I beseech you, do not thus immoderately grieve at my misfortune. Let us rather devise some means of rescue; for that physician who so zealously covets the possession of me, is no other than my greatest foe Lactantius, who desires to kill me. Therefore I implore you, do not give me into his hand, but feign to be indignant, and dash me against the wall: leave the rest to my care."

The following morning the physician again visited the king, who informed him that his daughter still persisted that she did not possess the ring. Lactantius much displeased, on hearing this, however, positively asserted that the ruby was in the princess's collection.

Thereupon the king again sent for the princess, and in the physician's presence said to her: "Violante, thou knowest that I owe the restoration of my health to this man's skill and care. He requires no other recompense of me than that ring which he declares to be in thy possession, and which thou dost assert thou hast not. I should have thought thy love for me would have led thee not to give thy ruby alone, but thy very life. I beseech thee, by the obedience thou owest to me, by the affection I have borne thee, to withhold it from me no longer."

The princess, on hearing her father's will so decidedly expressed, returned to her room, collected all her jewels, amongst which she laid the ruby, and taking them one by one in her hand, in the presence of her father, showed them each in succession to the physician, who, the moment he saw the ruby, would have laid his hand on it, saying: "Princess, this is the ring I wish for, and which the king has promised me."

But the princess, repelling him, said: "Stay, master, you shall have it!" and holding the ring in her hand, exclaimed: "Then it is this precious jewel, so infinitely dear to me, that you covet: I must renounce this, for the loss of which I shall be inconsolable for life. But

I do not yield it willingly, but only because the king, my father, requires it of me."

With these words she flung the ruby against the wall. As it fell to the ground it instantly changed into a beautiful pomegranate, which burst as it fell, and its seeds were scattered all over the room.

The physician as quickly became a cock, in order to swallow all the seeds, and thus to destroy the unlucky Dionysius; but he had miscalculated: one of the seeds had so concealed itself that the cock could not discover it. The seed watched its opportunity, transformed itself into a fox, who throwing himself on master cock, seized him by the throat, and strangled and devoured him in the presence of the astonished monarch and his daughter Violante. Dionysius then resumed his human form, and related all to the king, who thought he could not do better than immediately give him his daughter in marriage. They lived long together in peace and happiness, and the good old father of Dionysius became, instead of an indigent man, a rich and powerful one; whilst, on the other hand, the cruelty of Lactantius had cost him his life.

FORTUNE'S FAVOURITE;

OR, THE VERY WONDERFUL ADVENTURES OF PISTA, THE SWINEHERD.

[Hungarian.]

———◆———

NEAR the centre of a thick forest once dwelt a forester with his beloved wife. The chase was his occupation, and he lived contentedly on the provision which his ever-active bow procured him from day to day. In this manner he passed two years very happily; although the blessing of children, which he earnestly desired, had been hitherto denied him. But the saying, "Patience brings roses," consoled him, and indeed the saying did at last prove true, and in so striking a manner, that it seemed as if destiny had exerted its utmost power to fulfil it, in his case, even to excess. In the third year, whilst the forester was away hunting in the wood, his family was increased by the addition of twelve fine, healthy sons, upon whom the attendant midwife bestowed every necessary care, and then placed them in a circle on the floor in the centre of the room, where the sturdy infants stretched their limbs and raised their voices for the first time in a tremendously loud Tutti.

Whilst these events were taking place, the day declined, and evening gradually threw its shade over field and mountain. The light-hearted hunter bethought him of his supper, and returned, laden with two or three hares, to his cottage.

But how thunderstruck was he when he heard that Heaven had showered down upon him such an abundant blessing. He entered, gazed, and at the sight of the liberal gift, at once lost his reason, and rushed raving out of doors back into the depths of the dark forest, never to return again.

The poor forsaken wife now remained in her hut with her twelve little sons, desiring nothing more ardently than to be able to leave her bed, in order to provide food for her children.

The midwife afforded her all the assistance in her power, and when at length she recovered, she prepared a bow and arrows, scoured the woods and hills, and daily brought home as much game as was requisite for the support of herself and her children. Thus she lived fifteen years; during which period the little ones grew strong and healthy, and learned from her to provide, by hunting, for their own necessities.

But before they reached their sixteenth year, it pleased Heaven to call their mother to itself, and now the youths, deprived of parental care, were abandoned to their fate. They continued to live as before, on the products of the chase, which they fraternally divided amongst them, and remained together in harmony and peace.

The distracted father meanwhile continued to wander incessantly through the forest. His habiliments had long been torn to rags, and his appearance terrified every one who beheld him. Although other foresters occasionally met him, and brought tidings of him to his sons, yet no one could ever lay hold of him, as he shunned the approach of everybody, and at the aspect of a human being he hastened like a frightened beast to hide himself in the thicket. But his unhappy fate was a daily increasing source of sorrow to his sons, who at length consulted seriously together, how they might get him into their hands, so as to be able to take care of him, and, if possible, restore him to reason.

They at length agreed to betake themselves, provided

with a roasted goose, a pitcher of brandy, and one large boot, to a certain spring in the forest, near which the foresters frequently saw him. With these things they went to the appointed spot, placed them close to the spring, and then concealed themselves in the bushes to watch for his arrival.

They had waited a considerable time when they heard the sound of foot-steps, and beheld a dark figure approaching the spring. With ardent curiosity they peeped from their concealment, and at length saw, with surprise and horror, a being more like a ghost than a man, but who, however, perfectly corresponded to the description which the foresters had given them of their unfortunate father.

When he approached the spring to slake his thirst he started on perceiving the unaccustomed objects which were beside it, and prepared to start off at the moment, should he perceive a human form. But as the youths kept themselves entirely concealed, and made not the least noise, his alarm subsided, and he ventured to drink from the spring.

After he had refreshed himself, the roasted goose, the little pitcher, and the large boot seemed again to attract his attention, and he could not resist the desire

284

to make himself master of them. He laid himself down quite leisurely by the boot, devoured the goose with the greatest avidity, and emptied the pitcher with a satyr-like expression of countenance.

The liquor seemed quickly to affect him ; for almost as soon as he had swallowed it he manifested his satisfaction by fantastic leaps, and all kinds of ridiculous antics. He soon laid hold of the boot, examined it attentively on all sides, and nodded his head knowingly, as if in self-approval for having devised its purpose.

Thus satisfied with himself, he again seated himself on the ground, and endeavoured to draw the boot over both feet at once; and although it was large enough to admit the foot of a demi-giant, it cost the lunatic extraordinary efforts to effect his object. Overpowered by fatigue, and the strength of the liquor he had drunk, he gradually sank down by the stream, and fell asleep.

His sons, when they perceived this, hastened with the greatest caution from the bushes, raised the intoxicated sleeper from the ground, and carried him home. But before they had half reached the hut, they discovered with horror that the burthen, which at every step had appeared to grow heavier, was a corpse. Whether it was the effect of the too hastily swallowed drink, or the too rapid satisfaction of his appetite after long fasting, in either case, the father lay dead in the arms of his sons. With tears of regret, and self-reproaches for their ill-advised attempt, the afflicted sons buried the beloved corpse, under an oak not far from the cottage.

They lived together for some time after this event, but at length, being imbued with the desire of seeing foreign countries, they resolved to renounce their hitherto rude mode of life, and each to set out in a different direction to seek his fortune.

When they had fixed the day for their separation they once more went hunting together, in order to provide so much food as they might require for at least the first day of their wandering. On the day appointed for their departure they went to the oak which shaded their father's grave, swore eternal brotherly love to each other, and after mutually taking an affectionate leave, each pursued his separate way.

To relate what occurred to each of these twelve brethren, and how each fulfilled his appointed destiny, would be a very tedious task, and the more so as the fate of the younger brother was alone sufficiently remarkable to deserve attention.

286

FORTUNE'S FAVOURITE.

This youth had from his earliest years an aversion to all kind of labour and trouble; hence, in all his necessities he always relied on the favour of Fortune, and the more so as he had more than once had reason to surmise that she was favourably inclined towards him. Whilst his brothers laboriously pursued their game under every disadvantage of time, place, and weather, he would lie at his ease, with his weapons beside him, on a grassy hill, beneath the shade of the trees; and it generally came to pass that whilst his brothers pursued some poor hare, in the sweat of their brow, a roebuck would come, as if at his call, so near to him that he could shoot it without the least exertion. Owing to this, he had to endure many a jeer from his brethren, whose jealousy was excited by his good luck, and they called him in derision Lazy Bones.

His confidence in the favour of the blind goddess guided him prosperously on his way. By day he shot all kinds of game, which came in abundance towards him, kindled a fire, roasted and eat it; at night, he stretched himself on the soft grass, and slept refreshingly till the next morning. After he had pursued his way in this manner for six days, he arrived at a royal city altogether unknown to him. He entered one of the best inns, and offered the host a hare in exchange for a draught of wine, to refresh himself with after the fatigue of his journey. The host gave him credit for more than he was able both to eat and drink, offered him a bed, and charged him the most moderate price.

Just as he sat down to table, a multitude of persons assembled in the room of the inn, and conversed with each other about a most remarkable occurrence which had just taken place. The affair was indeed one of no trifling importance, for it concerned the royal establishment. The king had had ninety-nine swineherds, who one and all had disappeared, and in all probability would never again be heard of. The nine-and-ninetieth of these had been missed only the night before, and it was much doubted whether the king would be able to find any one again who would be willing to undertake so perilous a charge. For although the highest wages were offered to any one who would undertake to tend the royal swine but for a single day, yet no one throughout the whole kingdom had yet offered himself, and the illustrious owner of the swine was in great risk of losing them all.

The young stranger listened to this narration with surprise, but could not conjecture what could be the difficulty attached to the service. As the host had for some time

288

been employed in looking out for swineherds for the king, he asked his young guest whether he would undertake the office, adding at the same time, that the king would give a year's wages for a single day's service.

"Why not?" replied Pista, (that was the young adventurer's name) and he declared himself quite willing to undertake the charge, as he thought the business of a swineherd did not demand more skill and trouble than he was accustomed to exert. His consent thus given, the host joyfully conducted him to the king and praised throughout the whole city the courageous resolution of his guest.

The monarch received them both graciously, and not only confirmed the offer made by the host to the youth, but promised him a gratuity into the bargain, in case of his discharging his duty with zeal and perseverance.

He commanded a capital supper to be placed before him, and appointing him to drive the swine in the morning to the heath, he dismissed him with the most gracious wishes for his welfare.

Before the dawn of day, Pista was already at his post. The heath lay in a pleasant district, inclosed on the one side by mountains, and on the other by a thick forest. On his arrival there he found all tranquil, and could not imagine what danger was to be apprehended.

He passed the day in expectation, and the evening approached as peacefully as the day had departed. The moon and stars shed their light over the district, and the refreshing coolness of the air invited the care-free herdsman to repose. He lay calmly down near his herd, commended them and himself to fortune, and slept in peace.

He had not slept an hour, when the most extraordinary of all night visions awakened him. The oldest patriarch of the herd stood before him, and thus addressed him: "Fear not, for I am thy friend, and come to thee as a well-intentioned counsellor, to warn thee of the danger that awaits thee. As I have selected thee for my protégé, I will assist thee to the best of my power. When thou drivest us home to-morrow, mind to request the king to give thee a loaf of bread and a flask of wine, for the following day. These shall preserve thee from all misfortune. A great dragon who rules this forest, will endeavour to overthrow and swallow thee. But if thou givest him these gifts, thou wilt not only be able to resist him, but after he shall have drunk the wine thou mayest destroy him."

Pista was not a little astonished at this apparition; he rubbed his eyes, pricked up his ears, and collected all his senses, to convince himself that he was really awake and not dreaming. But when he saw the boar standing bodily before him, and distinctly heard every word, he at last returned him grateful thanks for his friendly admonition, and promised punctually to observe his instructions.

The following evening he drove the herd home. The king met him, not without astonishment, caused the year's wages to be paid to him immediately, and gave him permission further to ask some favour. Pista, well pleased, put the money in his pocket, and for the present asked for nothing more than bread and wine for the following evening.

The cock had scarcely crowed to welcome the first hour of the morning, when our herdsman again passed out at the city gate with his herd. He betook himself to the same heath where he had passed the foregoing night, and had had the strange *tête-à-tête* with the boar.

As soon as he reached the spot, his bristly Mentor again approached him and said :—

" Up and mount me without fear,
Swift on my back I thee will bear ;
So that, ere many minutes' space,
Thou shalt reach the appointed place."

291

The youth bestrode the boar, and in a trice found himself in the neighbouring wood, and deposited under an enormous oak. The boar then repeated what he had said to his protégé the preceding day, and hastened back to the herd.

Pista prepared himself for his adventure, and before he could accurately reconnoitre the field of battle, so dreadful a noise proceeding from the interior of the forest pierced his ears, that all the trees round him creaked and rustled as in a storm. It came nearer and nearer, and he soon perceived a monstrous dragon, rapidly making towards him, tearing the bushes and trees as he passed, and even throwing them to the ground. Mindful of his Mentor's words, Pista took courage, offered the bread and wine to the dragon, and besought him to spare his life.

This liberal offer astonished the dragon more than the resistance of a whole band of herdsmen would have done. He quietly received the gifts, devoured the bread with much satisfaction, and as the wine speedily took effect, he drowsily tumbled on the earth. Pista did not delay to avail himself of the opportunity. When he perceived that the dragon slept, he drew out his knife and cut the throat of the drunken monster;

292

FORTUNE'S FAVOURITE.   P. 292.

before, however, he had completed the operation, he saw a copper key fall out of his jaws, which he picked up and put in his pocket.

In the meantime, the herd had gradually moved towards the interior of the forest, to a considerable distance from the spot where the dragon had met his death. Pista, fearing he might lose the objects of his charge, resolved to cut across the bend of the forest, and to go in a straight line, the same by which the dragon had come, to look after them.

He had not gone far, when a new overwhelming surprise banished them from his thoughts. An immense castle, entirely built of copper, stood before him, far surpassing in splendour the residence of his king, and which seemed the more to invite him to enter, inasmuch as he could nowhere descry a single guard to forbid his approach.

Solitary and silent was all around him: not even the song of a bird broke the stillness. Hastening up to the castle, he found all the gates locked; but suddenly remembering the key in his pocket, he drew it out and tried it in the nearest gate, and discovered to his joyful surprise that it opened every lock. He soon found himself in the interior of a most magnificent palace, with such a number of state rooms opening round him, that he could hardly tell which he should first enter. He passed through the grand hall and went from room to room, until he at last reached a great saloon, the walls of which were mirrors, whilst all manner of gold and silver articles of furniture glittered round him. In the centre of the room stood a table of silver, whereon lay a golden rod. Without precisely knowing wherefore, he took up the rod and struck the table with it, upon which a young dragon immediately appeared, and with indescribable courtesy begged that he would honour him with his commands.

Recovering from his surprise, Pista expressed a wish to be shown the whole interior of the palace, with the gardens belonging to it. The obliging dragon immediately complied with, and requested his guest to follow him. He led him through all the chambers and halls of the palace, each of which seemed to contain the treasure of a whole kingdom; thence into the stables, where splendid coursers fed from silver mangers on golden oats, and who neighed loudly at the entrance of their visitors.

At last Pista and his attendant came into a garden full of marvellously beautiful flowers and delicious fruits, which seemed to the stranger like a second paradise. He could not refrain from plucking a rose, which he stuck in his cap.

When he had seen all, he inquired of the dragon for the lord of the palace. The dragon bowed before him with the greatest reverence, and begged him, as the

ISABEL THOMPSON

owner from thenceforth of the palace and its treasures, graciously to accept his homage, promising at the same time that he would guard all with the utmost vigilance, and endeavour to deserve his approbation.

Pista was not a little astonished at this address, but as all the events which had befallen him within the last few days, appeared to him to be nothing less than natural, he accepted the dragon's homage, and played the part of master as well as he could. Having nodded approbation to his new servitor, he left the castle with proud gravity. The portals closed of themselves after him with thundering noise; he then carefully locked all the gates with his key, and returned to seek his swine.

It was not long before he met the whole herd in the best order. The sun was already glowing in the west, and the shadows of the mountains stretched across the plains. It seemed time to turn homewards; he whistled; the herd put itself in motion; and before the evening star shone in the heavens, they were all at home again in their sheds.

Pista had no sooner housed his charge, than the king's daughters came running towards him with the most unusual friendliness. The youngest had seen from afar the rose in his cap, and as she could not resist the desire to possess it, she begged from him the lovely flower. The swineherd instantly presented it to the princess, and thought himself highly honoured when he saw his gift placed in the bosom of the most charming of the royal maidens.

The king, meanwhile, deeply amazed at the no less punctual than safe return of his herdsman, sent for him into his presence, and inquired particularly about all that had occurred to him on the heath. But Pista carefully avoided satisfying his curiosity; gave very brief answers to his questions; and said nothing that could betray his fortunate adventure.

" This rose," said he, " which I found already plucked, and lying on the stem of a tree, is all that I saw on my way. I stuck it in my hat that it might not fade quite unenjoyed."

The king again expressed his entire satisfaction and favour; and promised for the future days the same rich reward he had already enjoyed.

The herdsman thanked his patron and returned to his swine, in order to pass the night near them on his bed of straw.

Just about midnight the friendly boar awakened him

as on the preceding night, and said, "Pista must provide himself with bread and wine for the coming day also, as he would have to do with a still larger dragon than the former."

He advised him to double the measure of provisions, and told him he would have nothing to fear if he encountered the monster as courageously as he did that of the day before.

Before daybreak Pista supplied himself with two loaves and two flasks of wine, and went as usual with the swine to the heath. Arrived there, the boar again approached him and said :—

> "Up and mount me without fear,
> Swift on my back I will thee bear ;
> This day thou must higher go,
> And still higher fortune know."

The youth obeyed the boar, and sooner than if on a racer's back he found himself by an inclosure, considerably beyond the place where he stopped the day before. The boar again deposited him under an oak, repeated several times what he had before enforced, and left him to his destiny.

Pista had not long to wait ; he soon heard a terrible rustling descending from the tops of the trees. By degrees it grew darker around him, and at once a monstrous dragon, much larger than the first, came sailing through the air, whose out-spread wings shaded, like a thunder-cloud, the district beneath, as with furious haste he seemed descending on the herdsman. But Pista lost no time in offering him the two loaves and the two flasks, which so fortunately appeased the monster that he immediately stretched himself on the grass, and, much at his ease, swallowed the provisions, and then fell asleep and snored like thunder. Pista again seized the favourable moment and cut the dragon's throat, from whose jaws fell a silver key, which he put at once into his pocket.

Then he went, as on the preceding day, into the interior of the forest, and soon saw a palace built entirely of silver, which dazzled his eyes from afar by its brilliancy. All that he saw and did in the Copper Palace, he saw and did here; only the magnificence of the one far exceeded that of the other, and caused him to linger here much longer. After a very obsequious dragon had shown him all the treasures, and at last led him into the garden, he plucked there a silver rose, of which there were great numbers, and stuck it in his cap. He then locked the gates of his beautiful palace with the silver key, returned to his herd, and as the day was declining, drove them quietly home.

As before, the king's daughters came familiarly to meet him, and the youngest snatched the silver rose from him, and ran playfully with it to her father. The king sent for him as before, questioned him of all that had occurred, and having received satisfactory answers, expressed his entire approbation.

The same adventure occurred on the third day, with the sole difference that the herdsman this time entered a Golden Palace, and brought from the garden a golden rose, which the fair princess appropriated as before.

It happened that a festival which the king had long resolved to give to the suitors of his daughters, was just about to be held. He caused three golden apples of the same size to be made, on each of which he had inscribed the name of one of the princesses. These he ordered to be suspended by golden threads in the front court of his castle, as the prize of a trial of skill, for which the victor was to receive the hand of one of the princesses. Whoever, at full gallop, should succeed in striking down with his lance one of these apples, was to receive the golden fruit and the princess whose name it bore. As the three sisters were no less extraordinarily beautiful than rich, it may easily be guessed that the number of their suitors was not small. A countless number of princes from far and near were assembled in the royal city, and the king's brother was also present with his nine daughters. The whole kingdom took a lively interest in this festival, and young and old rejoiced at its commencement. Whatever the royal treasures could produce was exhibited there, and all the rich and noble flocked thither to contribute their share towards enhancing the pomp of the long looked for feast.

As it was to be supposed that Pista would not willingly be absent from such a grand sight, the youngest princess, out of gratitude for her three roses, invited him to witness it; advising him not to stay away if he had any curiosity to see all the most precious of her father's possessions, in horses, clothes, and jewels. But to the no small surprise of the princess, the herdsman thanked her for her invitation, but said he preferred remaining with his equals, and would tend the swine as usual.

The morning arrived, and all within and around the city was in motion. The streets swarmed with countless people: even the most helpless cripples dragged themselves along, anxious to see the show. Pista alone drove forth his swine with the utmost indifference, and did not evince the slightest curiosity.

Who could have guessed, however, what the homely youth had secretly determined, and what a trick he had resolved to play on all the princely suitors? He no sooner reached the heath than he hastened to the forest where his late adventures had occurred. He went to the Copper Palace, entered the hall, and with a stroke of the golden wand commanded the serviceable dragon to provide for him the most magnificent attire and the finest courser. The dragon rapidly obeyed his master's order, dressed him as expeditiously and handily as the most experienced valet could have done, and then as quickly cantered up a splendidly caparisoned steed, who seemed to breathe fire as he neighed with desire for the combat.

Pista mounted his horse, and the courts of the castle thundered beneath his tramp. He flew, as if borne on the lightning's wing, over the heath and road, and suddenly appeared in the lists of the royal disputants. The brilliancy of his attire, the swiftness and strength of his horse, and the costly jewels that adorned him, dazzled all eyes, and it could not have occurred to any one that in him they beheld the swineherd. The

302

king himself thought he must be his equal in dignity, and offered him the honour of precedence. But Pista declined this distinction, and requested, on the contrary, to be allowed to be the last on the list of suitors.

At last the signal was given. All pressed to the lists, and the race began. Riders and horses flew emulously towards the prize, but not one succeeded in even touching either of the apples with his lance.

Suddenly the unknown guest darted over the course like an arrow, and hit the first of the three apples so dexterously, that it, together with the golden thread to which it was fastened, remained hanging on his lance. The gaze of all was fixed upon him; but without vouchsafing a look on any, he flew with his prize straight across the lists and disappeared.

This unexpected circumstance created universal embarrassment amongst the disconcerted suitors, and determined the king to postpone the remainder of the festival until the following day. Meanwhile he sent some of his swiftest riders in search of the strange fugitive, in order to discover, if possible, whence he came. But before these were ready to start, our knight had already become invisible, and, in his herdsman's dress, had again rejoined his swine.

303

In the evening, as usual, he brought them home, and attended to them in the customary manner. But before he retired to rest, the youngest of the princesses descried him, and hastening to him, related in great agitation the untoward event which had that day deprived her of the apple destined to her, and at the same time of him who should have been her bridegroom. The herdsman expressed his great sympathy, and tried to console her, by saying that no one could tell whether the misfortune that had happened might not in the end turn out to her advantage.

The next day, before the ceremonies recommenced, Pista was again on the heath with his herd. This day he went to the Silver Palace, attired himself still more splendidly, and mounted a yet finer horse. Swift as the wind, and resplendent in gold and jewels, he again sprang to the lists. All were astonished at this second apparition. All inclined themselves before him, and no one recognised in him the same guest who had so distinguished himself on the preceding day.

But, as yesterday, all eyes were riveted on him; he set spurs to his horse, and sprang with hanging bridle to the prize, then flew like an arrow, bearing the second apple across the lists, and disappeared from the sight of the astonished multitude.

The king and his illustrious guests now began to apprehend that some supernatural power influenced these events, and they had nearly determined not to renew the trial of skill till the following year. But as already two of the golden apples were lost, they could not resist their curiosity respecting the third and last. The king therefore appointed the conclusion of the festival for the next morning, and in the meantime endeavoured to tranquillise himself as well as he could.

As before, so was it on this third occasion. The herdsman had gone early to the heath, and now appeared in an attire, and mounted on a horse, this time procured from the Golden Palace, both of which infinitely surpassed the two former. He carried off the third apple, and fled, to the wonder of all, swift as the wind, far out of sight.

The festival was now over; the assembly separated; the suitors returned to their homes, and the king lamented the fate of his beloved daughters. The daughters shed many tears, and mourned over their fate as an appointment of Heaven, forbidding them ever to have a bridegroom.

As the very first of these occurrences had caused the

king entirely to forget to pay the herdsman his daily wages, the latter had now three days' hire due to him. Pista therefore availed himself of the pretext of demanding his wages as a good opportunity to learn what impression his three adventures had made at court. That same evening, when he brought home his herd, he presented himself before the king, but apprehending that, if he left his three apples in the stall, they might be purloined, he concealed them in his hat, which he retained on his head, although in presence of his monarch.

The king perceived this disrespectful conduct of his herdsman not without surprise; but, as he was exceedingly well disposed towards him, on account of his great services, he indulgently asked him what he required. Pista had scarcely prepared himself to make his request, when the youngest, and now exceedingly discontented princess entered, and with an air of highly offended pride, snatched his hat off his head.

The golden apples fell out of it, and rolled to the monarch's feet.

What was the astonishment of the whole court! The princesses recognised their names, and could not express their delight at finding their apples. The

306

king pressed the youth in the most gracious terms to explain how he had come by them.

Pista replied, with the utmost frankness, that he was the winner of the three apples, and therefore thought he had a full right to one of the princesses for his bride.

Now, as the king, mindful of the unexampled splendour, as also the extraordinary good fortune by which the stranger had distinguished himself in the lists, anticipated some still greater advantage behind the darkness of this mysterious occurrence, he admitted the herdsman's claim with very little hesitation.

The youngest of the princesses felt herself suddenly cheered, and so powerfully attracted to the metamorphosed swineherd, that in spite of his peasant's dress she threw her arms around his neck. The king immediately decided that he should become her husband, and the following morning the wedding was celebrated with the utmost magnificence, in presence of the whole court, at the Golden Palace in the forest, which Pista immediately selected for his residence.

When the banquet was over, the bridegroom commanded his faithful dragon, who had already the day before provided a numerous establishment of domestics of his own winged race, immediately to bring hither his eleven brothers, whose respective names he had furnished him with, and had described their persons as accurately as he could.

Before the sun went down the eleven brothers were seen coming at full gallop to the Golden Palace. By the care of the ever active dragon they were all splendidly dressed, and they rejoiced and wondered not a little at the unexpected change in their destiny.

Two of them married the sisters of their royal sister-in-law, and the rest married the nine daughters of the other king. They soon conquered for themselves as many kingdoms, and lived happily together till their dying day.

THE LUCKY DAYS.

[Italian.]

———◆———

A T Casena, in Romagna, lived a poor widow, a very worthy, industrious woman, by name Lucietta. She unfortunately had an only son, who, for stupidity and laziness, had yet to find his equal. He would lie in bed till noon, and when he did resolve to rise, he took a full hour to rub his eyes, and then he would be nearly as long stretching his arms and legs; in short, he behaved like the veriest sluggard upon earth.

This grieved his mother very much, for she had once hoped that he would some day become the support of her old age; and she never ceased to urge and advise him, in order to make him a little more active and industrious.

"My son," she often said to him, "he who would

see good days in this world must exert himself, be industrious, and rise at break of day; for good fortune favours the industrious and the vigilant, but never comes to the lazy and sluggardly. Therefore, my son, if you will believe my counsel, and follow it, then you shall see good days, and all will fall out to your heart's content."

Lucilio—that was the young man's name—the silliest of the silly, unquestionably heard what his mother said, but he did not understand the meaning of her words. He got up as if he were waking out of a deep and heavy sleep, and sauntered along the road before the city gate, where he stretched himself, in order to finish his nap, right across the pathway, so that all entering or leaving the city could not avoid stumbling over him.

It so happened that the very night before, three inhabitants of the city had gone out to bury a treasure which they had accidentally discovered. They had succeeded in finding it again, and were in the act of carrying it home, when they came upon Lucilio, who still lay across the road, but no longer sleeping. He had just waked up, and was looking round him for one of the good days his mother had prophesied to him.

310.

" Heaven send you a good day, friend," said the first of the three men, as he walked over him.

" Heaven be praised ! " said Lucilio, when he heard the words.   " Now I shall have a good day ! "

The man who had buried the treasure, conscious of his fault, fancied directly that these words bore reference to him, and that the secret had been betrayed.   This was quite natural; for whoever has a bad conscience, always interprets the most indifferent words as an allusion to himself.

The second man then stumbled over Lucilio, likewise wishing him, as his predecessor had done, a good day.   Whereupon Lucilio, still dwelling on the good days, said to himself, but half loud, " Now I have two of them ! "

The third followed and saluted him as the two others had done, also wishing that Heaven might send him a good day.   Up started Lucilio, overjoyed, and exclaiming, " Oh ! delightful !   Now I have got all three of them !   I am fortunate ! "

He alluded only to three lucky days ; but the buriers of the treasure thought he meant them ; and as they feared he might go and give information of them to the magistrate, they took him aside, told him the whole affair, and, to bribe him into silence, gave him the fourth part of the treasure.

Well pleased, Lucilio took his portion, carried it home to his mother, and said, " Dear mother, Heaven's blessing has been with me; for, as I did as you desired, so I have found the good days. Take this money, and buy with it all we require."

The mother was not a little pleased at the fortunate occurrence, and urged her son to go on exerting himself that he might find more such good days.

THE FEAST OF THE DWARFS.

[Icelandish.]

———◆———

OT very far from Drontheim, in Norway, dwelt a powerful man, blessed with all the gifts of fortune. A considerable portion of the land around belonged to him; numerous herds grazed in his pastures, and a numerous establishment of domestics contributed to the grandeur of his dwelling. He had an only daughter called Aslog, whose beauty was celebrated far and near. The most illustrious of her countrymen sought to obtain her hand, but without success; and those who arrived gay and full of hope, rode away in silence and with heavy hearts. Her father, who thought that his daughter's rejection of so many suitors proceeded from her anxiety to make a prudent choice, did not interfere, and rejoiced to think that she was so discreet. At length, however, when he perceived that the noblest and the most wealthy of the land were rejected equally with all others, he grew angry, and thus addressed her :—

" Hitherto I have left you at full liberty to make your own selection; but, as I observe that you reject all indiscriminately, and that the most eligible suitors are yet in your opinion not good enough for you, I shall no longer permit such conduct. Is my race, then, to be extinguished, and are my possessions to fall into the hands of strangers? I am resolved to bend your stubborn will. I give you time for consideration until the great winter nights' festival; if you shall not then have made your election, be prepared to accept him whom I determine upon for you."

Aslog loved a handsome, brave, and noble youth, whose name was Orm. She loved him with her whole soul, and would have preferred death to giving her hand to any one but him. But Orm was poor, and his poverty compelled him to take service in her father's house. Aslog's love for him was therefore kept secret, for her haughty father would never have consented to an alliance with a man in so subordinate a position. When Aslog beheld his stern aspect and heard his angry words, she became deathly pale, for she knew his disposition, and was well aware that he would put his threat in execution. Without offering a word in reply, she withdrew to her chamber, there to consider how to escape the storm that menaced her.

The great festival drew near, and her anxiety increased daily.

At length the lovers resolved to fly. "I know a hiding place," said Orm, "where we can remain undiscovered till we find an opportunity of quitting the country."

During the night, whilst all were asleep, Orm conducted the trembling Aslog across the snow and fields of ice to the mountains. The moon and stars, which always seem brightest in the cold winter's night, lighted them on their way. They had brought with them some clothes and furs, but that was all they could carry.

They climbed the mountains the whole night long, till they arrived at a solitary spot completely encircled by rock. Here Orm led the weary Aslog into a cave, the dark and narrow entrance to which was scarcely perceptible; it soon widened, however, into a spacious chamber that penetrated far into the mountain. Orm kindled a fire, and they sat beside it, leaning against the rock, shut out from the rest of the world.

Orm was the first who had discovered this cavern, which is now shown as a curiosity; and, as at that time no one knew of its existence, they were secure from the pursuit of Aslog's father. Here they passed the winter. Orm went out to chase the wild animals of the lonely region, and Aslog remained in the cave, attended to the fire, and prepared their necessary food. She frequently climbed to the summit of the rock, but, far as her eye could reach, it beheld only the sparkling snow-fields.

Spring arrived, the woods became green, the fields arrayed themselves in bright colours, and Aslog dared now only seldom, and with great precaution, to emerge from her cavern.

One evening Orm returned home bringing news that he had recognised, at a distance, her father's people, and that they had no doubt also descried him, as they could see as clearly as himself. "They will surround this place," continued he, "and not rest till they have found us; we must therefore instantly be off."

They immediately descended the mountain on the other side, and reached the sea-shore, where they fortunately found a boat. Orm pushed off, and the boat was driven into the open sea. They had, it is true, escaped their pursuers, but they were now exposed to perils of another kind. Whither should they turn? They dared not land, for Aslog's father was lord of the

whole coast, and they would so fall into his hands
Nothing remained, therefore, for them, but to commit
the boat to the winds and waves, which pursued its way
all night, so that at day-break the coast had disappeared, and they saw only sky and water ; they had
not brought any provisions with them, and hunger and
thirst began to torture them.   Thus they drove on for
three days, and Aslog, weak and exhausted, foresaw
their certain destruction.

At length, on the evening of the third day, they
beheld an island of considerable size, surrounded by a
multitude of lesser islets.   Orm immediately steered
towards it, but, as they approached it, a gale arose and
the waves swelled higher and higher; he turned the
boat in hopes to be able to land on some other side, but
equally without success. Whenever the bark approached
the island, it was driven back as if by some invisible
force.

Orm, gazing on the unhappy Aslog, who seemed
dying from exhaustion, crossed himself, and uttered
an exclamation, which had scarcely passed his lips,
when the storm ceased, the waves sank, and the little
bark landed without further obstruction. He then
sprang on shore, and a few muscles, which he collected,

so revived and strengthened the exhausted Aslog, that in a short time she also was able to quit the boat.

The island was entirely covered with dwarf mushrooms, and appeared to be uninhabited; but when they had penetrated nearly to the centre of it they perceived a house, half of which only was above the ground, and the other half under it. In the hope that they might find human help they joyfully approached it; they listened for some sound, but the deepest silence prevailed all around. At length Orm opened the door and entered with his companion; great was their astonishment, however, when they perceived everything prepared as if for inhabitants, but no living being visible. The fire burnt on the hearth in the middle of the room, and a kettle with fish hung over it, waiting, probably, for some one to make a meal of its contents; beds were ready prepared for the reception of sleepers. Orm and Aslog stood for a time doubtful, and looked fearfully about; at length, impelled by hunger, they took the food and eat it. When they had satisfied their hunger, and, by the last rays of the sun, could not discover any one far and wide, they yielded to fatigue and lay down on the beds, a luxury which they had so long been deprived of.

318

They had fully expected to be awakened in the night by the return of the owners of the house, but they were deceived in their expectation; throughout the following day, also, no one appeared, and it seemed as if some invisible power had prepared the house for their reception. Thus did they pass the whole summer most happily; it is true they were alone, but the absence of mankind was not felt by them. The eggs of wild-fowl and the fish which they caught afforded them sufficient provision.

When autumn approached, Aslog bore a son, and in the midst of their rejoicing at his arrival they were surprised by a wonderful apparition.—The door opened suddenly, and an old woman entered; she wore a beautiful blue garment, and in her form and manner was something dignified, and at the same time unusual and strange.

"Let not my sudden appearance alarm you," said she. "I am the owner of this house, and I thank you for having kept it so clean and well, and that I now find everything in such good order. I would willingly have come sooner, but I could not until the little heathen there—pointing to the infant—had established himself here. Now I have free access; but do not, I

319

pray you, fetch a priest here from the main-land to baptise him, for then I shall be obliged to go away again. If you fulfil my wish, not only may you remain here, but every good you can desire I will bestow on you; whatever you undertake shall succeed; good fortune shall attend you wherever you go. But if you break this condition, you may assure yourselves that misfortune on misfortune shall visit you, and I will even avenge myself on the child. If you stand in need of anything, or are in danger, you have only to pronounce my name thrice: I will appear and aid you. I am of the race of the ancient giants, and my name is Guru. Beware, however, of pronouncing, in my presence, the name that no giant likes to hear, and never make the sign of the cross, nor cut it in any of the boards in the house. You may live here the year round; only on Yule evening be so kind as to leave the house to me as soon as the sun goes down. Then we celebrate our great festival, the only occasion on which we are permitted to be merry. If, however, you do not like to quit the house, remain as quietly as possible under ground, and, as you value your lives, do not look into the room before midnight; after that hour you may again take possession of all."

320

When the old woman had thus spoken, she disappeared, and Aslog and Orm, thus rendered easy as to their position, lived on without disturbance contented and happy. Orm never cast his net without a good draught—never shot an arrow that did not hit—in short, whatever he undertook, however trifling it might be, prospered visibly.

When Christmas came they made the house as clean as possible, set everything in order, kindled a fire on the hearth, and on the approach of twilight descended to the under part of the house, where they remained quiet and silent. At length it grew dark, and they fancied they heard a rustling and snorting in the air, like that which the swans make in the winter season. In the wall over the hearth was an aperture that could be opened and shut to admit light, or to let out smoke. Orm raised the lid, which was covered with a skin, and put out his head, when a wonderful spectacle presented itself. The little surrounding islets were illuminated by countless little blue lights, which moved incessantly, danced up and down, then slid along the shore, collected together, and approached nearer and nearer to the island in which Orm and Aslog dwelt. When they reached it they arranged themselves in a circle round a great stone, which stood not very far from the shore, and which was well known to Orm. But how great was his astonishment, when he saw that the stone had assumed a perfectly human form, although of gigantic stature. He could now clearly distinguish that the lights were carried by dwarfs, whose pale earth-coloured faces, with large noses and red eyes, in the form of birds' beaks and owls' eyes, surmounted mis-shapen bodies. They waddled and shuffled here and there, and seemed to be sad and gay at the same time. Suddenly the circle opened, the little people drew back on either side, and Guru, who now appeared as large as the stone, approached with giant steps. She threw her arms around the stony figure, which at that moment received life and movement. At the first indication of this, the little people set up, accompanied by extraordinary grimaces and gestures, such a song, or rather howl, that the whole island resounded and shook with the noise. Orm, quite terrified, drew in his head, and he and Aslog now remained in the dark so quiet, that they scarcely dared to breathe.

The procession arrived at the house, as was clearly perceived by the nearer approach of the howl. They

322

THE FEAST OF THE DWARFS.   P 329.

now all entered. Light and active, the dwarfs skipped over the benches; heavy and dull sounded the steps of the giants among them. Orm and his wife heard them lay out the table and celebrate their feast with the clattering of plates and cries of joy. When the feast was over and midnight was approaching, they began to dance to that magic melody which wraps the soul in sweet bewilderment, and which has been heard by some persons in the valleys and amid the rocks, who have thus learnt the air from subterranean musicians.

No sooner did Aslog hear the melody than she was seized with an indescribable longing to witness the dance. Orm was unable to restrain her. " Let me look," said she, " or my heart will break." She took her infant and placed herself at the furthest extremity of the chamber, where she could see everything without being herself seen. Long did she watch, without turning away her eyes, the dance, and the agile and wonderful steps and leaps of the little beings, who seemed to float in the air and scarcely to touch the ground, whilst the enchanting music of the elfs filled her soul.

In the mean time the infant on her arm grew

sleepy and breathed heavily, and, without remembering the promise she had made to the old woman, she made the sign of the cross (as is the custom) over the child's mouth, and said, " Christ bless thee, my child ! " She had scarcely uttered the words when a fearful piercing cry arose. The sprites rushed headlong out of the house, their lights were extinguished, and in a few minutes they had all left the house. Orm and Aslog, terrified almost to death, hid themselves in the remotest corner of the house. They ventured not to move until day-break, and, not until the sun shone through the hole over the hearth, did they find courage to come out of their hiding-place.

The table was still covered as the sprites had left it, with all their precious and wonderfully wrought silver vessels. In the middle of the room stood, on the ground, a high copper vessel half filled with sweet metheglin, and by its side a drinking-horn of pure gold. In the corner lay a stringed instrument, resembling a dulcimer, on which, as it is believed, the female giants play. They gazed with admiration on all, but did not venture to touch anything. Greatly were they startled, however, when, on turning round, they beheld, seated at the table, a monstrous form, which Orm immediately recognised as the giant whom Guru had embraced. It was now a cold hard stone. Whilst they stood looking at it, Guru herself, in her giant form, entered the room. She wept so bitterly that her tears fell on the ground, and it was long before her sobs would allow her utterance; at length she said:—

"Great sorrow have you brought upon me; I must now weep for the remainder of my days. As, however, I know that you did it not from any evil intention, I forgive you, although it would be easy for me to crumble this house over your heads like an egg-shell.

"Ah!" exclaimed she, "there sits my husband, whom I loved better than myself, turned for ever into stone, never again to open his eyes. For three hundred years I lived with my father in the island of Kuman, happy in youthful innocence, the fairest amongst the virgins of the giant race. Mighty heroes were rivals for my hand; the sea that surrounds that island is full of fragments of rock which they hurled at each other in fight. Andfind won the victory, and I was betrothed to him. But before our marriage came the abhorred Odin into the country, conquered my father, and drove us out of the island. My father and sister fled to the mountains, and my eyes have never since beheld them.

Andfind and I escaped to this island, where we lived for a long time in peace, and began to hope that we should never be disturbed. But Destiny, which no one can escape, had decreed otherwise; Oluff came from Britain. They called him the Holy, and Andfind at once discovered that his journey would be fatal to the giant race. When he heard Oluf's ship dashing through the waves, he went to the shore and blew against it with all his strength. The waves rose into mountains. But Oluf was mightier than he; his vessel flew unharmed through the waves, like an arrow from the bow. He steered straight to our island. When the ship was near enough for Andfind to reach it, he grasped the prow with his right hand, and was in the act of sending it to the bottom, as he had often done with other ships. But Oluf, the dreadful Oluf, stepped forwards, and crossing his hands, cried out with a loud voice :—' Stand there, a stone, until the last day !' and in that moment my unhappy husband became a mass of stone. The ship sailed on unhindered towards the mountain, which it severed, and separated from it the little islands that lie around it.

"From that day all my happiness was annihilated, and I have passed my life in loneliness and sorrow.

326

Only on Yule evening can a petrified giant recover life for seven hours, if one of the race embraces him, and is willing to renounce a hundred years of life for this purpose. It is seldom that a giant does this. I loved my husband too tenderly not to recall him to life as often as I could, at whatever cost to myself. I never counted how often I had done it, in order that I might not know when the time would come when I should share his fate, and in the act of embracing him become one with him. But ah! even this consolation is denied me. I can never again awaken him with an embrace, since he has heard the name which I may not utter, and never will he again see the light until the dawn of the last day.

"I am about to quit this place. You will never again behold me. All that is in the house I bestow on you. I reserve only my dulcimer. Let no one presume to set foot on the little surrounding islands. There dwells the little subterranean race, whom I will protect as long as I live."

With these words she vanished. The following spring, Orm carried the golden horn and the silver vessels to Drontheim, where no one knew him. The value of these costly utensils was so great, that he was enabled to purchase all that a rich man requires. He loaded his vessel with his purchases, and returned to the island, where he lived for many years in uninterrupted happiness. Aslog's father soon became reconciled to his wealthy son-in-law.

The stone figure remained seated in the house. No one was able to remove it thence. The stone was so hard that axe and hammer were shivered against it, without making the slightest impression on it. There the giant remained till a holy man came to the island, and with one word restored it to its former place, where it still is to be seen.

The copper vessel which the subterranean people left behind them, is preserved as a memorial in the island, which is still called the Island of the Hut.

THE THREE DOGS.

[Frieslandish.]

—◆—

SHEPHERD who had two children, a son and a daughter, had, at his death, nothing to leave them but three sheep, and the little cottage they inhabited. On his death-bed he blessed them, and with his last breath admonished them to divide the legacy, and share it affectionately. When the children had buried their beloved father, the brother asked the sister which part of the inheritance she would prefer,—the sheep or the cottage? and as she chose the cottage, he said, " Then I will take the sheep, and wander out in the wide world; many a one has there found his fortune, and I am a Sunday child." With these words he embraced his sister, and with his inheritance left his native place.

Far and wide did he wander, and much did he suffer —fortune never once recognising him as her son.

Once, full of sorrow, uncertain whither to bend his steps, he sat down by a cross road, when all at once there stood before him a man accompanied by three large dogs, the one greater than the other, strongly built, and jet black.

"Well, my brave youth," said the man, "you have there three fine sheep, and if you choose we will exchange property; let me have your sheep, and you shall have my dogs."

In spite of his mournful disposition, the youth could not help laughing at the proposal. "What am I to do with your dogs?" demanded he; "my sheep feed themselves, but your dogs will want to be fed."

"My dogs are of a peculiar kind," answered the stranger; "they will provide for you, instead of your providing for them, and besides they will bring you great fortune. The smallest of them is called Bring-food; the second, Tear-to-pieces; and the great and strong one is named Break-steel-and-iron."

The shepherd, persuaded by the stranger, gave up his sheep; and now, to try their quality, he called out "Bring-food!" and forthwith one of the dogs ran away, and soon returned with a great basket full of the costliest and daintiest victuals. The shepherd was now much pleased at his exchange, and travelled far and wide over the land.

Once on his road he met a carriage hung all over with black crape drawn by two horses, which were covered with cloth of the same colour, and the coachman, too, was in deep mourning. In the carriage was seated a wondrously beautiful lady, also enveloped in the mournful colour of sorrow, and bitterly weeping; the horses, with drooping heads, paced slowly along. "What means this?" said he to the coachman; but the coachman gave an evasive answer; at last, however, after much pressing, he related as follows: "There dwells in this neighbourhood a ferocious dragon who caused great havoc and destruction; to appease him, and to secure the land against his devastation, a compact has been entered into with him, and he each year receives as tribute a fair maiden, whom he at one morsel devours and swallows. All the maidens in the kingdom at the age of fourteen draw lots between them, and this year the lot has fallen upon the daughter of the king: on this account the king and the whole state were plunged into the deepest grief; but such terror did the dragon inspire, that they dared not refuse him the sacrifice."

331

The shepherd felt pity for the beautiful young princess, and followed the carriage, which at last stopped at a high mountain. The princess descended, and, full of despair and anguish, went slowly onwards to meet her awful destiny. The driver, on observing that the youth followed her, warned him; the shepherd, however, was not to be persuaded, but followed her steps.

When they had thus advanced half-way up the mountain, the terrible monster approached from the summit, with an awful noise, to devour the victim. From its widely-extended jaws issued streams of burning sulphur, its body was encircled with thick horny scales, on its feet it had immense claws, and wings were attached to its long serpentine neck: already was it near enough to pounce upon its prey, when the shepherd cried out, " Tear-to-pieces ! " and his second dog threw himself upon the dragon, and attacked him with such strength and ferocity, that, after a short combat, the monster fell exhausted and dead at the feet of his antagonist, who, to finish his victory, wholly devoured him, leaving only two teeth ; these the shepherd put in his pocket.

The princess, overcome with the extreme emotions of

fear and joy, had fainted away; the shepherd by every means in his power tried to restore her back to life, in which he at last succeeded. When fully recovered, the princess threw herself at the feet of her deliverer, thanking, and imploring him to return with her to her father, who would richly reward him for having returned him his daughter, and saved the country from the scourge of the dragon.

The youth answered, he would first like to see and know a little more of the world; but in three years he would return, and by this resolution he remained. The maiden then returned to her carriage, and the shepherd continued his wanderings in an opposite direction.

Meanwhile the coachman, who had been a spectator of the whole, now meditated in his own black mind how to turn this fortunate conclusion of the tragedy to his own profit and aggrandizement. As they were passing over a bridge, under which flowed a great stream, he turned himself to the princess and said, "Your deliverer is gone, and was not even anxious for your thanks. It would be a noble action of yours to make the fortune of a poor man. If you, therefore, were to tell your father that it was by my hand that the dragon perished, this would be accomplished. But should you refuse to do so, I will throw you into this deep river, and no one will ever ask after you, being all convinced that the dragon has devoured you. The maiden cried and prayed, but in vain; she was forced to swear that she would proclaim the coachman as her deliverer, and never divulge the secret to any mortal.

They then returned to the capital, where all was rejoicing and gladness at their return. The black banners were removed from the steeples of the church, and gay coloured ones were hoisted to replace them. The king with tears of joy embraced his daughter and her supposed deliverer: "Thou hast not only saved my child," said he, "but thou hast also delivered my land from the greatest pestilence by which it ever has been scourged: to reward you royally for your undaunted courage, and in a manner commensurate with your great service, I intend to bestow my daughter in marriage upon you; but as she is yet too young, we will defer the ceremony for one year."

The coachman thanked the king, was forthwith richly apparelled, elevated to the rank of a duke, with the possession of a dukedom, and instructed in those polite manners requisite in his new and elevated station. The princess was much afflicted, and bewailed her mournful destiny most bitterly, when she was informed of the promise her father had made; but withal she feared to break her oath. When the year was at an end, in spite of all her entreaties she could not obtain from her father anything beyond the promise that the wedding should be delayed for another year. This also expired.

She again threw herself at her father's feet imploring for yet another year, for she well remembered the promise of her young and handsome deliverer, that in three years he would return. The king could not resist her entreaties, and acquiesced in her prayer on the condition that at the termination of that time she would wed the man he had chosen for her. The time again quickly elapsed. The auspicious day was already fixed, on the towers gay banners waved in the breeze, and the joyful shouting of the people mounted to the sky.

On the same day a stranger, with three dogs, entered the town. On demanding the reason of the public rejoicing, he was informed that the king's daughter, that very day, was to be united to the man that had delivered her and the country from the terrible dragon, which he had slain.

The stranger, in no very measured terms, pronounced this man an impostor, who had decked himself with other's feathers : the watch who, passing by, had overheard him, at once apprehended him and threw him into a strong prison guarded with doors and bars of iron. As he lay on his bundle of straw and sorrowfully contemplated his destiny, he thought he heard the whining of his dogs,—a gleam of hope suddenly burst upon him— "Break-steel-and-iron !" cried he as loud as he could, and hardly had he uttered the words when he saw the paws of his biggest dog hard at work on the bars of his window, tearing and breaking them down as if they had been reeds ; the dog then jumped down into the cell and bit the chains with which his master was fettered, to pieces; whereupon both left the prison by the window as hastily as possible. He was now again at liberty, but the thought painfully oppressed him that another should have reaped the benefit of the deed of which he deserved the merit and reward. He felt also very hungry, and he called to one of his dogs, " Bring-food," which dog soon returned with a napkin full of costly food; the napkin was marked with a royal crown.

The king was seated at table, with all the great men of his land around him, when the dog made its appearance, and, as if in supplication, licked the hand of the princely maiden. She at once recognised the dog, and tied her own napkin round his neck, looking upon his appearance as foreboding her deliverance. She then prayed her father for a few words in private, when she disclosed to him the whole of the secret: the king sent a messenger to see whither the dog went, and the stranger was soon after brought into theroyal presence. The former coachman, pale and trembling at his appearance, fell upon his knees imploring mercy; the princess at once recognised the stranger as her saviour, who moreover proved his identity by the two dragon teeth that he yet carried about with him. The coachman was thrown into a deep dungeon and his dignities were conferred on the shepherd, who was the same day wedded to the princess.

The youthful pair lived a long time in the greatest happiness. The former shepherd often thought of his sister; and, that she might participate in his felicity, a carriage and servants were sent to fetch her, and before long she was pressed to the breast of her affectionate brother; then one of the dogs said to his master, "Our time is now expired; you need us no longer; we remained thus long with you to see whether in fortune also you would remember your sister, or whether the sudden acquisition of wealth and power would make you proud, forgetful, and austere. You have not proved guilty of such wickedness, but have shown yourself virtuous and affectionate." The dogs then changed into birds and vanished in the air.

THE COURAGEOUS FLUTE-PLAYER.

[A traditional tale in Franconia.]

THERE lived once a gay-hearted musician, who played the flute in a masterly style, and earned his living by wandering about, and playing on his instrument in all the towns and villages he came to. One evening he arrived at a farm-house, and resolved to stay there, as he could not reach the next village before night-fall. The farmer gave him a very friendly reception, made him sit down at his own table, and after supper requested him to play him an air on his flute. When the musician had finished, he looked out of the window, and saw by the light of the moon, at no great distance from the farm, an ancient castle, which was partly in ruins.

" What old castle is that ? " said the musician ; " and to whom did it belong ? "

The farmer then related to him, that many, many

years ago, a count had dwelt there, who was very rich, but also very avaricious. He had been very harsh to his vassals, had never given any alms to the poor, and had finally died without heirs, as his avarice had deterred him from marrying. His nearest relations had then taken possession of the castle, but had not been able to discover any money whatever in it. It was, therefore, supposed that he must have buried the treasure, and that it must still be lying concealed in some part of the old castle. Many persons had gone into the castle in hopes of finding the treasure, but no one had ever appeared again; and on this account the authorities of the village had forbidden any access to it, and had seriously warned all people throughout the country against going there.

The musician listened attentively, and when the farmer had finished his narration, he expressed the most ardent desire to go into the castle, for he had a brave heart, and knew not fear. The farmer, however, entreated him earnestly, even on his knees, to have regard for his young life, and not to enter the castle. But prayers and entreaties were vain : the musician was not to be shaken in his resolution. Two of the farmer's men were obliged to light a couple of lanterns and accompany the courageous musician to the old and dreaded castle. When he reached it, he sent them home again with one of the lanterns, and taking the other in his hand, he boldly ascended a long flight of steps. Arrived at the top, he found himself in a spacious hall, which had doors on all sides. He opened the first he came to, entered a chamber, and seating himself at an old-fashioned table, placed his light thereon, and began playing on his flute. Meanwhile, the farmer could not close his eyes all night, through anxiety for his fate, and often looked out of the window towards the tower, and rejoiced exceedingly when he heard each time his guest still making sweet music. But when, at length, the clock against the wall struck eleven, and the flute-playing ceased, he became dreadfully alarmed, believing no otherwise than that the ghost, or devil, or whoever it might be that inhabited the castle, had, doubtless, twisted the poor youth's neck. The musician, however, had continued playing without fear until he was tired, and at length finding himself hungry, as he had not eaten much at the farmer's, he walked up and down the room, and looked about him. At last he spied a pot full of uncooked lentils, and on another table stood a vessel full of water, another

341

full of salt, and a flask of wine. He quickly poured the water over the lentils, added the salt, made a fire in the stove, as there was plenty of wood by the side of it, and began to cook soup. Whilst the lentils were stewing, he emptied the flask of wine, and began playing again on his flute. As soon as the lentils were ready, he took them off the fire, shook them into the plate that stood ready on the table, and eat heartily of them. He then looked at his watch, and saw it was about eleven o'clock. At that moment the door suddenly flew open, and two tall black men entered, carrying on their shoulders a bier, on which lay a coffin. Without uttering a word, they placed the bier before the musician, who did not interrupt himself in his meal on account of them, and then they went out again at the same door, as silently as they had come in. As soon as they were gone the musician hastily rose from his seat, and uncovered the coffin. A little old and shrivelled man, with grey hair and a grey beard, lay therein; but the young man felt no fear, and lifting him out of the coffin, placed him by the stove, and no sooner did the body become warm, than life returned to it. Then the musician became quite busy with the old man, gave him some of the lentils to eat, and even fed him as a

342

mother does her child. At last the old man became quite animated, and said to him, " Follow me ! "

The little old man led the way, and the young flutist, taking his lantern, followed without trepidation. They descended a long and dilapidated flight of steps, and at last arrived in a deep gloomy vault.

On the ground lay a great heap of money. Then the little man said to the youth, " Divide this heap for me into two equal portions ; but mind that thou leave not anything over, for if thou dost I will deprive thee of life ! "

The youth merely smiled in reply, and immediately began to count out the money upon two great tables, laying a piece alternately on each, and so in no long time he had separated the heap into two equal portions ; but just at the last he found there was one kreutzer over. After a moment's thought he drew out his pocket-knife, set the blade upon the kreutzer, and striking it with a hammer that was lying there, cut the coin in half. When he had thrown one half on each of the heaps, the little man became right joyous, and said : " Thou courageous man, thou hast released me ! It is now already a hundred years that I have been doomed to watch my treasure, which I collected out of avarice,

343

until some one should succeed in dividing the money into two equal portions. Not one of the many who have tried could do it; and I was obliged to strangle them all. One of the heaps of gold is thine; distribute the other among the poor. Thou happy man, thou hast released me!"

When he had uttered these words, the little old man vanished. The youth, however, re-ascended the steps, and began again to play in the same chamber as before, merry tunes on his flute.

Rejoiced was the farmer when he again heard the notes; and with the earliest dawn he went to the castle and joyfully met the youth. The latter related to him the events of the night, and then descended to his treasure, with which he did as the little old man had commanded him. He caused, however, the old castle to be pulled down, and there soon stood a new one in its place, where the musician, now become a rich man, took up his abode.

THE GLASS HATCHET.

[Hungarian.]

———◆———

IN a remote land there dwelt, in former days, a wealthy count. He and his consort most ardently wished for a child, to whom they might bequeath their riches; but a long time passed ere their wish was gratified. At length, after twelve weary years, the countess bore a son; but short was the time granted her to rejoice at the accomplishment of her desire, for she died the day after the child's birth. Before she expired, she warned her husband never to allow the child to touch the earth with his feet, for, from the moment he should do so he would fall into the power of a bad fairy who was on the watch for him. The countess then breathed her last.

The boy throve well, and when he had outgrown the age for being in the nurse's arms, a peculiarly-formed chair was constructed for him, in which ne could, unassisted, convey himself about the garden of his father's castle. At other times he was carried in a litter, and most carefully attended to and watched, in order that he might never touch the earth with his feet.

As, however, the physicians, in order to supply the absence of other exercise, prescribed riding on horseback, he was instructed in that art as soon as he was ten years of age, and soon became proficient enough in it to be allowed to ride out daily, without any apprehension of danger to him being felt by his father. On these occasions he was always attended by a numerous suite.

He rode almost every day in the forest and on the plain, and returned safely home. In this manner many years glided away; and the warning given by the late countess almost ceased to be dwelt upon, and the enjoined precautions were observed rather from old habit than from any immediate sense of their importance.

One day the youth, with his attendants, rode across the fields to a wood, where his father frequently took the diversion of hunting. The path led to a rivulet, the borders of which were overgrown with bushes. The riders crossed it; when suddenly a hare, startled by the tramp of the horses, sprang from the bush and fled through the wood. The young count pursued, and had almost overtaken it, when the saddle-girth of his horse broke; saddle and rider rolled together on the ground, and at the same moment he vanished from the sight of his terrified attendants, leaving no trace behind.

All search or enquiry was vain; and they recognised in the misfortune the power of the evil fairy, against whom the countess had uttered her dying warning. The old count was deeply afflicted; but as he could do nothing to effect the deliverance of his son, he resigned himself to fate, and lived patiently and solitary, in the hope that a more favourable destiny might yet one day rescue the youth from the hands of his enemy.

The young count had scarcely touched the earth before he was seized by the invisible fairy, and carried off by her. He seemed now transported to quite a new world, and without a hope of ever being released from it. A strangely-built castle, surrounded by a spacious lake, was the fairy's residence. A floating bridge, which rested only on clouds, afforded a passage across it. On the other side were only forests and mountains, which were constantly wrapped in a dense fog, and in which no human voice, nor even that of any other living creature was ever heard. All around him was awful, mysterious, and gloomy; and only on the eastern side of the castle, where a little promontory stretched out into the lake, a narrow path wound through a valley in the rocks, behind which a river glistened.

As soon as the fairy with her captive arrived on her territory, she commanded him fiercely to execute all her behests with the extremest precision, at the risk of being punished severely for disobedience and delay.

She then gave him a glass hatchet, bidding him cross the bridge of clouds and go into the forest, where she expected him to cut down all the timber before sun-set. At the same time she warned him, on pain of her severest displeasure, not to speak to the dark maiden whom in all probability he would meet in the forest.

The young count listened respectfully to her orders, and betook himself with his glass hatchet to the appointed place. The bridge of clouds seemed at each step he took to sink beneath him; but fear would not admit of his delaying; and so he soon arrived, although much fatigued by his mode of passage, at the wood, where he immediately began his work.

348

But he had no sooner made his first stroke at a tree, than the glass hatchet flew into a thousand splinters. The youth was so distressed he knew not what to do, so much did he fear the chastisement that the cruel fairy would inflict on him. He wandered hither and thither, and at length, quite exhausted by anxiety and fatigue, he sank on the ground and slept.

After a time something roused him; when upon opening his eyes, he beheld the black maiden standing before him. Remembering the prohibition he did not venture to address her. But she greeted him kindly, and inquired if he did not belong to the owner of the domain. The young count made a sign in the affirmative. The maiden then related that she was in like manner bound to obey the fairy who had by magic transformed her and forced her to wander in that ugly form, until some youth should take pity on her and conduct her over that river beyond which the domain of the fairy and her power did not extend. On the further side of the river she was powerless to harm any one who, by swimming through the waves, should reach the other shore.

These words inspired the young count with so much courage, that he revealed to the black maiden the whole of his destiny, and asked her counsel how he might escape punishment, since the wood was not cut down, and the hatchet was broken.

" I know," resumed the maiden, " that the fairy, in whose power we both are, is my own mother; but thou must not betray that I have told thee this, for it would cost me my life. If thou wilt promise to deliver me, I will assist thee, and will perform for thee all that my mother commands thee to do."

The youth promised joyfully; she again warned him several times not to say a word to the fairy that should betray her, and then gave him a beverage, which he had no sooner drunk than he fell into a soft slumber.

How great was his astonishment on waking to find the glass hatchet unbroken at his feet, all the trees of the forest cut down and lying round him !

He instantly hastened back across the cloud bridge, and informed the fairy that her behest was obeyed. She heard with much surprise that the forest was cut down, and that the glass hatchet was still uninjured, and being unable to believe that he had performed all that unassisted, she closely questioned him whether he had seen and spoken to the black maiden. But the count strongly denied that he had, and affirmed that he had not once looked up from his work. When she found that she could learn nothing further from him, she gave him some bread and water, and showed him a little dark closet where she bade him pass the night.

Almost before day-break the fairy again wakened him, assigned him for that day's task to cleave, with the same glass hatchet, all the wood he had felled into billets, and then to arrange them in heaps; at the same time she again warned him, with redoubled threats, not to go near the black maiden, or dare converse with her.

Although his present work was in no respect easier than that of the preceding day, the youth set off in much better spirits, for he hoped for the assistance of the black maiden. He crossed the bridge quicker and more lightly than the day before, and had scarcely passed it when he beheld her. She received him with a friendly salutation; and when she heard what the fairy had now required of him, she said, smiling, "Do not be uneasy," and handed to him a similar beverage to that of yesterday. The count again fell into a deep sleep. When he awoke his work was done; for all the trees of the forest were cut up into blocks and arranged in heaps.

He returned home quickly. When the fairy heard that he had performed this task also, she was still more surprised than before. She again inquired if he had seen or spoken to the black maiden; but the count had the prudence to preserve his secret, and she was again obliged to content herself with his denial.

On the third day she set him a new task, and this was the most difficult of all. She commanded him to build, on the further side of the lake, a magnificent castle, which should consist of nothing but gold, silver, and precious stones ; and if he did not build the said castle in less than one hour's time, he might expect the most dreadful fate.

The count listened to her commands without alarm, such was the confidence he reposed in the black maiden. Cheerily he hastened across the bridge, and immediately recognised the spot where the palace was to be erected. Pickaxes, hammers, spades, and all manner of tools requsite for building, lay scattered around; but neither gold, nor silver, nor jewels could he spy. He had, however, scarcely begun to feel uneasy at this circumstance, when the black maiden beckoned to him from a rock at some distance, behind which she had concealed herself from her

352

mother's searching looks. The youth hastened to her well pleased, and besought her to assist him in the execution of her mother's orders.

This time, however, the fairy had watched the count from a window of her castle, and descried him and her daughter just as they were about to conceal themselves behind the rock. She set up such a frightful scream, that the mountains and the lake re-echoed with it, and the terrified pair scarcely dared to look out from their hiding-place, whilst the infuriated fairy, with violent gestures and hasty strides, her hair and garments streaming in the wind, hastened across the bridge of clouds. The youth gave himself up for lost; each step of the fairy seemed to bring him nearer to destruction. The maiden, however, took courage, and bade him follow her as quickly as possible. Before they hastened from the spot she broke a stone from the rock, uttered a spell over it, and threw it towards the place from which her mother was advancing. At once a glittering palace arose before the eyes of the fairy, which dazzled her with its lustre, and delayed her by the numerous windings of its avenue, through which she was obliged to thread her way.

Meanwhile the black maiden hurried the count

along, in order to reach the river, the opposite bank of which alone could protect her for ever from the persecutions of the raging fairy. But before they had got half way, she was again so near them that her imprecations, and even the rustling of her garments reached their ears.

The terror of the youth was extreme; he dared not to look behind him, and had scarcely power left to advance. At every breath he fancied that he felt the hand of the terrible fairy on his neck. Then the maiden stopped, again uttered a spell, and was at once transformed into a pond, whilst the count swam upon its waters under the figure of a drake.

The fairy, incensed to the utmost at this new transformation, called down thunder and hail on the two fugitives; but the water refused to be disturbed, and whilst it remained calm no thunder-cloud would approach it. She now employed her power to cause the pond to vanish from the spot: she pronounced a magic spell, and called up a hill of sand at her feet, which she intended should choke up the pond. But the sand-hill drove the water still further on, and seemed rather to augment than diminish it. When the fairy found this would not answer, and that her art failed so entirely, she had recourse to cunning. She threw a heap of golden nuts into the pond, hoping thereby to entice the drake, and catch him; but he snapped at the nuts with his bill, pushed them all back to the margin, dived here and there, and made game of the fairy in various ways.

Finding herself again cheated, and unwilling to see the reflection of her face in the pond, glowing, as it was, with rage and mortification, she turned back full of fury to devise some other stratagem by which to catch the fugitives.

She concealed herself behind the very same rock which had served them for a place of refuge, and watched for the moment when they should both resume their natural form in order to pursue their way.

It was not long before the maiden disenchanted herself, as well as the count, and as they could nowhere perceive their persecutor, they both hastened in good spirits to the river.

But scarcely had they proceeded a hundred paces, when the fairy burst out again after them with redoubled speed, shaking at them the dagger with which she meant to pierce them both. But she was doomed to see her intentions again frustrated and derided;

for just as she thought she had reached the flying pair, a marble chapel rose before her, in the narrow portal of which stood a colossal monk, to prevent her entrance.

Foaming with passion she struck at the monk's face with her dagger, but behold, it fell into shivers at her feet. She was beside herself with desperation, and raved at the chapel till the columns and dome resounded. Then she determined to annihilate the whole building and the fugitives with it at once. She stamped thrice, and the earth began to quake. A hollow murmur like that of a rising tempest was heard from below, and the monk and chapel began to totter.

As soon as she perceived this, she retired to some distance behind the edifice, that she might not be buried under its ruins. But she was again deceived in her expectation; for she had no sooner retired from the steps, than the monk and chapel disappeared, and an awful forest surrounded her with its black shade, whence issued a terrible sound of the mingled bellowing, roaring, howling and baying of wild bulls, bears, and wolves.

Her rage gave way to terror at this new apparition, for she dreaded every moment to be destroyed by these

356

creatures, who all seemed to set her power at defiance. She therefore deemed it most prudent to work her way back through bush and briar towards the lighter side of the forest, in order from thence again to try her might and cunning against the hated pair.

Meantime, both had pursued their way to the river with their utmost speed. As this river resisted all kind of enchantment, consequently it was hostile to the black maiden whose hour of deliverance had not yet struck, and it might have proved fatal to her; she therefore did not let the moment for her complete disenchantment escape, but reminded the youth of his promise. She gave him a bow and arrows and a dagger, and instructed him in the use he was to make of these weapons.

She then vanished from his sight, and at the moment of her disappearance, a raging boar rushed upon him, menacing to rip him up. But the youth took courage and shot an arrow at him with such good aim, that it pierced the animal's skull. It fell to the ground, and from its jaws sprang a hare, which fled as on the wings of the wind along the bank of the river. The youth again bent his bow, and stretched the hare on the earth, when a snow-white dove rose into the air, and circled round him with friendly cooings. As by the directions he had received from the black maiden he was equally forbidden to spare the dove, he sent another arrow from his bow, and brought it down. Approaching to examine it more closely, he found in its place an egg, which spontaneously rolled to his feet.

The final transformation now drew near. A powerful vulture sailed down upon him with wide stretched beak threatening him with destruction. But the youth seized the egg, waited till the bird approached him, and cast it into its throat. The monster at once disappeared, and the loveliest maiden the count had ever beheld stood before his delighted eyes.

Whilst these events were occurring, the fairy had worked her way out of the forest, and now adopted her last means of reaching the fugitives in case they should not already have passed the river. As soon as she emerged from the forest, she called up her dragon-drawn car and mounted high in the air. She soon descried the lovers, with interlaced arms, swimming easily as a couple of fish towards the opposite bank.

Swift as lightning she bore down with her dragon-car, and regardless of all peril, she endeavoured to reach them, even though they were in the river. But the

THE GLASS HATCHET

P. 358

hostile stream drew down the car into its depths, and dashed her about with its waves until she hung upon the bushes a prey to its finny inhabitants. Thus the lovers were finally rescued. They hastened to the paternal castle, where the count received them with transport. The following day their nuptials were celebrated with great magnificence, and all the inhabitants far and near rejoiced at the happy event.

THE GOLDEN DUCK.

[Bohemian.]

DEEP in the bosom of a wood once stood a little cottage, inhabited by a poor widow. Her name was Jutta, and she had formerly lived in easy circumstances, but through various misfortunes, without any fault of her own, she had fallen into poverty.

By the labour of her hands she with difficulty contrived to support herself, her daughter Adelheid, and the two children of her departed brother, Henry and Emma. The children, who were good and pious, especially Henry and Emma, did their utmost to assist her by their diligence: the girls spun, and the boy helped the old woman to cultivate the garden, and tended the sheep, whose milk formed the principal part of their daily sustenance.

One evening they were all sitting together in the

little cottage, whilst a tremendous storm raged without. The rain poured down in torrents, and flash after flash of lightning followed the thunder, which broke over the mountains, and seemed as if it would never cease.

The old woman had just sung to the children the song of the water-sprite who danced with a young maiden till he drew her down into the abyss, when suddenly they heard a tap at the door. The startled children huddled close together, but the mother took courage and opened it, when a soft female voice begged her to give shelter to a traveller who had been overtaken in the forest by the storm.

The stranger was an elderly woman of a noble and dignified appearance, but so kind and friendly in her manner that all were anxious to show her some attention. Whilst the widow was regretting that her poverty did not allow her to receive such a guest in a more worthy manner, Henry lighted the fire, and Emma was anxious to kill her favourite pigeons for her supper, but the lady would not permit this, and took only a little milk.

The following morning, when Jutta and the children awoke, they were not a little astonished at beholding, instead of the aged woman who had entered the hut the night before, a youthful one of superhuman beauty, arrayed in a magnificent dress which sparkled with diamonds.

"Know," said the stranger to the widow, "that you yesterday received into your dwelling no mortal, but a fairy; I always try those mortals whom I desire to benefit, and you have stood the trial. To little Emma I am especially beholden, because she would yesterday have killed for my supper what she most values, her pigeons. For this she shall be gifted. Whenever she weeps, either for joy or sorrow, pearls instead of tears shall drop from her eyes, and the hairs she combs from her head shall turn into threads of pure gold. But beware that no ray of sun ever shine upon her uncovered countenance, for then a great misfortune will befall her; from henceforth never let her go into the open air without being covered with a veil."

The beneficent fairy having thus spoken, vanished; but Jutta, who was desirous to prove the truth of her words, hastily spread a large cloth on the ground, placed the little maiden on it, and commenced combing her long fair locks. Immediately the hairs that fell on the cloth became threads of gold, and when the old woman told the child how rich and grand she might now become, and what pretty toys she might buy, she

362

wept for joy, and the most beautiful pearls rolled from her eyes upon the linen cloth.

The next day the old woman betook herself to the nearest town, sold the pearls and the threads of gold, and bought a fine veil, without which Emma was never suffered to leave the house. She often combed the child's hair several times in the day, telling her all the time the prettiest tales, which drew from her eyes abundance of tears, either of pleasure or compassion, so that in a short time Jutta possessed a considerable treasure in gold and pearls.

At first she sold her treasures to Jews, and received but little for them, as they believed the goods were stolen. By and by, however, when she had become possessed of a small landed estate in the district, she traded with jewellers and goldsmiths, who paid her according to the value of her goods, and so at length she collected a very considerable treasure.

Meanwhile Adelheid and Emma grew into young women. But the increasing wealth of the old woman, whom her neighbours had formerly known to be in such straitened circumstances, and who knew not how she had acquired her riches, gave occasion for envious tongues to utter many an evil spceeh against her. Still further were their curiosity and ill-nature excited by the singular circumstance that Emma always went about veiled, and under these circumstances, what could be more natural than that the greater part of them were ready to swear without hesitation that old Jutta was a vile witch, and ought to be burned?

Now although these evil speeches were unable to do the widow any real injury, still she was not a little vexed and annoyed when they reached her ears, or when she perceived that she was looked upon with suspicious and wondering looks; and finding it impossible by obliging and friendly conduct, or even by conferring benefits, to win the hearts of her neighbours, or to stop their calumnies, she preferred to abandon altogether the place where she had been known in indifferent circumstances, and to go far away, where her riches would not excite suspicions against her. She therefore resolved to sell her estate, and to take up her residence in the city of Prague. In order, however, not to be too precipitate, she first sent thither her nephew, Henry, that she might become a little acquainted with their future residence, before removing from the former one.

So Henry went to the Bohemian capital, and, as he

was a personable youth, had good manners, and was richly provided with money by his aunt, so that he could live in as good style as any of the nobles of the land, he soon became on friendly terms with numerous counts and other illustrious persons. Judging by his personal appearance and expenditure they took him for one of their own station; nay, one of them, a young count, became his confidential friend, and, as wine often unlocks the secrets of the heart, it happened one day that Henry let out the whole secret concerning his sister, quite forgetting at the moment his aunt's strict prohibition ever to reveal it.

When the count heard so much of the extraordinary understanding, good heart, sweetness, and beauty of the young maiden who was possessed of such wonderful gifts, his heart at once glowed with love for her, and he said with great warmth :—

"I myself possess a domain of such great value, that I am in no need of the riches of another; but I have ever desired to have a wife distinguished above all others for her beauty, virtue, and other rare gifts; therefore I offer my hand to your sister, and I swear to you that I will do all in my power that I may call so wonderful a maiden my own."

Henry perceived his indiscretion now that it was too late, and he could not withstand the earnest entreaties of his friend to obtain for him the hand of his sister. In order, indeed, to lose no time, the count immediately caused to be constructed an entirely closed and well-covered carriage in which to transport Emma to him, without her being exposed to a breath of air.

Surprising as was his proposal, it was so honourable a one, that, after a few minutes' reflection, Emma could not think of refusing such an illustrious and amiable young man as Henry described the count to be. The brother, therefore, hastened back with the news of her consent, and the count immediately went to his residence, in order to make preparations for the reception of his bride, and for a magnificent bridal entertainment.

During the interval, Emma, accompanied by her mother and Adelheid, began her journey, and when they had proceeded about half-way, they came to a great forest. The heat was oppressive, and Emma happened to draw aside her veil, just as Jutta, in order to look after the attendants whom the count had sent to escort his bride on the journey, thoughtlessly opened the door of the carriage. No sooner did a sunbeam shine on the maiden, than she was suddenly transformed into a golden duck, flew out of the carriage, and vanished from the sight of her terrified aunt.

C.T. THOMPSON.

As soon as the old woman had recovered from her first alarm, she was greatly troubled how to escape the wrath of the count. They had still to traverse a considerable portion of the forest. So she sent the servants who had not perceived the occurrence, under some pretext, to a village at some distance, and during their

367

absence she covered her own daughter with Emma's veil. On their return they found the old woman in the greatest distress; she wrung her hands, and related with well simulated despair, that having gone with her daughter only a few steps from the carriage, armed men had surprised them, and carried off her Adelheid.

The count's servants, deceived by the despairing words and gestures of the old woman, searched the forest, in hopes of tracing the robbers, but as was to be expected, without success. Meanwhile Jutta instructed her daughter in the part she was to play, in order that she in Emma's place might become the count's wife. And as she feared she might not be able to conceal the cheat from Henry, she desired the servants not to go through Prague, but to take the direct road to the count's castle.

When they arrived, Jutta descended alone from the carriage, carefully closed it again, and besought the count, that until her niece had entirely recovered from the fatigue of the journey, he would permit them both to occupy a chamber from which all daylight could be excluded, and she forbade at first any visit from the bridegroom. Impatient as the latter was to see his bride, he yet submitted to this delay which the old

368

woman so earnestly requested of him. The most splendid apartments were now thrown open to the mother and daughter, and the most inner chamber of the suite was so hung with curtains that no daylight could penetrate. In this room dwelt Jutta with her daughter, and even Henry, who came to visit his supposed sister, was, under pretext of her being indisposed, not allowed to enter. As his aunt, however, provided him with plenty of money, and the merry life in Prague pleased him better than the retirement of the country, he soon returned thither.

The count, whom Jutta put off from day to day under various pretexts from visiting his bride, at length lost patience, and would not be longer withheld by the gold and pearls which Jutta continually brought him; he forced his way into the chamber, and clasped Adelheid in his arms.

Although the count could not but remark that Adelheid in no degree corresponded to the description her brother had given of her, he was still prepared to fulfil his word, and was therefore married, though with the greatest privacy, to the false bride. Very shortly, he became aware that neither her heart nor mind possessed the excellence that had been represented to him; and in consequence of this discovery, when he next met his brother-in-law, he overwhelmed him with reproaches. The contemptuous expressions which the count used respecting his bride, whom Henry had only known as the loveliest and most amiable maiden in all Bohemia, so incensed Henry, that he forgot all the consideration due to the rich and powerful man, and the count, who, besides this, believed himself to have been deceived by Henry, caused him to be seized, brought to his castle, and thrown into a deep dungeon.

The wife of the count, who was also most severely punished for the crime in which she had taken part, overwhelmed her mother with the bitterest reproaches. More than once she was on the point of confessing the fraud to her husband, but he drove her from him, and would not listen to her.

Whilst these women were thus suffering for their crime, Henry sat in his dungeon, hopeless of ever recovering his freedom, or of being able to take vengeance on him who had so unjustly treated him; when one day, as he lay in despair, a sweet voice reached him, which sang a song he had often listened to when his sister Emma used to sing it in former days.

The youth, who distinctly recognised his sister's

voice, uttered her name, and on looking upwards, he saw, by the light of the moon, a duck fluttering before him, whose feathers were of gold, and whose neck was adorned by a costly row of pearls.

Then said the golden duck to the astonished youth, " I am thy sister Emma, who, transformed into a golden duck, fly about without a home."

She then related to her brother what had occurred during the journey, and the deception her aunt had been guilty of. As she thus recounted her unhappy fate, which constrained her to fly about unprotected, her life exposed to the snares of the hunters, whilst her beloved brother was languishing in prison, she wept abundantly; and the tears rolled about the tower as costly pearls, and golden feathers fell from her, and glittered on the dark ground.

The brother and sister pitied and tried to console each other. Henry especially lamented his talkativeness, which had brought all this misfortune upon them. At daybreak the duck flew away, after promising to visit her brother every night.

After this intercourse had lasted some time, one night she did not make her appearance, which threw poor Henry into the greatest anxiety, for he feared she might, for the sake of her precious feathers, have been caught, or perhaps even killed. Then, for the first time, the door of his prison was opened; the count's superintendent entered, announced that he was free, and conducted him to the very same apartments which he had occupied in happier days.

Before Henry could recover from his surprise, the count himself entered, tenderly embraced him, and besought his forgiveness for all the suffering that had been inflicted on him.

The warder of the tower, it appeared, had remarked the golden duck, and heard with astonishment how she spoke with a human voice, and conversed with the prisoner; all of which he had disclosed to the count. The count thus discovered, by listening in secret to their conversation, the fraud which had imposed the false bride upon him instead of the true and beautiful one. Vain, however, were his efforts the following night to get the golden duck into his power; she escaped from all the attendants who endeavoured to catch her; and snares and nets and all the artifices they practised, and all the pains they took, were of no avail.

Then the count entreated the intercession of the brother. Since his hard fate had robbed him of such an amiable wife, he besought her at least in her present form to inhabit his castle. It was possible that his grief, his love, might move the offended fairy to restore her to her former shape.

Henry freely forgave the count, and promised to make his request known to his sister the next time she should visit him. Before, however, the duck's next visit, Adelheid expired, for the reproaches of her husband, and her own grief and remorse, had brought her to the grave. As soon as she was dead, the count banished Jutta to a remote place and forbade her ever to appear in his presence again. With Henry he lived on his former friendly terms.

Both lived in hopes of the reappearance of the golden duck. Long did they wait in vain, and they began to fear that the endeavours of the count to catch her had scared her from the place for ever, when one afternoon, as Henry was sitting alone in the dining-hall, she flew in at the window, and began gathering up the scattered crumbs on the table. How great was the brother's joy! He addressed her by the tenderest names, stroked her golden feathers, and inquired why she had remained so long absent.

Then Emma complained of the efforts to catch her,

which the count's servants had made, and threatened never to return should such be repeated. The entreaty which Henry made in the count's name that she would dwell in the castle she decidedly rejected; and as she heard a noise in the adjoining chamber, she hastily flew away.

For a long time the youth hesitated whether he should tell the count of his sister's visit; as, however, he knew the strong affection of his friend, and feared he might not refrain from fresh attempts against the liberty of the golden duck, he resolved to say nothing about it. But the count had seen the duck fly past, and when Henry said nothing about it, he conceived mistrust of him, and laid a new plan to get possession of her.

The following morning, when Emma flew into her brother's chamber, the window was suddenly closed, the count having fastened a cord to it from above, and in a few moments he entered the room thinking he had now made sure of the much-desired prize. But the duck fluttered about, and made her exit through the keyhole.

Henry was much distressed, for he feared that he should now see his beloved sister no more, and heaped reproaches on the astonished count, who returned them to him so liberally, that they separated in mutual disgust, and Henry resolved to quit the city and wander through the wide world.

One day after he had long travelled he found himself in a thick fir wood, when suddenly a female form of great dignity stood before him, in whom Henry at once recognised the fairy who had so richly gifted his sister.

"Wherefore," said she, with a reproachful look, "didst thou leave the castle at the time when thy sister's ill fortune, of which thou wert the cause, was beginning to turn to good? Hasten back immediately, confirm the count in the remorse for his profligate life which is now awakening in him, and the golden duck will then be released from her enchantment. And not only shall she retain the wonderful gifts she has hitherto possessed, but thenceforth she shall no longer have to fear air and sun-light."

The fairy disappeared, and Henry returned full of hope to the castle. On his way thither he met several of the count's servants, who told him their lord had sent them out with commands not to return until they found him. For they added, since Henry's departure had left the count so lonely and forsaken, he had fallen sick through sorrow and longing after his friend.

When Henry entered the count's chamber, he found

375

him lying on his bed really ill and unhappy. He comforted him with the fairy's promise, and the count solemnly vowed that he would never more return to his wild and sinful mode of life.

Scarcely had he uttered this solemn vow, when the window flew open of itself, the golden duck flew into the chamber, and, perching on the bed-post, said, "The period of my trials is completed. I may now return to my former figure and remain with you for ever."

Then the golden feathers dropped from her body; the long beak rounded into mouth and chin, above which gazed a pair of lovely eyes; before they could look round, a wondrously beautiful maiden stood before them, magnificently habited, and her joy at being re-united to her brother and her bridegroom drew the purest pearls from her eyes.

At the sight of her the count felt himself at once cured of his illness, and, a few days after, the nuptial feast was celebrated with all the pomp and magnificence befitting the high station and great wealth of the count.

GOLDY.

[From Justinus Kerner.]

————◆————

MANY a long year ago there lived in a great forest a poor herdsman, who had built himself a log cabin in the midst of it, where he dwelt with his wife and his six children, all of whom were boys. There was a draw-well by the house, and a little garden, and when their father was looking after the cattle the children carried out to him a cool draught from the well, or a dish of vegetables from the garden.

The youngest of the boys was called by his parents Goldy, for his locks were like gold, and although the youngest he was stronger and taller than all his brothers. When the children went out into the fields, Goldy always went first with a branch of a tree in his hand, and no otherwise would the other children go, for each feared lest some adventure should befall him; but when Goldy led them they followed cheerfully, one behind the other, through even the darkest thicket, although the moon might have already risen over the mountains.

One evening, on their return from their father, the children had amused themselves by playing in the wood, and Goldy especially had so heated himself in their games, that he was as rosy as the sky at sunset.

" Let us return," said the eldest, " it seems growing dark."

" See," said the second, " there is the moon ! "

At that moment a light appeared through the dark fir-trees, and a female form, shining like the moon, seated herself on the mossy stone, and span, with a crystal distaff, a fine thread, nodding her head towards Goldy, singing :—

> " The snow-white finch, the gold rose, for thee ;
> The king's crown lies in the lap of the sea ! "

She was about to continue her song when the thread broke, and she was instantly extinguished like the flame of a candle. It being now quite dark, terror seized the children, and they ran about crying piteously, one here, and another there, over rock and pit, till they lost each other.

378

Many a day and night did Goldy wander in the thick forest, but could find neither his brothers nor his father's hut, nor yet the trace of a human foot, for the forest had become more dense; one hill seemed to rise above another, and pit after pit intercepted his path.

The blackberries, that grew in profusion, satisfied his hunger and slaked his thirst, otherwise he must have perished miserably. At last, on the third day—some say it was not until the sixth or seventh—the forest became less and less dense, and at last he got out of it, and found himself in a lovely green meadow.

Then his heart grew light, and he inhaled the pure fresh air.

Nets were spread over the meadow, for a bird-catcher lived there, who caught the birds which flew out of the wood, and carried them into the city for sale.

"That is just such a boy as I want," thought the bird-catcher, when he saw Goldy, who stood in the meadow close to the net, gazing with longing eyes into the blue sky; and then in jest he drew his net, and imprisoned within it the astonished boy, who could not comprehend what had befallen him. "That's the way we catch the birds that come out of the wood," said the bird-catcher, laughing heartily. "Your red feathers please me right well. So I have caught you, have I, my little fox? You had better stay with me, and I will teach you how to catch birds!"

Goldy was well content; he thought he should lead a merry life amongst the birds, especially as he abandoned all hope of again finding his father's hut.

"Let us see how much you have learnt," said the bird-catcher to him, some days after. Goldy drew the net, and caught a snow-white chaffinch.

"Confound you and this white chaffinch!" screamed the bird-catcher; "you are in league with the evil one!" and he drove him roughly from the meadow, at the same time treading under his feet, the white chaffinch which Goldy had handed over to him.

Goldy could not conceive what the bird-catcher meant; he returned sadly, but yet not despairingly, to the forest, with the intention of renewing his endeavours to find his father's hut. Day and night he wandered about, climbing over fragments of rock and old fallen trees, and often stumbled and fell over the old black roots which protruded in all directions from out of the ground.

On the third day, however, the forest once more became

somewhat clearer, and he issued from it into a beautiful bright garden, full of the most delightful flowers, and as he had never before seen such he stood gazing full of admiration. The gardener no sooner perceived him —for Goldy stood beneath the sunflowers, and his locks glistened in the sunshine just like one of them— than he exclaimed: "Ha! he is just such a boy as I want!" and the garden-gate closed directly. Goldy was very well satisfied, for he thought he should lead a gay life amongst the flowers, and he had again lost the hope of getting back to his father's cottage.

"Off with you to the forest!" said the gardener to him one morning, "and fetch me the stem of a wild rose, that I may engraft cultivated roses on it."

Goldy went and returned with a rose-bush bearing the most beautiful golden-coloured roses imaginable, which looked exactly as if they were the work of the most skilful of goldsmiths, and prepared to adorn a monarch's table.

"Confound you, with these golden roses!" screamed the gardener; "you are in league with the evil one!" and he drove Goldy roughly out of the garden, as with plenty of abuse he trampled the golden roses on the ground.

Goldy knew not what the gardener could mean; but he went calmly back into the forest, and again set himself to seek after his father's cabin.

He walked on day and night, from tree to tree, from rock to rock. On the third day, the forest again became clearer and clearer, and he came to the shore of the blue sea. It lay before him without a boundary; the sun mirrored itself in the crystal surface, which glistened like liquid gold, and gay vessels with far-floating streamers floated on the waves. Some fishermen sat in a pretty bark on the shore, into which Goldy entered, and gazed with wonder out into the bright distance.

"We stand in need of just such a boy," said the fisherman, and off they pushed into the sea. Goldy was well pleased to go with them, for he thought it must be a golden life there amongst the bright waves, and he had quite lost all hope of again finding his father's hut.

The fishermen cast their nets, but took nothing.

"Let us see if you will have better luck," said an old fisherman with silver hair, addressing Goldy. With unskilful hands he let down the net into the deep, drew it up, and lo! he brought up in it—a crown of pure gold.

"Triumph!" cried the ancient fisherman, at the same time throwing himself at Goldy's feet. "I hail thee as our king! A hundred years ago, the last of our kings, having no heir, when he was about to die, cast his crown into the sea, and until the fortunate being destined by fate, should again draw up the crown from the deep, the throne, without an occupant, was to remain wrapt in gloom."

"Hail to our king!" cried all the fishermen, and they placed the crown on the boy's head. The tidings of Goldy and of the regained crown, resounded from vessel to vessel, and across the sea far into the land. The golden surface was soon crowded with gay barks and ships, adorned with festoons of flowers and branches; they all saluted with loud acclamations of joy the vessel in which was the Boy-king. He stood with the bright crown upon his head, at the prow of the vessel, and gazed calmly on the sun as it sank into the sea, whilst his golden locks waved in the refreshing evening breeze.

THE SERPENT PRINCE.

———◆———

HERE lived once a peasant's wife who would have given all she possessed to have a child, but yet she never had one.

One day her husband brought home a bundle of twigs from the wood, out of which crept a pretty little young serpent. When Sabatella, that was the peasant woman's name, saw the little serpent, she sighed deeply and said : " Even serpents have their offspring; I alone am so unfortunate as to remain childless !"

" Since you are childless," replied the little serpent, " take me in lieu of a child; you shall have no cause to repent, and I will love you more than a son."

When Sabatella heard the serpent speak, she was at first ready to go out of her wits from fright; but at length taking courage said : " If it be only for your kind words, I will love you as well as if you were my own child."

So saying, she showed the serpent a cupboard in the house for his bed, and she gave him a share, daily, of all she had to eat, and so the serpent grew; and when he was quite grown up, he said to the peasant, Cola Mattheo by name, whom he considered in the light of a father: "Dear Papa, I wish to marry."

"I am willing," said Mattheo; "we will look about for a serpent like yourself, and conclude the alliance at once."

"Why so," replied the serpent; "we shall then only become connected with vipers, and similar vermin. I greatly prefer to marry the king's daughter; so pray go forthwith, solicit the king for her, and say that a serpent wishes to have her for his wife."

Cola Mattheo, who was a simple-minded man, went without further delay to the king, and said: "The persons of messengers are always held sacred. Know, therefore, that a serpent desires to have your daughter for his wife; and I am come hither in my capacity of gardener to see whether I can graft a dove upon a serpent."

The king, perceiving that he was somewhat of a booby, in order to get rid of him, said: "Go home, and tell this serpent that if he can turn all the fruit in this garden into gold, I will give him my daughter in marriage," and laughing heartily, he dismissed the peasant.

When Cola Mattheo reported the king's answer, the serpent replied: "Go early in the morning and collect all the fruit kernels you can find throughout the city, and sow them in the royal garden; then you shall behold a wonder."

Cola Mattheo, who was a great simpleton, said nothing, but as soon as the sun with his golden besom had swept away the shades of night, he took his basket under his arm, went from street to street, carefully picking up every seed and kernel of peach, pomegranate, apricot, cherry, and all other fruits he could find. Then he sowed them in the royal garden as the serpent had desired him,—which he had no sooner done than he perceived the stems of the trees, together with their leaves, flowers, and fruit, all turn into shining gold; and the king, when he saw it, went almost out of his senses, and could not tell what to make of the affair.

But when Cola Mattheo was sent by the serpent to request the king to perform his promise, the king replied: "Not so fast! For if the serpent really desires to have my daughter in marriage, he must do something more; and, in fact, I should like him to change the walls and the paths in my garden into precious stones."

386

On this new demand being reported to the serpent, he said: "Go early in the morning and collect all the potsherds you can find on the ground; strew them in the paths and on the walls of the garden; then we shall soon make the king perform his promise."

And when the night had passed away, Cola Mattheo took a great basket and collected all the bits of broken pots, pans, jugs, cups and saucers, and all similar rubbish; and when he had done with them as the serpent desired him, the garden was suddenly covered with emeralds, rubies, chalcedonies, and carbuncles, so that its brilliancy dazzled all eyes, and astonished all hearts. The king was almost petrified at this spectacle, and knew not what had befallen him.

When, however, the serpent caused him to be again reminded of his promise, he answered: "All this is nothing yet. I must have this palace quite filled with gold."

When Cola brought this further put-off from the king, the serpent only said: "Go and take a bunch of green herbs, and sweep the floors of the palace with it; then we shall see what will happen."

Mattheo directly made a great bunch of purslain, marjoram, rue, and chervil, with which he swept the floors of the palace, and immediately the rooms were filled with gold in such quantities, that poverty must have fled at least a hundred houses off.

Now when the peasant went once more in the name of the serpent to demand the princess, the king found himself constrained at last to keep his promise. He called his daughter, and said: " My beloved Grannonia, in order to make sport of an individual who requested you in marriage, I required things of him which seemed impossible. As, however, I now find myself obliged to fulfil my promise—I entreat you, my dutiful daughter, not to bring my word to disgrace, but that you will resign yourself to what Heaven wills, and I am constrained to do."

" Do as you please, my lord and father," answered Grannonia, " for I will not depart one hair's breadth from what you desire."

On hearing this the king desired Cola Mattheo to conduct the serpent to his presence; who accordingly repaired to court in a carriage made entirely of gold, drawn by four elephants, also of gold. As they passed along, however, everybody fled before them, from terror at seeing such a dreadfully large serpent.

When the serpent reached the palace, the courtiers shuddered and trembled; even the very scullions ran away, and the king and queen shut themselves up in a remote chamber. Grannonia alone retained her self-possession; and although her royal parents called to her, saying: "Fly, fly, Grannonia!" she stirred not from the spot, and merely said: "I will not flee from the husband whom you have given me."

No sooner had the serpent entered the apartment,

than he encircled Grannonia with his tail, kissed her,

then drew her into another chamber, locked the door, and stripping off his skin, was transformed into a remarkably handsome young man, with golden locks and bright eyes, who immediately embraced Grannonia with the utmost tenderness, and paid her the most flattering attentions.

The king, on seeing the serpent lock himself into another room with the princess, said to his wife: "Heaven have pity on our poor daughter; for, unquestionably, all is over with her. This confounded serpent has, no doubt, by this time swallowed her up like the yolk of an egg." And they peeped through the key-hole to see what had happened.

But when they beheld the surprising elegance and beauty of the young man, and perceived the serpent skin, which had been thrown down on the ground, they burst open the door, rushed in, and seizing the skin, threw it into the fire, where it was instantly consumed. Whereupon the young man exclaimed: "Ah! you wretched people, what have you done to me!" and changing himself into a pigeon, he flew with such force against the window glass, that it broke, and he flew through, although very much injured.

390

THE SERPENT PRINCE.

Grannonia, who in one and the same moment beheld herself thus rejoicing and grieving, happy and unhappy, rich and poor, complained bitterly at this destruction of her happiness, this poisoning of her joy, this sad change of her fortune, all of which she laid to the charge of her parents, although these assured her they had not intended to do wrong. She, however, ceased not to bemoan herself until night drew in, and as soon as all the inmates of the palace were in their beds, she collected all her jewels, and went out at a back door, determined to search till she should again find her lost treasure. When she got beyond the city, guided by the moonshine, she met a fox, who offered to be her companion; to which Grannonia replied: "You are heartily welcome to me, neighbour, for I do not know the district very well."

They went on together a considerable way, and reached a forest, where the tops of the lofty trees met on high, and formed an agreeable canopy over their heads. As they were weary with walking, and wished to repose, they went under the thick leafy roof, where a rivulet sported with the fresh grass, sprinkling it with its clear drops.

They lay down on the mossy carpet, paid the debt of

sleep to nature for the wear and tear of life, and did not wake until the sun with his wonted fire gave notice that men might resume their avocations; but after they had risen, they stood awhile listening to the song of the little birds, as Grannonia took infinite pleasure in hearing their twittering.

When the fox perceived this, he said: " If you understood, as I do, what they say, your pleasure would be infinitely greater."

Excited by his words—for curiosity as well as love of gossip is a natural gift in all women—Grannonia begged the fox to tell her what he had learned from the birds.

The fox allowed her to urge him for a considerable time, in order to awaken still greater curiosity for what he was going to relate; but at length he told her that the birds were conversing about a misfortune which had befallen the son of a king, who, having given offence to a wicked enchantress, had been doomed by her to remain for seven long years in the form of a serpent. The period of his enchantment arriving at its close, he had fallen in love with the daughter of a king, and having, on finding himself in a room alone with her, stripped off his serpent's skin, her parents had broken in upon them and had burnt the skin; whereupon the

392

prince, by flying through a window in the form of a pigeon, had so severely injured himself, that the surgeons had no hope of his recovery.

Grannonia, on hearing the history of her beloved prince, immediately inquired whose son the prince might be, and if there were any means by which his cure could be effected. The fox replied, that those birds had said that he was the son of the King of Ballone-Grosso, and that no other means existed of stopping up the holes in his head, so that his reason should not evaporate through them, but to anoint the wounds with the blood of those very birds who had narrated the circumstance.

On hearing these words, Grannonia besought the fox to be so very kind as to catch the birds for her, that she might get their blood, and promised to share with him the profit she would make by curing the prince.

" Softly to work," said the fox; " let us wait till night, and when the birds are gone to roost, I will climb the tree and strangle them one after the other."

So he passed the day talking alternately of the beauty of the king's son, of the father of the princess, and of the misfortune that had befallen her, till at length night came on. When the fox saw all the little birds asleep on the branches, he climbed very quietly and cautiously up, and caught all the chaffinches, gold-finches, and fly-catchers that were on the tree, killed them, and put their blood in a little flask he carried with him, in order to refresh himself on the road.

Grannonia was expressing her delight at this success, when the fox said to her: "My dear daughter, your joy is all in vain; for you have gained nothing at all, unless besides the blood of the birds you also possess mine, which I certainly do not mean to give you;" and so saying, off he ran.

Grannonia, who saw that all her hopes were about to be annihilated, in order to obtain her desires, had recourse to cunning and flattery; so she cried out to him: "Dear daddy fox, you would be quite in the right to take care of your skin, if I were not so much indebted to you, and if there were no more foxes in the world. But since you know how much I have to thank you for, and that in these fields there is no lack of creatures of your kind, you may rely without uneasiness on me, and therefore do not act like the cow who kicks down the pail after she has filled it with her milk. Stand still, do not leave me, but accompany me to this king's city, in order that he may hire me of you for a servant."

The fox into whose head it never entered that a fox could ever be duped, found himself, however, deceived by a woman; for he had scarcely given his assent to accompanying Grannonia, and had not gone fifty paces with her, before she ungratefully knocked him down with the stick she carried, killed him, and poured his blood into the flask.

She then ran off as fast as she could," until she reached Ballone-Grosso. There she went straight to the royal palace, and caused the king to be informed she was come to cure the prince's wounds.

The king had her immediately brought into his presence, greatly surprised that a young maiden should promise to do that which the most skilful surgeons in his kingdom acknowledged themselves incompetent to effect. But as there would be no harm in trying, he gave her permission to make the experiment.

Grannonia, however, said : " If I fulfil your wishes, you must promise to give me your son for my husband." The king, who had lost all hope of seeing his son restored, replied: "Only restore him to health and spirits, and you shall have him just as you make him. For it is not too much for me to give a husband to one who gives me a son."

So they went into the prince's room, and no sooner had Grannonia anointed him with the blood than he was entirely cured.   Now when Grannonia saw him well and cheerful, she said to the king that he must keep his word; whereupon the latter turned to his son, and spoke thus: "My dear son, but lately I looked upon you as dead, and now, when I least expected, I see you again living and well; and since I promised this young maiden in case she restored you, that you should become her husband, and as heaven has been so gracious to me, enable me, if you have any regard for me, to fulfil my promise, for gratitude constrains me to recompense this service."

The prince replied: "My lord and father, I wish my will were as free as my love for you is great.   But since I have already given my word to another woman, you would not wish that I should break my promise; and this young maiden herself will not counsel me to act so faithlessly to her whom I love, therefore I must remain true to my choice."

When Grannonia heard these words, and perceived that the prince retained the memory of her so vividly in his heart, she felt unspeakable joy, and said, whilst she blushed to crimson: "But if I persuade the maiden whom you love, to renounce her claim on you, would you then comply with my wish?"

"Far be it from me," replied the prince, "that I should ever efface the fair image of my beloved from my breast. Whatever she may do, my desire and my sentiments will remain unaltered; and were I to risk my life for it, still I never would consent to the change."

Grannonia, who could no longer conceal her feelings, now made herself known; for the darkness of the chamber, where all the curtains were drawn on account of the prince's illness, and her own disguise, had entirely prevented him from recognising her. The moment he perceived who she was, he embraced her with indescribable joy, and then related to his father who she was, and what she had done for him.

Then they sent for the parents of the princess, and the marriage festival was celebrated with great rejoicings, so that it was again made manifest that for the joys of love, sorrow is ever the best seasoning.

THE PROPHETIC DREAM.

[Oral.]

———•———

N a little obscure village, there once dwelt a poor shepherd, who, for many years, supported himself and his family upon the very trifling wages he earned by his labour. Besides his wife he had one only child, a boy. He had accustomed this boy, from a very early age, to go out with him to the pastures, and had instructed him in the duties of a faithful shepherd, so that as the child grew up he could entrust the flocks to his care, whilst he himself could earn a few pence by basket weaving. The young shepherd gaily led his flocks over the fields and pastures, whistling or singing some cheerful song, or cracking his whip, that the time should not pass heavily with him. At noon he lay down at his ease by his flock, eat his bread, and quenched his thirst at the rivulet, and then slept for a short time before he drove it further.

THE PROPHETIC DREAM.

One day when he had lain down under a shady tree for his noontide rest, the young shepherd slept and had a remarkable dream. He was journeying on, far, far on—he heard a loud clinking sound, like to a heap of coins incessantly falling on the ground—a thundering noise like the report of incessant firing—he saw a countless band of soldiers, with glittering armour and weapons—all these sights and sounds encircled him and resounded about him. Then he seemed to wander on, constantly ascending a mountain until he arrived at the summit, where a throne was erected on which he seated himself, leaving beside him a vacant place, which a beautiful woman who suddenly appeared, immediately occupied. The young shepherd still dreaming, rose up, saying in a solemn and earnest voice: "I am King of Spain;" and at that moment he awoke.

Pondering on his strange dream, the youth led on his flock, and in the evening, whilst he assisted his parents in their work as they sat before their cottage door cutting fodder, he related it to them, and concluded by saying: " Verily, if I dream that again, I will be off to Spain to see whether I shall be made king."

" Foolish boy," murmured the old father; " thou be

made king? Don't go and make yourself a laughing-stock."

His mother laughed outright, rubbing her hands, and repeating in amaze, "King of Spain! king of Spain!"

The next day at noon he lay down again under the same tree, and oh, wonder! the same dream took possession of his senses. He hardly had patience to watch his flock till evening; gladly would he have run home, and at once set out on his journey to Spain. When at length his work was done, he again related his romantic dream, saying: "If I do but dream this once again, I will go off directly, on the very same day."

The third day he lay down again under the same tree, and the same dream again visited him for the third time. The youth raised himself up in his sleep, exclaiming: "I am King of Spain," and thereupon he awoke. He gathered up his hat, his whip, and his provision bag, collected his sheep, and went back straight to the village. When he got there the people began to chide him for returning so long before vespers; but the youth was so excited that he paid no heed to the reproofs either of the neighbours or of his parents, but packed up his Sunday clothes, hung the bundle on a hazel

400

stick, and throwing it over his shoulder started off without another word. He put his best foot foremost, and ran so fast that one would have thought he hoped to reach Spain that same night.

He got no further however that day than to the borders of a forest, and not a village nor even a solitary cottage could he descry; so he resolved to take his night's rest in a thick bush. He had scarcely fallen asleep when he was disturbed by a great noise. A company of men, conversing loudly, passed before the bush which he had made his bed. The youth crept softly forward, and followed the men at a little distance, saying to himself: "Perhaps thou mayest still find a lodging; where these men pass the night, thou surely mayest also sleep." They had not gone much further before they came to a house of considerable dimensions, which, however, was situated in the centre of the dark forest. The men knocked, and were admitted, and the young shepherd unperceived slipped in with them into the house. Another door was then thrown open, and they all entered a large and very imperfectly lighted room, on the floor of which lay numerous trusses of straw, beds and coverlids, which seemed ready prepared for the men's night repose. The shepherd boy crept quickly under a heap of straw, which was scattered near the door, and lay in his concealment on the look-out for all he might see and hear. As he was a very sharp boy, with all his senses about him, it was not long before he made out that he was amongst a band of robbers, whose captain was the owner of the house. This latter, as soon as the newly arrived members of the band had stretched themselves on their couches, ascended an elevated seat, and said in a deep bass voice: " My brave comrades, give me an account of your day's work; where you have been, and what booty you have got ! "

A tall man, with a coal black beard, was the first to raise himself from his bed, and answered: " My good captain, early this morning I robbed a rich nobleman of his leathern breeches; these have two pockets, and as often as they are turned inside out, and well shaken, a heap of ducats falls on the ground."

" That sounds well, indeed ! " said the captain.

Then uprose another, and said: " I stole from a great general his three-cornered hat; and this hat has the property, that so long as it is turned round upon the head shots are fired off incessantly from its three corners."

"That's worth hearing," replied the captain; upon which a third man sat up, saying: "I have deprived a knight of his sword, and when you stick the point of this sword into the earth, up starts at that very moment a regiment of soldiers."

"A brave deed," exclaimed the captain; as the fourth robber then began: "I drew off the boots of a traveller whilst he slept, and whoever puts on those boots goes seven miles at every step."

"I commend a bold deed," said the captain, highly pleased; "hang up your prizes against the wall, and now eat and drink heartily, and sleep well." So saying, he left the sleeping apartment of the robbers, who caroused lustily, and then slept soundly. When all was still and the men in deep sleep, the young shepherd stole from his hiding-place, put on the leathern breeches, set the hat upon his head, girded on the sword, drew on the boots, and slipped softly out of the house. As soon as he was outside the door, the boots, to his infinite delight, at once manifested their magic virtue, and it was not long before the youth entered the great capital of Spain; it is called Madrid.

He asked the very first person he met to direct him to the most considerable hotel in the city; but received for answer, "You little urchin, get off with you to some place where such as yourself lodge, and not to where great lords dine." A shining gold piece, however, soon made his adviser a little more courteous, so that now he willingly conducted the youth to the best hotel. Arrived there, he at once engaged the best apartments, and said to his host: "Well, how goes it in your city? What is the latest news here?"

The host made a long face, and replied: "My little gentleman, you must be indeed quite a stranger here. It seems that you have not yet heard that his majesty, our king, is on the eve of departing for the wars with an army of twenty thousand men. You must know we have enemies, powerful enemies. Oh, these are, indeed, dreadful times! Is your little worship disposed to join the army?"

"No doubt!" said the stripling, whose countenance beamed with joy.

No sooner had the host left him, than he quickly drew off his leather breeches, shook out a heap of gold pieces, and purchased for himself costly garments with arms and accoutrements, dressed himself in them, and then craved an audience of the king. As he entered the palace, and was being conducted by two chamberlains through a spacious and magnificent hall, he was met by a young and wondrously beautiful lady, who graciously saluted him, and whom he beheld surrounded by courtiers, who bowed to her as he passed, whilst they whispered to him, "That is the princess—the king's daughter."

The young shepherd was not a little enraptured by the beauty of the princess; and he was so inspired by his admiration and delight, that he was able to speak boldly and confidently to the monarch.

"I come," said he, "most humbly to offer to your majesty my services as a warrior. The army I bring to you shall gain the victory for you; and it shall win for your majesty whatever you may be pleased to desire. But I ask of you one recompense, namely, that if I gain the victory for you, I may receive your lovely daughter in marriage. Will you grant me this, my most gracious king?"

The king was astonished at the youth's bold address, and answered: "Be it so—I agree to your request. If you return home a conqueror, you shall be my successor, and I will give you my daughter in marriage."

405

THE PROPHETIC DREAM.

The *ci-devant* shepherd now betook himself all alone
to the open plain, and began to strike his sword here
and there in the ground, and in a few minutes there
stood on the plain many thousand well-armed combatants, and the youth himself, richly armed and
adorned, sat as their leader on a noble horse decked with
gold embroidered housings and a lustrous bridle. The
young general led his troops against the foe, and a
bloody battle was fought. Unceasing death-shots
thundered from the commander's hat, and his sword
called up one regiment after another from the ground,
so that in a few hours the enemy was vanquished and
scattered, and the flag of victory waved above the conquered camp. The victor pursued and conquered from
his foe a considerable portion of his country. Victo-
rious, and crowned with glory, he returned to Spain,
where his greatest good fortune still awaited him.
The fair daughter of the king had been no less struck
by the handsome youth whom she met in the hall, than
he had been by her; and the most gracious monarch
knew how to value duly the great service rendered to
him by the brave young man. He kept his word—
gave him his daughter in marriage, and made him heir
to his throne.

THE PROPHETIC DREAM   P. 406.

THE PROPHETIC DREAM.

The nuptials were celebrated with the greatest magnificence, and he who had so shortly before been only a shepherd youth sat now in high estate. Soon after the wedding the old king resigned his crown and sceptre into the hands of his son-in-law, who, seated proudly on the throne, with his beautiful consort beside him, received the oath of allegiance from his people.

Then he thought of his so quickly-fulfilled dream and of his poor parents, and when he was alone with his wife, he thus addressed her : " My beloved, know that I have parents living still, but they are very poor ; my father is a village herdsman, dwelling far away in Germany, where I myself, as a boy, looked after cattle, until a marvellous dream revealed to me that I should become king of Spain. Fortune has been favourable to me ; I am now a king, but I would willingly see my parents also prosperous, therefore with your kind consent I will return to my former home, and bring my parents hither."

The young queen was well content that her husband should do as he proposed, so he set off and travelled of course very fast, being possessed of the seven-mile boots. On his way the young monarch restored the

407

magical articles which he had taken from the robbers to their rightful owners, retaining only the boots; he carried back with him his parents, who were almost beside themselves for joy, and to the former owner of the boots he gave a dukedom in exchange for them. After that he lived happily and worthily all the rest of his days.

THE END.

LONDON:

BRADBURY AND EVANS, PRINTERS, WHITEFRIARS.

www.ingramcontent.com/pod-product-compliance
Lightning Source LLC
Chambersburg PA
CBHW031142050726
47495CB00018B/381

* 9 7 8 1 4 3 5 7 4 9 3 1 3 *